THE REVELATION

BEGINS . . . *With*

the Mercy Tree

By

SHIMIRA COLE

DEDICATION

I wrote this story for you. To the person who seeks God's presence, word, and mercy for internal and external healing.

" For I will restore health to you, and your wounds I will heal, declares the LORD,"
Jeremiah 30:17 (ESV)

To those who believe God has called them to be servants and to

spread the Gospel of Christ.

"For many are called, but few are chosen."
Matthew 22:14 (ESV)

And for those who struggle with unbelief and have wondered,

"Where is God?" during difficult seasons in life.

". . . for he has said, "I will never leave you nor forsake you.""
Hebrews 13:5 (ESV)

Lastly, to those who want to read an adventurous Christian novel with unpredictable twists, turns, and surprises, I hope you enjoy!

ACKNOWLEDGMENTS

To my mommy; Magnola "Wilson" Cole for encouraging me to live my dreams.

THE REVELATION

BEGINS . . . *With*

the Mercy Tree

«CHAPTER ONE»

I REMEMBER *it like it was yesterday.*

I stood inside the elevator that slowly ascended floor to floor, my fingers combing through my dark hair before patting down my wrinkled shirt. The elevator's voice-activation announced each level.

"Fourth floor," it said easing to a stop. My reflection on the doors doubled, opening to the name Pharmaceuticals Plant Discoveries (PPD) and the slogan, 'Dedicating Our Lives to the Formula' arched like a rainbow over the entrance to the executive suites.

My feet stuck to the floor with no courage to move. They kept me from entering the most sacred part of the facility where true plant scientists coexisted. I signaled the word *move* to my brain with no luck. Words like *failure* and *disappointment* held me hostage. I hoped for a gust of wind to push me out, but nothing came. I felt for the handwritten letter from Mama tucked inside my back pocket that read quite differently from the others. It wasn't filled with the usual questions about why I had stayed away after college or why I hadn't visited home for Christmas, but instead, it bragged about my brother Wheatly's accomplishments. Her letters had turned into telegrams about the Kole family's affairs as if I was stuck on a different planet or maybe inside an elevator somewhere with nothing to celebrate of my own.

Chatter from people approaching the elevator broke my daze. I held open the doors and dragged my feet forward to the shiny red floor where my reflection greeted me again. The floor reflected a tall, dark, nerdy, young man ready to ask for a long-overdue promotion—a big one that could make me co-partner of PPD or even the headmaster of my scientific organization—that would be worth celebrating. I winked at my reflection on the shiny floor and strolled through the hallway, glancing into various senior scientists' offices, envisioning myself sitting behind their desks, and admiring my honorable discovery plaques on the wall.

I stopped and read a plaque near an open door, "The Thom-o-nous Knell Plant founded by Dr. Thomas Knell in 1992."

Dr. Thomas sat in his office, nose in a textbook, scanning every word on the page and comparing his research to the pile of data on his desk. His eyes rose, and I leaped forward down the hallway.

I passed scientists dressed in fancy suits and ties, avoiding eye contact as I rubbed my hands against my casual button-up shirt to straighten out the wrinkles.

Trixie, the receptionist, twisted two strands of hair and worked on the computer when I approached her with my best smile.

"My name is—"

"Yes, you're the intern." She frowned and her face displayed unflattering lines.

"Ah? No . . . Maybe a few years ago, but I'm—"

Trixie pointed to an uncomfortable bench near Dr. Frazier's office— the CEO of PPD—and said, "Please take a seat. Dr. Frazier will be right with you."

I nodded and wandered towards a large cabinet in the corner that displayed framed plant fossils from various eras in history. A circular gold stamp on each frame read, "Pharmaceuticals Plant Discoveries (PPD) in association with the Scientific Allegiance Agency (SAA); a government sector formed in 1950 for extraordinary discoveries." The fossils gave me a second dose of motivation to wait the entire afternoon on the uncomfortable bench. I reviewed my goal list on the back of Mama's letter:

Number one; get a promotion.

Number two; brag about the promotion.

Number three; start my own scientific company and end the family's curse.

My reputation depended on the promotion because I knew Mama and Wheatly missed me.

I rested my head against the wall and took a deep breath that soothed the nerves dancing in my whole body. I tapped my feet while I waited. Then my hands joined the rhythm, and before I knew it, I had created a musical beat. However, Trixie pouted at me, and I quickly stopped. I cracked my knuckles and yawned. I heard the birds chirping next to the open window, and I whistled. Trixie dropped the pencil and massaged her temple. I held up Mama's letter and whispered, "I'm going to read," calming Trixie from going over the edge.

I reread Mama's handwritten letter. The date, September 30th, 1999, was the only thing I repeated to myself. Today's date was December 1st, 1999, and I still hadn't responded to her request to attend my brother's celebration dinner. Not my first time. Once, she mailed me a letter that took me over six months to reply to because I was busy with work and college. She used to call my house phone, but I was never home, and at work, I was too busy to talk. She knew I didn't purposely dodge her calls because I had always been the kid, locked away in the bedroom with my head lowered in a science book or tending to my plants in the garden. And I bet she didn't have anything to say but asked questions about my life in Georgia.

The letter encouraged me to wait outside Dr. Frazier's office for more than two hours and urged me to achieve an old family promise, returning home as a professional Plant Scientist. Trixie gave me a nasty stare as she pounded on the computer's keyboard, hoping that the wait would scare me off.

"Dr. Frazier will be with you in a second," she slurred and rolled her eyes, having said that twenty minutes ago and before that, an hour ago. I smirked. Nevertheless, Dr. Frazier took a phone call, and another forty minutes passed. Finally, the door swung open while I sat with my back against the wall and butt on the floor to save it from the bench. Dr. Frazier stared down at me with his small, grey, wolf-like-eyes and glossy sideburns, which made me more edgy about my request.

"Wellington, come inside." He marched ahead of me as I brushed myself off. He sat behind his desk. The large portrait of him on the back wall stopped me. It was gorgeous, and I admired the dark vibrant colors mixed throughout the painting. I jammed my hands into my pockets, and I slowly moved farther into his newly extended office. The royal burgundy drapes decorated the window. His brand new wooden desk—grander than the last one—had stacked folders in red, blue, green, and brown on top of it.

He replaced the old grey carpet with white carpet, genuinely resembling the United States president's Oval Office. I stood before his desk like a deer in a car's headlights using its nose to sniff out the danger. Massive pictures of a younger Dr. Frazier accepting awards and at archaeological sites from around the world spiked my confidence. Dr. Frazier noticed my curiosity and pointed to a black-and-white photo in the far corner.

"You remember that?" he asked. He blushed with memories.

"Yes, sir. One of the proudest moments of my life." I smiled proudly at the black-and-white photo of me, my church's youth group, and Dr. Frazier—an archeologist at the time—in Israel cheesing for the camera.

Dr. Frazier interrupted my daydream. "It's a shame that discovery became useless." He adjusted himself in his seat, removed his smile, and tapped his nails on top of his desk. The old photo of us gave me my last dosage of courage, so I cleared my throat.

"Sir, I received a letter from my mother—"

"Oh, great. How is everyone?" he interrupted me. He never allowed a person to get their thoughts out before offering his own words.

"They are great, sir. I received a letter from her." I waved it in the air. "She's having a celebration dinner for my brother and—"

"Go! You deserve the time off." He slammed his hand on his desk and shooed me away.

"That's not why I am here, sir," I declared.

"Okay?" He leaned back, halfway intrigued, in his oversized chair.

"I promised my family when I left for college that I would return home as a scientist, and—"

"You are. Everyone working here is considered a scientist."

"Not on the second floor, Dr. Frazier," I explained.

His eyebrow rose instantly, wrinkling his forehead. Pharmaceuticals Plant Discoveries was a three-story building, and the first two floors were administrative support.

"What I am trying to say is, I don't feel like a scientist. I've been sitting behind a desk for six years, and that's considered entry-level work compared to what I could be doing in the field."

Dr. Frazier froze for a moment, stood up, closed his grey blazer with the middle button, and slowly walked to the window. There wasn't anything outside, but a street and a field of grass, however, he endlessly stared as if it was the unending ocean.

"Wellington," he said while facing the window and fidgeting with his blazer.

"Sir? I can't help, but to think that you do not want to promote me? You know I am the smartest person in this company." I paused and realized that I might have been too conceited, so I reassured him, "Next to you of course, and you even said that I have a hot pot of brains." I glanced back at the black-and-white picture of us. "Right there, you said that to me, there." I pointed.

Quickly, he resented the picture and then turned to me with a frosty look. "Wellington, I told you that ten years ago—" he struggled to find his next words. "You were smarter than the kids in your age group back then. Now, you're average, and I have to promote the best in the company."

My heart leaped forward, and my desires of working for PPD faded.

"Mr. Alex Frazier," I commanded, and his eyebrow rose again. He knew I hadn't called him by that name in over seven years. "You said if I attended your college, you promised that I could work as a staff scientist on my discovery."

"And that discovery became useless . . . like I said in the beginning—"

"Granted. The school stopped investing in the experiments. However, you told me that you would start a company and get funding from the Scientific Allegiance Agency to invest in the soil experiment." I spread my arms. "And that I would be a partner and get admitted into the SAA's network, only if I worked my way up from office clerk. Sir, my discovery helped you build this company, and I still haven't got promoted."

"I've offered you an office coordinator position."

"Sir, I don't want to be a professional assistant. I want to be a professional scientist with his own office, with a title: doctor or headmaster before his name, and conducting scientific experiments like you said I would. That's what you promised me, and that is what I promised my mother and brother that I will be before I return home."

"You've been working on a lot of projects—" His anxiety danced around the request as his face turned bright red.

"If I don't get a promotion, then I will have to find a company that appreciates my—"

Filled with rage, Dr. Frazier emerged forward and shouted, "Wellington, the board wanted me to fire you a long time ago!" He pounded his fist on the desk. His voice thundered, and I knew for sure that everyone outside of the door heard us arguing.

I felt shocked, confused, and disappointed. I dedicated a majority of my twenties to this company and to be a scientist—eight years of college to get my bachelor, masters, and doctorate while working six years at Pharmaceuticals Plant Discoveries as an office clerk.

My heart broke into pieces, and he made sure it stayed that way.

"The Headmaster of Botany told me that your monthly research reports sound arrogant, foolish, and unrealistic."

Rage boiled inside of me. I reflected on past disputes with scientists in the organization, but none resulted in foul play. I only knew that I tried to help them collect data and make deadlines. They asked for my help, and I dedicated my time to their projects. Tears welled my eyes while Dr. Frazier rubbed his sweaty palms together and stepped closer with an awkward grin. "But I believe in you, and I know your potential. That is why I kept you here, as an office clerk for so long until the right time came along."

"You should have told me this," I muttered as my chin touched my chest.

"I couldn't. I couldn't break your heart and ruin your dreams." He stepped even closer to me, and I moved away to stare out the same window. This time the grass and street were not boring but gave me the strength to move my feet apart.

A double knock interrupted us, and the door slowly opened to Trixie blushing. "Your afternoon appointment has arrived." She giggled as she covered her mouth and moved to the side.

"Thank you, Trixie." A tall fair skinned man with sharp features walked inside and rested his heavy-duty hands-on Trixie's shoulder—she melted away while closing the door.

"Ah, Wellington, I would like you to meet—"

"Gary Foster?" I finished his statement. Gary approached us at the window, and his brown-slicked-back-hair glimmered in the sunlight.

"So you do remember Detective Gary?"

"Wellington, it's been a long time." Gary hurried towards me and pulled me between his massive arms. I pulled away.

"Detective Gary kept in contact with me after the discovery for all these years. Wait a minute . . . " Dr. Frazier rambled through the folders on his desk as I wondered what he had to talk to Gary about. "Wellington?" An airy sound came from Dr. Frazier as he held a green binder filled with paperwork. "You're right. I haven't been using you as a resource. That discovery in Israel is still extraordinary, and I know something good can come from it. If you can create applicable medicine from it, I bet that will show the SAA's headmaster board that you have the potential to be a scientist." His eyes avoided mine as he gave me the folder, and he retracted back to the window. I held the green binder with both hands to support all the documents inside. The front cover had a big question mark on it.

"I don't understand. You already said that this discovery was useless. And why choose me, an average guy, to solve it?" I mocked him.

"Because two heads are better than one. You guys discovered it together. You guys make some use out of it." Dr. Frazier glowed from ear to ear revealing his greed. He stormed back to his desk and sat down. "We spent thousands of dollars testing the soil, and if nothing happens soon, the Scientific Allegiance Agency will have our backside, and Pharmaceuticals Plant Discoveries will go to the biggest buyer. I made them a promise ten years ago, and I better deliver soon."

"But he's not a scientist." My voice quaked, and my muscle quivered.

"Well teach him how to be."

"But it took me six years to learn everything that I know."

Gary rested his hand on my shoulder.

"I may not be a scientist, Wellington, but I am an excellent investigator." He winked and tapped his silver and gold badge pinned on his jacket.

"There you have it. Detective Gary can help you research." Dr. Frazier waved me off.

"If I solve this, I want to become a member of the SAA and be promoted to VP of Pharmaceutical Plant Discoveries?" I reconfirmed the promise. My eyes scanned his desk to find a piece of paper to get a written agreement.

Dr. Frazier grasped his fingers together. "If you solve this." He pointed to the green binder in my hand. "You will get more than a promotion. You'll receive worldwide recognition."

I took a step back, shocked. My head spun at the thought of me accepting a Nobel Prize in Medicine in front of my family. Me, being recognized for creating medicine from a plant that I have discovered just like I imagined as a child.

"But Wellington, you can't leave anything out of the equation." Dr. Frazier leaned forward to me as Gary slowly crossed his arms.

"Of course not!" I smiled. Thoughts of awards and fortune still danced in my mind.

"Good! Go take some time off. See your mother and brother. Revisit your old childhood memories of you collecting plants," he said deviously. Suddenly, my dream of accepting a Nobel Prize broke because of one thought.

"I can't solve this before I go home. It's going to take months or maybe years."

"Well, you and Detective Gary better get started. You guys work from Virginia," he suggested and waited. "Or will you be too busy with family life? Because to be a scientist, you have to dedicate your life to the formula." He quoted the company's slogan.

"Of course, no. I—I've wanted this my whole life, so I choose this, and I choose to do it alone."

"Wellington, Detective Gary is—"

"It's fine, Dr. Frazier," Gary said, "Wellington, I am here if you need me."

"Okay then. You better get started." Dr. Frazier stood and stuck his hand towards me. "Wellington Kole, welcome to the first phase of becoming a scientist."

I shook his hand with a stone face and headed towards the exit. "Oh, Wellington." He displayed a cellphone in his hand. "Every scientist needs one of these."

"Ah? I have a beeper. So I'll be fine."

"Now you can have both." He laughed as I slowly took it from out of his hand and nodded, thank you, and I didn't know whether to feel grateful or agitated.

* * *

Once again, the splitting of the elevator doors resembled how I felt. Half satisfied with my meeting and unsatisfied with the result. Bright lights bounced off the dingy-white floors and bared-solid walls. I stormed angrily down the hallway thinking about what conspired. The nerve of Gary interrupting my meeting with Dr. Frazier, and the nerve of Dr. Frazier giving Gary a scientific job with no experience.

My failures and the impossible task of developing medicine from the soil distracted me because it would take years to conduct a new experiment. I wandered around fighting Dr. Frazier's voice in my head, which delayed the trip to my desk. I sought the men's bathroom to let out my frustration. I tried my best to hide the green binder behind my back as I traveled down the aisle between the cubicles where the junior researchers sat. Being assigned a green binder determined your value at the company. The fear of getting one kept people from asking for a promotion, and for the people who did get a green binder, they disappeared. Green binder cases were unsolvable for a reason, and this thought made me angrier. I took a shortcut through the staff scientist's research department and saw them enjoying their job. I loudly grunted as they conversed and laughed among like-minded scientists because I was jealous that I spent my days laughing with assistants and interns— all five years younger than me.

A few young scientists around my age headed my way, and I quickly changed course, too embarrassed to face anyone but the water fountain in the corner. I desperately gulped as they passed by. My fist wanted to hit someone, but the cold calmed my rage.

The water fountain kept me stable as tears flowed down my cheeks. I caught them with my sleeves while away from the sight of onlookers and took my time to regain my composure and to calm my heartbeat. I wondered if I should give Pharmaceuticals Plant Discoveries another try or if I should start over somewhere fresh. I hurried to the men's bathroom, splashed water on my face, wiped my tears with a paper towel, and looked in the bathroom mirror at my light brown eyes.

I worked so hard for this promotion.

I smoothed my hair and tossed the paper towel into the trashcan. Then I hurried to my desk and slammed the green binder on top of it. I flopped down on to my chair, took a deep breath, and opened my backpack to jam all of my personal research notes, books on plant intelligence and life, and random office supplies inside of it. My hands moved with speed, determined to not return to Pharmaceuticals Plant Discoveries because of Dr. Frazier's unsolvable assignment.

"You followed the red brick road to the Wizard of Pharmaceuticals?" A voice chuckled from behind me. Charlie Newman sat in his chair holding a coffee mug. I shook my head. He continued, "Did it glisten as you skipped down it?" He joked, and then he noticed the green binder on my desk. "That jerk!" He placed his coffee mug on his desk and then grabbed the folder.

"Anyone given a green binder discovery might as well quit or die. It's impossible to get funding for these experiments and to have scientists lend their expertise to something that had already been researched and tried multiple times." He laughed off his statement as he flipped through the sheet-protected pages in the folder.

"That is why I need to focus more on proving to my family that I didn't abandon them for all these years—so he can forget about me wasting time doing that assignment." I lifted my stuffed backpack.

"You're quitting? No . . . no . . . I was kidding. You can't leave me here with these stuck up scientists. Dude, I will blow my brains out if you leave," Charlie said and slapped his forehead. Instantly, he turned red, and his freckles disappeared.

"I don't know if I am quitting, yet. I'm just going to take a long break and go home with nothing to show for." Finally facing my failure, I grabbed the letter out of my pocket and revealed it to Charlie. He snatched it and my book bag from my hands, and I frowned at him.

He read the letter silently for a moment.

"Your mom will be happy to see you. I bet she wouldn't ask about your job or title." He grinned.

"She will if I told her that is why I've stayed away for so long. It will devastate her to know that I wasted years as an office clerk this whole time." Charlie observed the documents inside of the green binder pressed against his lap, ignoring my self-pity. My nose became congested, and my eyes rested in the palm of my hands.

"There is hardly anything in here: A camping site, a cave, and soil?" He squinted at me, confused. I pouted and took a deep breath to explain everything while my face rested comfortably in the palm of my hands.

"The soil was found in a cave in a mountain near the Dead Sea." I pointed to the black-and-white picture of the pile of soil formed in an angular position in the middle of the cave's floor. "It tested for numerous of substance. A curable natural substance found in fruit, herbs, plants, and roots used to fight off big virus and diseases such as Cancer, Aids, and sickle cell. If this soil produces all substances, then we found the cure to all things," I explained.

Charlie leaned back in his chair and combed his fingers through his hair.

"Dude. This assignment could put you on the map. This company will owe its whole existence to you if you crack this."

"Yeah, to me . . . and this weird guy named Gary." Charlie scratched his head, and I explained, "He was with me the day I found the soil. It's kind of funny though." I giggled and then said, "From the last time we spoke, he accused me of stealing a magical tree and his parents forced him to see a therapist for stating that it glowed."

"Wow, that's insane."

"Yeah . . . but the whole soil-healing-thingy is a myth. The soil can't cure all things if it tried."

"Hey! That's how you got your scar?" He quickly pointed at the small mark on the inner part of my hand.

Confused, I gently massaged it. "Ah?"

"Is this the camping trip?" He tapped the binder.

I suddenly remembered the exaggerated tale that I had told everyone. "Oh, yes. That's when I almost lost my hand," I took a deep breath and finished gathering my things.

"Did you test everything?" Charlie held the pages from the green binder up to the light to examine it. "Roots are covering the soil." He pointed and asked, "Roots come from trees, right? Where are you hiding the mystical tree?" He mocked me as he leaned closer to the photo trying to find the missing tree. My eyes rose forward. Thump . . . thump, my heart filled my ears. I quickly turned to the next page in the folder, mistakenly brushing Charlie's face with it and he moved away.

"It's from the vines." My voice squawked. I cleared my throat and pointed to the vines spread over the cave's walls in the photo. "However, it all did not test well, and our many experiments did not pass. So, it became a green binder, an unsolvable and worthless case." I paced with thoughts of feeling like a failure to Mama and Wheatly. "Therefore, I'll return home with nothing to celebrate."

"So what? Things change. Take your girlfriend, Janice, home. That will make everyone forget all about the scientist promise." Charlie winked at me and then a light bulb went off in my head. Janice, my beloved girlfriend for over three years, could replace the old promise and create a new one that produces little Kole grandbabies for Mama. A gift that every mother would enjoy.

I jumped and clapped my hands and said, "You're right. I can take Janice home to meet my mother. She'll be happy to see a girl on my arm, anyway." I walked and talked it out, remembering a few letters from Mama asking if a woman kept me warm at night. I ignored the question because I felt weird for answering it. However, if I took Janice home with me, then that would be saying yes, I do have a woman in my life. I did have a woman in my life.

My excitement disappeared because I then recalled that Janice and I got into a huge argument a week ago, and we broke up.

Nevertheless, still pumped, excited, and filled with fuel, I swayed to one knee and said to Charlie, "I will ask Janice to marry me, and that will replace the coming home as a scientist promise to coming home as a soon-to-be-married man for now." I lifted my fist in the air as if I cracked a case and then snatched my book bag out of Charlie's hand. However, Charlie yanked my bag.

"Wait, that's not what I meant when I suggested for you to take Janice home." He stuck out his leg to stop me from leaving our desk area. I tried stepping over them, but he blocked me again with the other.

"I was planning on asking her to marry me sooner or later. I got the ring already." I raised my eyebrow with an annoyed smile, and he grunted and sized me up hoping I told the truth.

"As long as you are ready for that type of commitment." He lowered his legs.

"Of course, I am. I love Janice." I grinned, convincing myself that I'm doing the right thing.

"Okay. Let's hear the proposal." Charlie jumped up, pushed the chairs back.

"Oh, no way." I blushed as everyone on the other side turned to us.

"Yeah, way!" he shouted and clapped his hands.

A few people walking by cheered and whistled.

"Okay . . . okay, but the proposal is going to be a little awkward. We broke up last week and—" My face completely turned bronze-red.

Charlie grabbed his head and sat down. "Back to work everyone . . . this guy is a failure at life," he joked and flipped open his planner.

I waved off Charlie's statement.

"Wait and see!" I grabbed my backpack and the green binder off Charlie's desk, and I side skipped towards the door. "I'll return as an engaged man!" I shouted as the assistants and interns cheered me on.

"You suck at promises. Stop while you're ahead!" Charlie shouted back.

I waved goodbye and headed out of the building, feeling as if I solved my problem.

* * *

A few hours later, paper, clothes, and books muddled the floor of my master bedroom. I took another item out of my drawer and threw it over my shoulder to join the rest of the mess. I couldn't find the ring, and I wondered if I should use it for the proposal.

My grandfather proposed to my grandmother with the ring, and then my grandmother gave it to my father to propose to my mother. My father couldn't afford an engagement ring at age eighteen, and since my father had passed away, Mama had no use for it. Therefore, she continued the little family-tradition and gave the ring to me before I left for college in case I needed to pop the question. I rammed through the smaller items in my chest drawer and then pondered if the ring sat in a case or not.

"Where are you, beautiful ring?" I whispered. "You wonderful ring," I flirted. I sorted through the less used items: batteries, old remotes, bankbooks, and pens and pencils in the top.

I examined the unpleasant mess. It was almost time, and I needed the ring and a broom to reorganize my bedroom before Janice happened to come snooping upstairs. Already, she never liked my earth tone theme bedroom—it made her feel as if we lied inside of a grave. She preferred vibrant bright colors like yellow, sky blue, gray to dark colors like maroon, brown, and green. The forest green walls, beige curtains, and brown carpet resembled a forest theme. Mama crocheted a flower pattern quilt with green, gold, and bronze colors and mailed it to me a few years ago.

Nevertheless, sleeping among nature relaxed me and soothed my inner soul. My body trembled, and sweat formed on my brow as thoughts danced within me; thoughts of my inner peace and plant collection tossed out on to the curb moments after pledging *I do* to Janice.

My stomach heaved with fear. But I wiped my brow, forged my way through the doubt, and continued the ring search. I convinced Janice to stop by on short notice. I removed the junk drawer from the dresser and poured everything onto the floor. A big crash rang, and I squinted my eyes to bear the noise. If the ring hid inside, it probably relocated to the floor. Determined, I fiddled through each thing-a-bob and placed each item back into the drawer. Suddenly, a tiny black box underneath coins, screws, and a pencil froze me.

My heart filled with joy as my hands quickly snatched it and examined the gold letters, M.K., which stood for May Kole, my grandmother's name. My thumb popped the case open, and the uniquely odd ring sparkled. It had a gold rim with greenish yellow rubies, and it mostly resembled a moon ring.

"I thought you were bigger," I said to the ring, "but I hope she likes you." I kissed it, giving it my best of luck. While bent down on one knee, I practiced. I held the ring up into the air with both hands attached to it and said, "Janice Marie McCoy, I realized how important you are to me in my life. Therefore, would you be my wife?" I paused, embracing the silence in my bedroom and imagining her crying and jumping into my arms. I practiced my happy smile, my excited smile, and my sincere smile as if Janice stood in front of me.

After a few seconds, I giggled to myself for talking to an imaginary Janice. *Ding Dong.*

The doorbell rang, and my heart skipped a few beats. I quickly got off my knees, hid the ring in my back pocket, and took one last disappointing look at the mess in my bedroom. I exhaled and rushed down the stairs and to the front door. I admired Janice's beautiful frame on the porch through the window's curtains, nervous to see her beautiful brown dimpled face.

My sweaty hands held the doorknob tight, ready to start the mission when I noticed the three unlit candles on the dining room table.

My eyes widened as my feet tiptoed to the table dressed with red cloth, fine silverware, and three tall skinny candles in the middle. Candles lit, I waved my hands over them trying to spread the cinnamon scent. Back at the front door where my sweaty hand grasped the knob, I took deep breath. I opened the door slowly and greeted Janice with a welcoming Kole smile engraved on my face, but she folded her arms and tilted her head to the side.

"Took you long enough," she said.

She's small and petite with kinky black hair and beautiful lips.

Speechless from admiring her natural beauty, I opened the door wide enough for her to enter. She slowly walked inside and saw the romantic setup to her left. Immediately, her eyes twinkled, and she thrust out her chest as she gazed at the glimmering table, set with red linen and napkins, and shining wine glasses.

"What is this for?" Curiosity fluttered within her mind.

"It's to say I appreciate you." Her fingers roamed on top of the table, and she entered the kitchen. I followed behind her like a lost puppy. She stared at the two bowls filled with food on the kitchen counter.

"So, you cooked dinner for me?" She lifted the top off a pot on the stove. Nervous to answer wrong, I said, "Just heating up some mashed potatoes." I blushed. "I sort of did something."

She squinted at me from behind her shoulders, and her eyes fell upon the trashcan, which revealed the red and white Kentucky Fried Chicken box inside.

"Go figure." She stormed out of the kitchen, but I caught her before she made it to the front door.

"Babe, look. I did this for you. Only you. I wanted you to feel special." I gave her that Kole family smile, the one that caught her eyes when we first met and the one that she fell in love with but it did not work.

"Wellington, you say this every time." And then she became weak as if she couldn't stand. I quickly grabbed the chair from the table and sat her down.

"Here. Drink this." Grabbing the red wine, I poured it into a glass and handed it to her. She wrinkled her forehead but took it and sipped.

"Welly, I can't do this with you anymore." She forced out the words before coughing again. I rubbed her back as I lowered myself to gaze into her eyes.

"Janice, baby. I know I am not the best man to pick when it comes to relationships, but I love you, and I can't see myself living without you." Moving closer to touch her thigh, I stared hopelessly into her eyes. I swayed on to one knee. "I started to realize how much you mean to me in my life."

"Oh, Wellington, cut the crap. If I did, then why didn't you visit me in the hospital? You didn't even stop by." Janice took another sip and crossed her legs.

"Janice, I told you I had a work thing."

"Yeah. A work thing." She sneered while creating bunny ears as if I lied. I shot up on to my feet and paced around.

"Janice, I took on a few research projects because I thought Dr. Frazier was going to give me a promotion if I did. I had to stay late and complete the work, babe," I pleaded and swayed back on one knee. "And, baby, I regret not coming to see you in the hospital that day, but you're alright? It was a small asthma attack, right? You didn't need me there, but if I could go back in time, I would have left that stupid work on my desk and came."

"You say that now." She glared.

I held her hand in mine and took a deep breath, and said, "Janice, I realized that you mean so much to me and—"

"And what? Want me to help you with another scientific project that will leave me tired, drained, and stressed out." She twisted her head to the side, and the muscle in my jaw twitched as my mouth curved into a smile.

"It was a simple project with plants, babe." I scowled.

"Plants are boring." She stuck her tongue out and then smirked.

"You're childish." I scorned and then forced a smile. She giggled and battered her lashes and my smile became genuine.

I grabbed one of her hands again. "Can you please let me finish?"

She nodded as she sipped the wine I wished I had never given to her. I took a deep breath and hopelessly romantically said, "Janice, you mean the world to me. I know I haven't been the best man in your life, but from this day forward, I promise to be the better man in your life. That will provide for you, put you first, and be the father of our future children. Therefore . . . " I reached in my back pocket, and her eyes grew as I revealed the engagement ring. "Will you do the same for me and be my wife?" The Kole's famous smile beamed, and Janice's heart fluttered.

"Oh, Wellington." She caressed my cheek. "Are you serious?" Tears formed as she admired me. Suddenly her face went blank as she said, "Umm, I don't know, Wellington?" she released my cheeks. Her mood changed quickly.

"What do you mean? I love you."

"I know, but." She frowned at the ring still between my two fingers.

"Look, the ring was passed down from my grandmother to my mother and now to you . . . if you accept. I promise to buy you a better-looking one." My heart palpitated.

"No, it's not the ring." She squeezed herself from between the chair and me, and I flew to my feet to read her mixed emotions.

"Well, if it's not the ring, then is it another he?"

"No, it's just . . . nothing." She gently pushed me away.

"No, it's something, Janice. Tell me, please." My eyebrows knitted, and she fidgeted with her clothes.

"Welly, when I came here today, I planned to break things off completely." She hid her face and quivered with fear.

My forehead wrinkled. "You're going to throw three years away like that?" My nostril flared as she searched for the nearest exit.

She stuttered. "It's time I put myself first and—" she stumbled over her words, and I crossed my arms.

"Oh, my goodness Janice. It was one mistake!" Every muscle tensed in my body.

"I should go." Janice rushed to the front door, and my hand slammed it shut.

"Wait. You can't leave. . . not like this." Tears formed and Janice finally revealed herself to me.

"Welly? I'm sick." Her hands quickly clutched her mouth, and she sobbed. A train blasted through and wrecked my mind when she said those words. I paused and then my body naturally embraced her. A familiar pain of loss developed in my chest.

Our heartbeat thudded together, and I asked, "What is it?"

She sniffed. "They think it is ovarian cancer."

I held her tight. I fiercely blinked to hold back my tears. Her head rested on my chest for a few seconds and then she said, "They discovered it when I was at the hospital."

"I should have been there... We'll figure this out. I promise," I said to her as she cried in my arms. "We'll figure this out," I said again, soothing her like a newborn baby.

"That is why I can't marry you. I know this will be hard for you to handle because your father's death was difficult for you." She tried to take a breath. "I need less stress in my life and more support from family than ever," she said.

"No, I get it. My father was a strong man, but you're stronger. So marry me regardless."

She smiled and finally nodded yes. I jumped and punched the air, and I slipped the ring on to her finger. I wiped her eyes with my shirt and stepped back.

"So, our first engagement outing is to meet my mother. She invited me home next week, and I want to show you off," I excitedly said. Janice's expression sobered, and she massaged the back of her neck.

"I knew it." She sniffed with frustration.

"Knew what?"

"I know you, Wellington! You did not get that promotion at work, so you're not a 'scientist.'" She created bunny ears around the word scientist. "And now you need something that will trump the old promise to your family and bringing home a fiancée sounds doable. You're disgusting." She struggled to take off the ring.

"Janice! I was going to propose to you, anyway." My body leaped forward to stop her.

"We've been together for three years. Kind of overdue, don't you think?" She lashed out.

"I had a plan, and it didn't work the way I thought it would have after college... babe?"

She finally pulled the ring off her finger. "Wellington, you need to do more soul-searching than using things or people to fulfill your needs. You need to find why your father's death made you abandon your family for all these years. You need to rebuild your relationship with your family without using me as a distraction," she yelled. My mood plummeted, and my body felt leaden. Tears dripped from her eyes. My heart shined a light on unsolved problems that I had avoided for ten years.

"You're right," I confessed, and she slowly melted with guilt. "That is why I need your support. Maybe I am not ready to go back home? Going back to that place brings up so many memories of my father. He was a great man."

Her words finally broke me, and I felt weak with the thought of neglecting Mama and Wheatly.

I confessed, "When I left for college, I did return to Virginia a few times. I even took a bus to the street, but couldn't get off it. I couldn't go back, and I shouldn't ever!" I held my tongue and slapped my fist into my hand. "It's hard to blame Him, you know?" I pointed upward.

She sighed and told me, "Wellington, you're not cursed. God wouldn't curse anyone he loves." She rubbed my shoulder, trying to loosen the bitterness I had with God.

"How do you know that? You don't understand. It's better that I stayed away, to protect my family. I rather stay here with you, anyway."

"No. This is not about me. It's about you reconnecting with your family." She counseled as if I trotted into her clinical office from off the streets.

"No, I am not leaving you here. Are you crazy?" I paced back and forth for a moment and blurted out, "Janice. I love you, and I can't lose you, ever!"

She calmly approached me. She nodded and focused on my every word as I continued, "Of course I figured my mom needed me more than ever now that she's getting older and my brother will be leaving for college, maybe soon. But I can't leave you here to deal with this on your own," I panicked.

"And I can't leave this earth without making sure you patch things up with your family, even the dark things deep inside of you. You sleep talk, and I've noticed." She giggled, and I blushed. A thought popped into my mind: me, a young boy, staring at my bloody hand. I shook the idea out of my head and hid my face. "Are you okay, Welly? It's fine to discuss the different outcomes to this—"

"You're not going to die." I turned to her. "There may be a way to save you. I will do everything in my power to find a cure for you, even if I have to risk it all."

"Stop talking foolish!"

"No, I am serious. I work at the biggest pharmaceuticals plant company in the world. There has to be something that I can find in a vault or in that green binder." The binder sat on the couch. The question mark captivated me with thoughts of the miraculous soil. I shook the thoughts out of my head and saw a huge smile on Janice's face. "But I need your support. Come with me to see my family," I said. I never asked her for her counsel, let alone acknowledged her expertise as a therapist.

"I will go and support you, but I will not accept your proposal, right now." She smiled and dropped the ring into my hand, and I placed it on a nearby shelf.

I stepped closer to her, and roamed my fingers against her cheek.

"Janice, I meant what I said. I will find something to cure you and not let anything get in the way again."

"Not even a work project?"

I thought for a moment about the same promise I made to Dr. Frazier. "Not even Pharmaceuticals Plant Discoveries."

She sparkled with excitement as we kissed and wrapped our arms around each other. "Okay, let's eat," she said.

I pulled her chair out, and she sat. I headed to the kitchen and uncovered the food, but fear crept up inside me. My grin now faced the floor. I rolled my shoulders back and took a deep breath wondering why I felt a sudden change of anxiety and nerves. My day recapped in my mind as I held on to the edge of the kitchen sink for support. Pain fluttered my chest, and my head spun with fear.

"Do you need help with anything?" she asked.

"Nope. I'm getting plates and will be there in just a moment," I reassured her. I rested my forehead in the palm of both hands and massaged the dark thoughts out of it. Each bowling ball of disaster struck against me, but none leveled up to the inner, unexplainable gut torment playing fight club inside me. The wall supported my back as my head hung low. Tears formed, and I rushed to splash water onto my face when a decorated plate, fixed over my sink, caught my attention. It displayed a painted tree—brown trunk and colorful sprout given to me by Wheatly for my birthday four years ago. I slowly stood up straight, star-struck at the resemblance of the colors, splashing off the plate.

I paced back and forth, fighting and accepting my past mistakes. Again, the decorative plate froze me and memories shivered all over me. My heart revealed that today's steps, setbacks, and decisions led me to one thing. I roamed my fingers across the hand-drawn depiction of my family's best-kept secret, The Mercy Tree.

«CHAPTER TWO»

VIRGINIA BEACH changed a lot. The roads led to various shopping outlets and restaurants. Houses expanded upward and outward with lavish landscaping, newer high schools and businesses appeared every fifteen miles, and I relied on the street names to know my whereabouts. My feet tapped the bottom of the taxi's floor, and my fingers joined the dance. A warm hand touched my lap. Janice cuddled up close to me and wrapped her arm around mine.

"It's going to be all right. Your mom is going to be happy to see you."

I hid my face and mumbled, "I am still a disappointment. I just know it. What do I say?"

"Hi, Mom," she joked, and then said, "Say nothing."

Failure, fear, and disappointment danced in my mind because I had been gone for so long with nothing accomplished. The taxi took a sharp turn down a familiar street, and my heart leaped. I was almost home, and for the first time in a long time, I felt at ease. I guided the taxi driver every bit of the way as I pointed out familiar places where I used to hang out to Janice.

"There. That's where Aaron and I used to play this game called Boat." I giggled. "We used to stand on that green box and push each other off." I referred to the green electrical box between the alleyways of the townhouses.

Janice chuckled.

The taxi slowed down as we passed a few houses. We turned onto the block, and I watched for the crab apple tree and red fence. The taxi stopped in front of a house, an older home with no crab apple tree and with a white fence.

"We're here." The taxi driver tilted his head backward, and I quickly reached into my pocket for my wallet.

"You're ready?" Janice asked.

"Umm, I am not sure."

The taxi driver opened Janice's door, opened the trunk, and rested our bags on the curve.

"Is everything okay?" Janice asked.

"No. I don't think so." The house looked completely different, so I took the letter out of my back pocket and skimmed for a new address. However, it was sent from this address.

"I'm sure everything is okay. Let's go knock." Janice grabbed my hand and off we went, leaving our bags on the driveway. My legs jiggled like Jell-O as the smell of newly cut grass filled my nose.

"Sir," The taxi driver yelled at me, and I quickly turned around. The green binder slouched inside of his hands.

"Don't want you to forget this."

"Yes, of course. Thank you, sir." I took it and joined Janice as she knocked. I took a deep breath, and we waited silently. We heard chatter and then a gentle touch of the doorknob.

"Who's there?" a mature woman's voice hummed. A big smile wiped across my face.

"Wellington," I said with tears in my eyes.

The door latches clicked off one by one. The door swung open, and two surprised eyes stared back at me.

"My baby!" she hollered and ran into my arms. Her eyes burst with tears, and I could hardly hear anything that came out of her mouth.

"Wheatly!" she screamed into the house.

"Hi, Mom." My nose flared, and I cried. Janice covered her mouth. Happiness and reassurance filled me.

We moved inside of the foyer between the stairs, the kitchen, and living room. "This is unexpected. Why didn't you call? I could have prepared a meal for you and your…" Mama noticed Janice and a bright smile covered her face. "I am sorry, Wellington, who is this?"

"This is … my girlfriend." I stepped backward, and she hugged Janice.

"Hi, baby. How are you?" Mama asked.

"I'm fine. I am happy to be here. You have a lovely home."

"Well, thank you. You can help me prepare lunch, and we can talk." She guided her to the kitchen.

"Ah. Mom, be gentle and Janice … " I tried to remind Janice to not say too much, but they chatted, and I hoped my career and job faded to the back of their minds. Excitement swept into me as I held the green binder tightly.

"I can do this. I know I can." I convinced myself when a short, stocky man with brown hair and a goatee walked into the room. He wore a gray sweater and jeans. He stood there with his arms crossed over his powerful chest and with a stone-cold face.

However, I smiled. I smiled big. Happiness flickered inside me as if I had butterflies dancing in my stomach. "Wheatly? You are grown." I stepped back to check out my little brother.

He raised an eyebrow trying to maintain his mean composure, but soon his cheeks spread revealing his white teeth. I gave him a long overdue hug. We wept and sniffled.

"I'm sorry for sending you all those hate letters. I was mad that you just left and never looked back."

"No… I deserved all twenty-five of them. I missed you," I admitted.

"You didn't act like it." Wheatly wiped with the back of his hand. "But I understand why you did it. It's better than being here."

"No. There is no excuse to not return home for all these years."

"Yes. You're a scientist that cures people. That's amazing."

I released him and said, "Ah, Wheatly I know when I left, I promised that I will be… well, I'm—I am not exactly." I lifted the green binder up and said, "I am working on doing that now."

He rested his hand on my shoulder. "Wellington. You'll always be my hero because you take chances and always kept your promises." He patted me on the shoulder and walked into the kitchen. My heart sucked into my stomach. I flipped through the green binder while my mind raced with memories of Israel, but I re-focused my thoughts on the delicious, southern, homemade food that Mama and Janice started to prepare and the nicely decorated living room, which seemed smaller than I remembered.

It was the only place where our family came together to decompress from the day, putting our differences and worry aside. Wheatly and I would sit on the green carpet that had now been replaced by brown hardwood floors. I tapped my foot against it and wondered how anyone could be comfortable sitting on it to watch television. The couch had been replaced with leather, which was more comfortable than the old fabric couch.

However, I missed the old white fabric with printed flowers decorations. I stretched my arms to the ceiling. My hands touched it. I walked over to the pictures displayed on the wall, bigger to smaller. One was of Wheatly and me at our school's science fair and the other of us outside digging in my garden. Dad held a shovel in his hand, wearing a sunhat that halfway covered his face.

Mama held an award in one photo while standing next to an older man dressed in a suit. His arms wrapped around her and they cheesed for the camera. However, before I could get more in depth in thought, I saw the black-and-white photo that Pastor Patrick took of Dad, Wheatly, Aaron, and me in Israel. My heart fluttered as I remembered how simple life was back then and how motivated I was to discover a plant at that camping site.

«CHAPTER THREE»

TEN YEARS AGO, in the spring of 1989, the dry heat and sweat stuck to my skin in the Judean Desert. I sat on a huge round rock with my arms wrapped around my knees gazing into the distance at the mountains as I thought about my purpose in life. *What divine plan did God have for me on this earth and what was it that was manifesting inside of me and consumed my dreams?*

I wanted it to be big, like solving life's biggest problem, death, and disease. I wanted it to surround my passion, plants because my granddad owned a vegetable garden. The smell of fresh water grass, and the wind brushing through trees calmed me. A lot of medicines come from natural substances, and that is why studying plants seemed purposeful. I felt the sunshine upon my face, and I imagined it was God approving my purpose in life. I meditated on Dad and me exploring the hills in the distance.

I saw the sun's shadow slowly creeping over the land, and the caves in the distance began to vanish. I envisioned ancient armies traveling on foot during the night to take over palaces while the villagers slept. The next morning, three thousand warriors stood outside of their gates ready for battle.

"Grab the wood!" someone yelled in the distance.

No wildlife. No sign of life at all except the hotel in the far distance, the chatter from the camping ground, the buzzing from the bugs, and the bubbling and salty fragrance of the Dead Sea. Nothing that I hadn't seen already. I toyed with a rock inside of my hand, and then threw it at the ground. *Thump*. It echoed back, and my imagination went wild again.

The red rock covered the Judean Desert for miles and miles and what lay underneath it interested me. Explorers found lost cities and ancient artifacts all over Israel. My heart thumped with excitement as if God led me here for a reason. Maybe He wanted me to find something great on this ancient land.

"What are you staring at?"

Someone's knuckles tapped the rock that I sat on. I turned around, and It was my cousin, Aaron. He was several inches shorter than my five feet seven inches, but when he stood next to me, his broad-shouldered and muscular chest made me look like a tall, bony beanpole.

"The mountains. They don't have any vegetation, no green, no plants." The words slithered out of my mouth with pain because I hoped that when Dad and I explored, I would find a plant to take back home. However, the rays of the sun slowly shifted, and the moon and stars came into sight. I fixed my blue tank top and wiped my sweaty hands on my blue jeans.

"I bet they have a lot of rocks. Ancient people used rocks for everything," Aaron replied. He tapped the rock that I sat on with his knuckles. "This one is solid."

Wheatly, with a high-pitched and less mature voice, said from the left side of the rock, "I wondered if ancient people used chemicals?" Wheatly collected dirt into his hands. He wore blue jeans, hi-top sneakers, and a bright green T-shirt that said, 'I love Israel.' "If we create a fire, then maybe we can perform an experiment on something around here." Wheatly jumped up, throwing the dirt into the air, and I turned my face from it.

"Hey," I said, ruffling his wavy hair. "Dad is not going to let us create our own fire experiment. Besides, we're going to be too busy exploring," I grunted and pushed the white T-shirt wrapped around my head up.

"He's never going to go exploring in the dark," Wheatly said, and he was right.

I rolled my shoulder back and said, "If you want to find an ancient rock for your rock collection, Aaron, if you want to find something to experiment on, Wheatly, and if I want to find at least one plant species in this desert, then I say let's go exploring without Dad." They jumped with excitement. Then I said, "Aaron," while gesturing that I meant that he and I should go, but not Wheatly.

"What! Come on." Wheatly widened his arms, disgusted and mad.

"You're too young, and you will hold us back."

"No, I won't. I promise I won't. Please let me go." He fell on to his knees and begged.

"No, Wheatly."

"Welly, it's dark. We will get lost or something." Aaron shivered.

They squabbled on and on, and I asked, "Guys, do you even know your purpose in life?"

"What?" Aaron squinted, and Wheatly scratched his head, wondering what purpose meant.

"Go figures. For example, God wants me to own my own plant scientific company that cures diseases."

"How do you know that?" Wheatly yelled.

"Shut up!" I snapped. "Because I feel it, I want it, and I know it." I cleared my throat, "Why can't I find out a way to stop diseases from happening?"

"Oh, me next!" Wheatly waved his hand as I pushed his hands away from me. "I want my purpose to be a hero ... a superhero. I want to save the world."

"You can't be a superhero without powers, Wheatly!"

"Sure I can. What if I haven't discovered my powers yet?"

"Boys!" a voice shouted. Dad stood outside of the camping ground as the teenagers behind him gathered wood from the truck.

"Saved by the bell," I puffed. He motioned us to come over.

"Geez, Uncle Robert's going to give us the talk again." Aaron pouted. He never liked being in trouble, especially from my father.

I hopped off the rock, and we all raced to Dad who stood with both fists glued to his hips.

He rested his massive arm on my shoulder and said to us, "Boys, I need you guys to participate in the activities." He eyed us. "Please?" he begged us as we gave him a pleasant grin.

The rest of the youth group participated in the activities. Each year, Olive Baptist Church planned a ten-day camping expedition for the youth boys to explore the ancient sites where Jesus traveled.

A farmer discovered the scroll of Isaiah in the Qumran Caves a few miles from Masada and from our camping site. During the ten days, we visited monuments and then prayed. We visited museums and then prayed.

We visited Christian's homes and then prayed. Rode camels and blah blah . . . then prayed. Then there was Dad's famous campfire story on the last night, that he trapped me into performing every year.

"Is everything okay, Robert?" Youth Pastor Patrick joyfully waved his hands at us, and we all waved back. "Yeah! Just having a talk with my boys."

"Say cheese!" He snapped a quick picture of us smiling together before walking off.

Dad, an elder at Olive Baptist Church, and one of the leaders of this expedition said, "Participate. Make friends. Less science talk," he grumbled and pushed Aaron and Wheatly forward while holding me back.

"Wellington, you promised me that you would try this year. This whole trip you were grumpy and antisocial." He crossed his arms.

"Maybe because you said we would go exploring and find cool desert plants this time around."

"We will."

"When? We leave tomorrow," I whined, and Dad lifted his head.

"Okay. Once we finish setting up, we have an hour to kill before the sunlight completely fades. Just you and I, but we can't go too far." He smiled and moved me towards the campsite, and I staggered to the rest of the group.

Wap. Wap. The wind slammed against the tents making them bounce in and out.

"I guess it's going to be a windy night. Let's make sure our tents are tied down, or we'll be sleeping in the caves tonight," Youth Pastor Patrick joked as he pointed to the caves in the hill.

No one could see them, but I curiously wondered if cave men lived inside and watched us like ants at night. And during the day, black-polka-dots, caves, covered the hills. *Do caves have hidden treasures or plants?* I pondered

"Don't worry. I'm sure the mad black scientist would save us," a squeaky voice from a few feet over cracked a joke. A red-curly-haired boy named Christopher Forrest hit fists with his friends as they laughed at us. The other teenagers made fun of us and called us geeks, nerds, and weirdos. However, they didn't call us punks. I took my finger and outlined my throat as Aaron took his fist and smashed it in the palm of his hand. Christopher's giggles went to quivers as he quickly tied down the tent.

"I kind of liked the name Mad Scientist," I said to Aaron and Wheatly.

"Yeah, it makes us sound crazy for science." Wheatly rolled his head around in a circle.

"Christian scientist," Aaron spoke up. "Because science can prove things." We fist bumped in the middle and made a secret handshake. Wheatly immediately ran off to help with setting up the tents as Aaron collected rocks from the fire pit.

"No sense of letting this burn," he murmured as he used the bottom half of his shirt to carry them back to our tent.

A few people carried firewood from the jeep and dumped it into the fire pit as some helped with setting up the tents. They sorted bags of food on the navy-blue blanket: hot dogs there, buns here, and marshmallows, gram crackers, and chocolate for the dessert over there. They placed the thicker logs twenty feet away and around the fire pit for us to sit on when we sang and shared stories.

Our time had come to an end in Israel, and from what I heard, everyone enjoyed touring King Herod The Great's abandon palaces, and seeing ancient monuments, hearing stories of King David, and praying where Jesus stood. However, I did not care because I had experienced it, seen it, tasted it, and felt it for the past five years. I begged Dad for me to not to come on the trip, but he convinced me that Wheatly and Aaron would make this one more exciting.

"Hey Wellington, give us a hand over here," Pastor Chris called me. He had a hammer in his hand, and one kid held down a large nail.

I headed over to him, and he said, "Hold on to this rope, we want to make this is tight and steady." I grabbed the rope as Pastor Chris hammered. The kid released the nail and watched it go deeper and deeper into the ground. A big gust of wind scattered the plates, cups, and a few hats around the camping ground, and without warning, the rope popped, and a piece of strand deeply punctured my hand.

"Ah!" I cried. I held my hand tight to stop the pain from raging, but blood oozed out, and I panicked. The adults quickly ran over to me and tried to comfort me. The kids tried to explain what happened.

"The wind, then *pop*," A kid stuttered. But my hero, Dad, ran over with a first aid kit and a water bottle. He poured water on to my wound, poured alcohol, which stung, and then bandaged my hand.

"Hey, you're all right, big man. Just a small cut." He patted me on my shoulder and left just like a superhero completing a heroic act.

"Wellington." Pastor Chris's hand rested on my shoulder. "How are you? You're hanging in there?" he questioned, feeling sorry for almost chopping my hand off with his lousy tent.

"Yes, sir." I smiled and positioned my hand awkwardly on my lap.

"Great!" He began to walk away.

"However," I said. "Repetition on ancient grounds is an aspiring boy scientist's worst best friend." I grinned, hoping to lure him into an enticing conversation.

"Is that right?" He stopped, knowing I wanted to share more.

"Of course. The same routine of visiting the same places. Gathering wood to add to the bonfire. Setting up the tents in a circle, resembling our own colony is boring. What we should be doing is exploring the grounds."

He squinted with amusement. "You firecracker." He hurried away.

"I can't find a shrub anywhere!" I was forced to come here and agitated that I left my plant collection in the hands of my mother at home. I thought of how thirsty my plants might be.

"Where are all the cactus, right?" I yelled louder, hoping that someone would agree with me. However, they ignored my plea.

Gary Foster tapped me on my shoulder. "So, you're going to college next year. Which school?" He beamed from ear to ear.

"I am not going to college."

"You're not? I would think you of all people would—"

"I applied to the Elite Scientific Program," I bragged, referring to the most highly respected federal government program. They developed and trained aspiring scientists to use their knowledge and skills to help the Federal Government and The Scientific Alliance Agency to make the world a better place through science. They prepared trainees to study environmental cases that are indescribable and considered unknowable to the public.

"Oh cool. Sounds super hard," Gary said.

"Only if you're not smart." Silence remained between us for a moment as he waited for me to ask the same question.

"Umm. Did you get into college?" I asked.

"You're funny. Of course, I did. I'm going to Old Dominion University to study law and criminal justice. I want to be a detective someday," he proudly declared as he tapped an imaginary badge.

"Good for you."

"I would ask you the same question, but I think I know you're going to study earth science." He cringed and hoped he guessed right.

"Just plants."

"Oh, so is it a program or a college program thing?"

"Both. I will be working for the government while studying plant paleobotany or plant morphology." I paused, giving him an opportunity to leave the conversation.

He quickly sighed, "Oh . . . okay. I'm going to help out over there." He pointed.

I nodded and whispered, "Yep."

He hurried away to join the campfire games.

"What you talking to him about?" Aaron asked. He and Wheatly shared a log. Aaron already had a plate of food on his lap with a half-eaten hot dog and chips.

"Nothing much," I said because Aaron's attention span couldn't handle my plant theory.

"Oh, you're thinking about what to study in college?" He took another bite and munched. "Study the traveling one." Ketchup squeezed out the corner of his mouth.

"Study paleobotany?" I turned away from him for getting the name wrong. "That would be my dream to study historical plants." I thought about my purpose as an archeologist traveling the world digging up lost and forgotten flowers and trees fossils. To know that these plants once dominated the earth's surface millions of years ago until the weather turned on them, forcing them beneath the soil and rock, smashing them like gum on the sidewalk.

"No! I like the genetics and slimy stuff. You can be a hero if you create medicine." Wheatly leaned over Aaron and reached his dirty hands toward my face. I smacked them away and explained, "Studying plant morphology will be my better solution because I'll be able to explore plant species' genetic similarities." I imagined myself discovering medicine on a petal that can cure a rare disease or studying why diverse leaves have the same genetic coding.

"They are both my dream jobs," I confessed to the both of them.

CLAP CLAP CLAP. "Amazing Grace how sweet is the sound ..." The youth leaders sang and motioned everyone on the logs.

"I once was lost, and now I am found." Dad's singing voice vibrated the air and overshadowed the other leaders' voices. Dad, more mature and wiser than the bunch, always shared stories of the good ole days in summer Bible school.

"Dad!" I grunted. He pointed to his palm and mouthed, *Sorry*.

"Your hand is hurt," Aaron translated his message and my heart sunk. Another wasted trip, and I refused to participate in the group activities.

"Here." Aaron gave me a tiny twig that he found during his rock search. I broke it in half with my two fingers and dropped it. His mouth fell open and then his face crumbled into a fake cry that made me laugh.

"Shut up." I knocked his shoulder with mine.

I grabbed dirt from the dusty ground and repositioned away from the group.

I noticed critters crawling on the log, and I imagined them entering my pants. I refocused my attention to the sand trickling out of my hands and between my fingers. The texture was cold, dry, and lifeless, glistening in the moonlight. To relax my thoughts from insects, I followed the dirt as it flew out of my hand and into the night's breeze. The breeze mixed its nightly potion with the smoke from the bonfire, burning hot dogs, marshmallows, and the smell of salt from the Dead Sea. However, all of this soothed my senses.

The bonfire's orange and yellow flames danced in the wind as if they praised the stars above. The Big Dipper and David's Belt beautified the campsite above. The stars grew brighter and very noticeable by the minutes and the moon dominated the night.

Usually, I would nudge Aaron to stop staring up at the sky, but now, I understood why. The solar system and the universe created a sense of a whole new world that needed to be explored.

Suddenly, I heard nothing. The chatter among the group stopped. I lowered my head forward, and everyone stared at me. I used my senses to figure out what happened and nothing but giggles were directed at me. Dad, who stood on the other side of the bonfire, caught my eyes with his. His face shined with embarrassment. I smiled back, unaware of the situation. *Was he talking to me?*

My mind entertains the thought of plants, especially when there's nature all around me, and how precious plants and now, stars are. Did you know that plants could live up to—See! I did it again. I slowly turned my bright smile to Aaron and Wheatly sitting next to me so they could fill me in on what I missed, but their guilty giggles turned my smile sour. I knew exactly why their grin stretched from ear to ear and why their tummies burst with laughter. The joke was on me.

Dad's famous campfire story had begun. Stories that he wouldn't let twiddle away but told as a tradition each year. The time when he bought two parakeet birds named Chat and Rabbit for our home garden.

"Come on, son, we don't have all night." He urged me as twelve youth kids chuckled at him and me. He fidgeted with the script in his hand, and everyone probably thought that his own sons had enough of his imagination, and I questioned if they were wrong.

"But my hand. Remember?" I translated the same message that he sent to me.

"Ah, this will do you some good. Get up here now." Everyone sat silently, and the mood became tense.

I struggled with disobedience and quickly relented, "Wheatly gets jealous when you pick me for stuff." I grabbed Wheatly by his left arm, purposefully squeezed Aaron in the middle, and I whispered, "If you want to go on the adventure with Aaron and me, then you'll do the stupid show." Wheatly's head lifted with joy.

"You promise?" he held up his pinky.

"Pinky swear." Risking the pain from my hand, I hooked mine around his.

"Dad, please!" Wheatly begged.

"Well, if it's okay with Wellington, then get up here and lets begin the show." The kids cheered on Wheatly as he pumped his arms up into the air, getting them hyped for another Chat and Rabbit tale. Pastor Patrick and Chris clapped, relieved.

He told the story of how he bought me my first pet birds at age five and how I named them Chat and Rabbit. Apparently, I was terrible at naming things back then. He would tell Aaron and I that Chat and Rabbit would escape during the night to solve mysteries. Aaron and I used to believe these stories until we realized that animals do not talk, but Dad insisted Chat and Rabbit did. He claimed that he heard them one night discussing their next adventure and when he poked his head into my bedroom, they started chirping again.

As a thirteen-year-old kid, I attended these camping trips and acted out the scenes from my Dad's Chat and Rabbit scripts. Now, as an aspiring eighteen-year-old scientist, I was too old for make believe, so passing on the torch only seemed right. Plus, Wheatly seemed perfect for the role. Wheatly followed five years behind me, and he enjoyed every moment of it. He gracefully hopped from one side of the fire pit to the next as Dad read from the script.

"Adventure?" Aaron whispered to me. "What about your hand?"

"It's not broken."

"What about Uncle Robert?"

"He didn't say we couldn't go."

"Where are we going? Is it safe?" He glimpsed over his shoulder at the darkness that surrounded us, and he stuttered, "I hardly can see anything."

"I'm sure they'll be plenty of rocks for you to collect if you go." I showed him a pebble in the palm of my hand and watched Aaron's scary thoughts vanish into thin air. He picked up the pebble and analyzed. He stared at rocks for hours and wondered how each type of rocks had been formed. Aaron lifted the pebble up to the sky to measure it against the moon. "Do you think the moon is composed of the same minerals that this rock has?" he marveled, and I squinted and thought how Aaron's overwhelming rock collection didn't compare to my small plant garden back home.

Aaron's dad, my uncle, would have enjoyed Aaron's appreciation for nature. He died in a car crash a week after Aaron graced this earth. Ever since then, Aaron's eyes have been glued to the sky, gazing up into the heavens. Thankfully, Dad stepped up and practically raised Aaron within our family. In fact, the story of Chat and Rabbit becoming natural scientists to save the farm from producing bad crops established Aaron's and my love for science. I guess that story molded my and Aaron's life.

Our whole life we dreamt of solving diseases, determined to discover rare things in the world and to make a name for ourselves. We both wanted to make it in the World Book Encyclopedia and most of all, receive a Nobel Prize before we reached the age of thirty. Suddenly, I remembered that Aaron ignored my purpose question, so I asked again. "What is your purpose in life?"

"Oh, jeez, I don't know."

"Come on, Aaron. Don't you want to be a scientist too? You like rocks, and you love the moon. Those are big goals there." Aaron twitched from side to side as he tapped his heel against the log. Finally, his mouth opened, and I waited for something amazing, creative, or challenging to fall out, but he said, "To survive, I guess." And he shrugged.

I grumbled, "That isn't a purpose."

"Chill. I see my mom struggle to provide for her and me every day, so I just want to survive through life. It's hard you know."

I rested my arm on Aaron's shoulder and said, "To survive and to be my partner in science."

We both smirked at each other when Wheatly sat next to Aaron and leaned over to me. "Mission Completed."

"Okay, boys." Pastor Patrick stood up and smacked off the dirt from his pants. "We will wake up bright and early tomorrow, eat breakfast, and visit Jerusalem for shopping. Then we will head home."

I stretched my arms to the sky and then swung them from side to side to loosen up my back. Curiosity filled my mind as darkness completely covered the land, mountains, and caves. Everyone helped clean up before running towards the tents.

"Come on, boys." Dad motioned for us to get inside; one adult supervising four kids in a tent. We shared a tent with my father and Gary; they slept like logs and snored every night, and I hoped they would do the same again tonight.

Dad stopped me before entering the tent. "Welly, I know I promised that we would explore more this trip." He grinned, feeling guilty for breaking his promise. "But, look at it this way. We can always try again next year."

"I'm going to be in the Elite Scientific Program and wouldn't have time to come back next year."

"Well, just maybe." He patted my shoulder and went inside of the tent.

I grabbed Aaron and Wheatly by the arms before they entered and whispered, "Bright and early we explore."

«CHAPTER FOUR»

THE RAYS OF THE SUN crept into our tent's four corners as I waited all morning for dawn to make an entrance. It wasn't too bright to wake the adults but enough to see the fields. Dad loudly snored, and Gary was tucked deep into his sleeping bag wheezing as well. I checked my watch, and it read 6:30AM.

I rolled over to a goofy grin and two white eyeballs with crust between each corner staring back at me.

"You ready?" Wheatly whispered.

"Shush," I said, as I quietly stood up, stretched, and motioned for him to tap Aaron gently who snored. Aaron peeled open his eyes as I stood towering over him. I secretly motioned for them both to meet me, quietly, outside of the tent. I took Dad's belt and made a sling for my arm and wrapped my hand in a fatigue bandana. I grabbed my khaki pants, a white T-shirt, and quietly tiptoed out of the tent.

I cradled my hand against my body as the cold air soothed the pain that tickled all around it. The smell of last night's fire and the Dead Sea still roamed the atmosphere. I slipped on my pants and my shirt, and I opened my book bag and made sure that my *Back to the Future* exploring kit lay inside. It came with a mini flashlight, a compass, a plastic pocketknife, and small plastic jars for samples. Finally, Wheatly and Aaron joined me wearing thermal underwear underneath their sweat pants and shirt.

"Where are we going?" Aaron whispered as he focused on the empty plains under the rising sun. As the sun grew brighter, the shadows slowly disappeared off the beautiful red rock.

"And what are you wearing?" Wheatly giggled at my sling.

"Shut up." I shoved him and approached Aaron and exclaimed, "There." I pointed to caves in the distance.

"Caves? Wellington, why not explore the dirt over there . . . much closer? The caves are super far. We will never make it."

I juggled Aaron's suggestion against my desire.

"No. Since we only have an hour or so, let's explore the hill in the middle. Right there!" I pointed to the left of the mountain. My imagination went wild, and I started running towards it when a voice yelled, "Wait for me." We turned to see Gary running towards us.

"I thought you were sleeping?" I mumbled and wondered how he knew about our plan.

"I was, but I had to take a leak and saw you guys running away. What you gonna do over there?"

"Exploring and we don't have room for another person." Wheatly stepped forward protecting his spot in the pack.

"What Wheatly is trying to say is exploring might not be your style."

"Sure it is." His finger tapped his head. "Detective, remember?" Then Gary patted my shoulder and headed towards the hill. "If you find something, I want to find it too."

"Okay." I took a deep breath, hoping that no one from the campsite saw us heading to the hill. "Let's hurry up."

"Last one there is a rotten egg," Gary teased. He ran towards the hill and Wheatly took on the challenge.

* * *

We were all sweaty from the sunlight beaming down on us, and we had come too far to turn back. We followed the steep winding path up the hill. From the peak, the campsite and the tents looked like tiny blocks. I followed Wheatly up the dirt trail and steps that led us to the closet caves, but I wanted to go to the middle cave that had a unique shape.

"Welly." Aaron's voice made me cringe because I knew he wanted to go back.

I turned to him very calmly, and he scolded, red in the face from the sunlight beating down on him, "Why are we skipping all of these caves? Explore them!"

The middle cave called my name; its strange origami shape drew my curiosity.

"Can we please stop here?" Aaron begged.

"You need to man up, Aaron," I yelled back at him. He had become more and more scared lately.

Wheatly stood ahead of us, inches from the middle cave. "Hurry," he yelled down to us as we traveled quicker up the trail. He poked his head in and then vanished. Suddenly, thoughts of *what if* popped in my mind.

"Wheatly!" I shouted and wondered if he had entered a mountain lion's den. Dad would never forgive me if I allowed something terrible to happen to Wheatly. Aaron and I quickly ran up the hill. I poked my head inside of the cave, and there was nothing, but red rocks. Aaron walked in collecting samples into his pocket. I flopped down on to my butt as everyone examined the empty cave.

Gary lagged behind, "Nothing in here! Let's go to the top." He ran out as Wheatly raced passed him. I hopped on to my feet because those words sounded like angels singing in my ears. I followed them to the very top, to the cave shaped like a triangle. I ran past Gary and Wheatly and hoped that the cave contained everything that I wished for.

I entered, and the smell of wet rock filled my nose. A small amount of soil covered the ground. The cool moisture clustered the air, and the desert heat was nowhere inside. *Where is the moisture coming from in this arid environment?* I wondered.

"Wow, it's beautiful." Wheatly stepped inside gazing at the hard shiny rocks.

"Not much in here either. No hidden treasures." Gary stepped in for a moment and then headed back outside. "Hey! Over here." He waved to everyone at the campsite. I rushed over to him.

"Be quiet. What are you doing?" I stopped his arm from waving like a maniac.

"Why?" he questioned as he yanked back his arm. We watched the kids from our youth group stampede towards us from the camping site, and below where I stood, Aaron struggled to make it to the top. I went to the back of the cave to collect some native shrubs from the corner before the rest of the group came inside and destroyed it with their touchy-feely hands.

"Wellington," someone called my name. My heart pounded.

"Over here," the voice said again. I followed the sound to a curved wall hidden from the cave's entrance. At first glance, it seemed just like a wall, but once I roamed my hands upon it, I felt emptiness. "Come over here." Wheatly poked his head out to me.

"Wheatly. Come from out of there now."

"Come on, Welly." He squeezed his body further into the next section, and my heart skipped a beat. My body trembled, and I dropped everything as nerves trickled down every layer of my skin. I couldn't see him anymore, and his voice faded away behind the rock layer. I couldn't help but think *what if something awful waited for Wheatly, or what if someone left an ancient trap or a hole?*

"Wheatly, come back! I can't see you." I reached inside, but I couldn't feel him. I quickly opened my bag and grabbed a flashlight.

"Where's Wheatly?" Aaron huffed and puffed as he leaned against the wall.

"Behind the rock."

"What!"

"Calm down." I turned the toy light on and pointed it into the dark, afraid to witness what lurked behind my brother. I just knew something scary like a mountain lion or an anaconda or—"Plants?"

The light fell upon Wheatly's grin as vines and leaves dangled over him and up and down the wall. Immediately, I took off my sling and squeezed my body between the walls into the next section with Wheatly.

"You got to be kidding me!" Aaron shouted from the other side of the wall. His voice sounded so far away.

"Hello over there." My voice echoed as Wheatly laughed to himself.

"Come on, Aaron," Wheatly pleaded with him.

"Oh, no way. Not me."

As Wheatly pleaded with Aaron, I examined the healthy leaves covering the cave's walls. They amazed me. I wondered how they grew in complete darkness and where they were getting their sunlight and water? Before I walked further into the cave, I listened for sounds of growling and snarling and heard nothing.

"It's safe, Aaron. Come on!" I yelled behind me.

Once Aaron made his way inside of the cave's hidden section, we both pointed our flashlights towards the middle of the den.

"Wait!" I grabbed Aaron's flashlight to point in the same direction as me.

"What is it?" Wheatly stepped forward, but I stopped him before he invaded *its* personal space.

"Looks like a tiny tree to me," Aaron answered and waited for confirmation.

My facial expression revealed my own cluelessness. I twitched and scratched my chin as the little tree glowed like a lava lamp. We stepped backward, ready to escape. Our flashlights beamed upon the tiny tree, and we slowly took another step back. However, I stopped my feet from moving backward and forced them to inch forward.

"Wellington, what are you doing?" Aaron whispered. "It looks poisonous."

The tree glowed with a reddish orange color. My hands trembled as I shined my flashlight two inches from the tiny tree, discovering that it sat on a pile of dirt that came to my thigh. Aaron pointed his flashlight downward.

"It's sitting on a hump," Wheatly said. He stepped forward, and then Aaron inched toward us with one leg back ready to run at any moment.

"Here, Wheatly." I handed him my toy flashlight as I searched in my backpack for Dad's heavy-duty flashlight. Three flashlights illuminated the hidden section of the cave's walls. Roots went from the tiny tree's hump, across the cave's floor and up the walls with small leaves covering the area.

"What the heck is it?" Wheatly asked.

"Help me count the roots." I counted five, no ten, maybe twenty roots spreading from the dirt hump and creating thick lines on the ground. I stepped even closer to the tiny tree and measured its size against my fingers and felt the heat from the reddish-orange colors changing to bluish and greenish.

Tiny Tree's whole trunk could fit in the palm of my hand and small leaves filled the branches. It was not an ordinary tree, but mature, grand in stature, and confident of its own existence. My fears disappeared, and a gentle sensation covered us all. Tiny Tree stood tall despite its size, and it twinkled like a star in the middle of the night.

"Can trees grow in the dark?" Wheatly asked me.

"Or live in the dark?" Aaron wondered.

I answered my previous question, "I'm going to study paleobiology."

"What?" Aaron questioned.

"I'm going to be a plant paleobiologist."

The tiny tree changed my perspective of plant life by its glorious presence. Aaron's shoulder touched mine, and I immediately knew the little tree made us all feel safe.

"How could this be left alone here?" I admired.

Aaron replied, "Well, it was waiting for someone to discover it. It's your purpose remember?" He knocked shoulders with me. I smiled. I had always dreamt of discovering a plant and naming it after me. My heart jumped with joy, and my spirit rejoiced.

At that moment, shimmery green and blue light from the tiny tree exploded all over the walls, and we watched in awe. Different colors reflected and beams bounced between the walls.

"Look." Wheatly held his hands up at the light, and he and Aaron made images with their hands, laughing and enjoying the moment.

I sensed the tree enjoyed our presence too as it sparkled and celebrated our presence.

"Whoa." A curious voice snapped us out of our daze, and both flashlights turned to Gary behind us. "Hey, it stopped glowing," he blurted. We turned back to the tiny tree, which hid in the darkness.

Aaron shined his flashlight on it, and everything returned to normal.

"What's making it glow?" Gary examined. Aaron and Wheatly both looked at me, and we realized trees do not glow. So, we all searched for the light source.

Wheatly and Aaron followed the roots up the wall with the flashlight when their light fell on a sketch figure with two lines across it.

"Guys?" Aaron's voice quivered. He stepped backward towards the exit.

We turned to a giant, eerie mark on the wall.

"Here's another one." Wheatly pointed with his flashlight on the opposite wall.

"And another." Aaron found another creepy sketch on the back wall that was bigger than the two on the sidewall of the cave. The sketch markings on the rear wall stuck out like a statue. Gary walked closer and stood underneath the abnormally shaped figure. He pointed his finger up, traced the markings that looked like a head, and then outlined the bigger circle that resembled a body.

"It's not human." He determined because the figure had no arms or legs.

He used his finger to show where the two lines intersected beneath the small circle on the bigger circle.

"It looks like an X," Gary explained with his finger still pointed at the figure.

"X, like do not enter?" Aaron panicked.

"Or X marks the spot." Gary clapped his hand and ran past us. "Wait until everyone sees what I found!" He vanished to the other side and screamed for the leaders to hurry up.

Aaron and Wheatly rushed to exit. Fear crept back inside of them, and they forgot the joy we had experienced moments before Gary climbed in. However, I didn't forget. It was my discovery, and I needed to take Tiny Tree with me. I fell to my knees and sawed the roots with my pocketknife.

"What are you doing?" Aaron yelled from halfway out of the hidden cave.

"I can't leave this here. You even said it was meant to be discovered by me," I pleaded. Aaron and Wheatly saw blood draining from my hand and my teeth gripping my lip.

Wheatly ran towards me. "It's going to die if you cut it like that, right?" He pondered.

His words didn't faze me. The thought of adding the tree to my plant collection back home gave me zealous faith. Wheatly dug deeper into the ground. He picked up my pocketknife to slice Tiny Tree's roots from the wall. Aaron kicked his feet against the ground and grunted, and then he helped remove Tiny Tree's roots from the hump.

"I have to cut it far enough so it can still grow." I grabbed the pocketknife from Wheatly and measured the roots as if performing surgery. I held the knife in my hand, took a deep breath, counted to three, and then cut.

We heard voices from the other kids getting closer.

"We have to hurry." I sliced the ground away from the roots up to the tree. Wheatly reached, but I yelled, "Stop!" and my voice echoed.

"Don't touch it. It might be dangerous," I explained as Wheatly stepped back with both hands up. I reached into my backpack and grabbed a comic magazine.

"Hey, that's mine!" Wheatly yelled.

"I'll buy you another one." I ripped the pages and wrapped the tree inside of it, pulled it away from the hump that it sat, on and immediately placed it into my backpack. I scooped dirt into my bag and dusted the sides off. A sense of accomplishment and defeat at the same time wrestled inside of me, but I shook it off. I glanced at the figure on the back wall, and I saw it clearly through the darkness.

The human-like-figures, held swords across its body in a running stance—ready for war. The figures on the sidewalls stood in the same position but carried a torch. Small pins-and-needles went from my head all down my body.

"What's wrong?" Aaron wondered why my joyful expression went away. However, if I told him what I saw and felt, he would never let me keep the tree, so I kept quiet.

"You boys okay?" Pastor Patrick poked his flashlight and head inside, snapping me out of my trance.

"Yes, sir," Aaron and Wheatly yelled together, hiding me behind their back as I gently zipped up my bag and placed in on my shoulders.

We followed Pastor Patrick's voice, and Aaron, Wheatly, and I squeezed our way back to the other side. I struggled to get back through, and everyone wondered how I was able to squeeze through the little hole in the first place.

"Kids, are you guys okay?" They patted us on the back, dusting off the layers of dirt.

"You guys look like coal miners," Pastor Chris teased, eliminating the awkwardness of the rescue.

"We found a glowing tree," Gary exploded with excitement. I searched around for Dad, but he wasn't near us.

"I'm going to go find my dad," I blurted. Aaron and Wheatly followed me out of the cave, down the hill, and towards the campsite, proud that we found something unique, and leaving Gary to explain everything to the leaders.

When Pastor Patrick reported the findings to the Israel Antiquities Authority, police cars, news vans, reporters, and archeologists arrived in less than an hour. We watched as the archeologist gently analyzed and discussed the markings on the wall in their work van. They showed us how to collect natural samples and how to store them.

"Yep, high energy," we overheard one scientist tell authorities and then pointed back to the campsite. The medical team tested our whole group for signs of fevers, but we all passed.

We sat inside of the ambulance waiting for the journalist to interview me when Wheatly said, "Welly, your hand?" I held my hand up and examined the lines. No blood, no open wound but a scar. Nevertheless, my hand was perfectly healthy again.

"Did it heal you?" He stepped forward and gripped my legs.

"Ouch and no! The paramedics did it. They gave me some type of medicine," I lied, and his smile turned sour.

I held on tight to my backpack with the precious tree inside as the Tel Aviv journalist interviewed the four of us for the newspaper. We explained how we found the sacred place and what we each saw. After the interview, we noticed Dr. Alex Frazier, an Italian American and senior archeologist admiring the hillside near our campsite. He squinted at us, blocking the sunlight from his eyes, and watched us as we helped take down the tents.

"You boys may have found something unique. I can smell how rich the nutrients are and the story it may tell," he yelled to us and smirked. We smiled back, afraid of leaking knowledge about the tree, but he walked towards us.

"How old are you guys?"

"I'm sixteen," Aaron spoke up.

"Eleven," Wheatly mumbled.

"Seventeen," I whispered. I covered my mouth and swung my backpack behind my shoulders.

"He'll be attending college next year," Aaron said.

"You don't say? You know where you'll be going?"

I scowled at Aaron because I wasn't good at not bragging.

I uncovered my mouth and said, "Elite Scientific Program… well, once I get in."

"You're kidding? That's not college, that's work. They only take the best."

"I got twelve offers from universities that I did not apply to. I think I got it."

"Really?"

"Oh, sorry thirteen. I spoke to my mother yesterday, and she told me I got another offer letter."

"You must have quite a hot pot of brain there. Listen, I'm a professor at the University of Georgia, if the Elite Scientific Program doesn't work out, attend that college, and you could assist me on your own discovery." He winked and continued, "Ask for Dr. Alex Frasier."

One journalist motioned everyone to stand tightly together for the newspaper photo. Our church group, the team of archeologists, and Dr. Frazier smiled for the camera.

"Say Cheese." She took the photo.

Pastor Chris announced, "Okay. We have a flight to catch in two hours!"

Dad squeezed my shoulder. "Boys, meet me in the car. We need to talk." He meandered to the car.

Gary yanked my arm. "I know you took it!" he yelled, and his face, red.

"Took what?" I answered.

"The glowing tree. You stole it. And you're going to be in big trouble because that's a felony here because it's probably ancient."

"An ancient tree?" Aaron replied and scratched his head.

"A glowing tree!" Gary pouted.

"Glowing tree?" Wheatly crossed his arms and tilted his head.

"Oh, don't you guys do it!"

"I think you need a nap, Gary. You had a long day." I wrapped my arms around my two best friends and brother and cousin and headed towards the jeep where Dad waited for us. I opened the jeep's trunk, placed my backpack inside, and checked if Tiny Tree was safely wrapped in the magazine paper.

"Wellington, get in the car before everyone comes inside," Dad called.

I slammed the trunk and hurried to the front seat as Aaron and Wheatly jumped in the back seat.

"What's up, Dad?"

He snapped his head towards me. "DON'T YOU EVER DO THAT AGAIN, DO YOU HEAR ME?" His voice rang through the desert grounds.

I lowered my head, and Aaron's and Wheatly's eyes grew wide.

"Dad. I'm sorry," I whispered. Leaving the campsite without his permission was a black kid's felony in my home.

"I came here with three sons, and I expect to leave here with three. Do you understand me?"

"Yes, sir."

"Do you two hear me?" His eyes struck the rearview mirror at Wheatly and Aaron in the backseat.

"Yes sir," they agreed quickly together.

"Wellington, are you out of your mind? You didn't know what lived in those caves? You could have been bitten or, worse, killed!"

"Dad, I know. I—"

"It's time that you made better decisions now that you're going to college. Adventure this and adventure that is over! That only leads to doing time at the city jail, and I won't have that happen to you." We all sat in silence for a bit. Dad's rage calmed down. I wanted to tell him about the tiny tree, but I didn't have the guts to.

Dad covered his mouth with his handkerchief and coughed repeatedly. He moved it away, and I caught a glimpse of blood.

"Dad?" I whispered.

He balled the handkerchief up and shoved it between the seats. He didn't make a sound but focused on the car's shifters.

"I promise, I will be more responsible." I apologized.

Dad stopped tinkering with the radio and rubbed the back of my neck. "I know you will."

"Sorry, Dad," Wheatly said.

"Sorry, Uncle Robert," Aaron followed. The rest of the kids entered the car, and I gave a shy glimpse of the mountain where Tiny Tree had lived.

"What do you think they will do to it?" I asked Dad.

"Probably dig to see what was buried there. At least the reporters have your four names, the kids who discovered the ancient cave. Great to put on your college application." He winked at me and drove off leading the two vans behind us.

* * *

I tapped my feet while Dad inserted the key into the front door to the house. I was nervous because I wondered if hot climate kept the tiny tree alive, and I didn't know how it would survive in a bipolar state like Virginia.

Dad opened the front door, and I zoomed inside of the house, passing Mama and ran up the stairs. They both shook their head as they embraced one another.

"How was the trip?" Mama felt Dad's sweaty forehead.

"Long," he declared.

"You're hot, are you okay?" She pressed her hand harder against his head, and he nodded a yes.

"I had to keep up with these boys for a whole week." He winked at Wheatly and Aaron.

"Oh, is that what's wrong with Welly?" She yelled up the stairs to me.

"I think Welly was more concerned about you killing his plant collection, Aunt Molly," Aaron innocently mentioned.

"Oh, he was?" Mama frowned.

When I entered my bedroom, my plants stood tall, fed and given sunlight. I felt each plant's leaf in my plant collection: *The ZZ Plants, Jade Plants,* and *my Ponytail Palm Plant* sat on my windowsill.

"I want to introduce you to the newest member of the Kole's plant family," I announced.

I slowly pulled apart my backpack and admired Tiny Tree, carefully wrapped. I showed it off to each plant like a newborn baby.

"Oh, don't be shy." I urged them to wave. The thought of plants having an imaginary language that humans cannot understand kept me intrigued.

"No, no, this is a tree, and it belongs outside with the other trees." Staring through the window and into my garden, I wondered if the plants in my bedroom envied the ones in my yard. Various plants occupied my garden like arborvitae bushes, crabapple and flowering trees, and Asiatic Lily flowers that I nurtured since birth, from little seeds in the palm of my hand.

"Hey, look at the goody-two-shoe plants in Wellington's bedroom, they hardly get any sunlight as we sit here dying for thirst. I bet he waters them every day." I imitated the garden plants as well as the houseplants in my bedroom. "Look at them down there, they look like they are having so much fun in the sunlight, but we are stuck next to the window fighting for sunlight."

My belly rumbled with laughter once again, imagining my plants talking. "Don't worry, this plant will not be in here or in the garden but kept somewhere safe where no one can find it." I grabbed my *Back to the Future* science kit, ready to use it for my first project in the program.

"Well, hello!" I twisted around, and Mama blocked my bedroom door. I dove onto the floor where my backpack laid and stuffed Tiny Tree inside. "I'm searching for some . . . ah . . . money in my bag . . . that I lost, I think," I sneered.

"Congratulations, Mr. Wellington." She wiggled a letter right in front of my face.

"That's fourteen!" I shouted and zipped my bag.

"I lost count." She beamed with happiness as I grabbed the letter, read congratulations, and placed it in my drawer with the rest. I gave her a warm hug that moved her away from the door.

"I have to tell Dad." I threw the bag onto my shoulders, rushed downstairs, and out the back door.

Aaron and Wheatly raced towards me as I lingered outside of the shed.

"So what now? Are you going to plant it in your garden?" Aaron pondered.

"Too much sunlight. It needs to be planted in a dark place."

"Over there in the shade." Wheatly pointed to the corner of the fence where the neighbor Oak tree's branches dangle over. "You can plant it behind the shed."

"That's perfect," I shouted.

I went to the shed, and I cupped my face against the window to see inside of the shed.

"What are you doing?" Aaron wondered as I knocked my knuckles against the shed's door.

"I'm going to plant my tree in here." I opened the shed and entered.

"In the shed?" Wheatly scratched his head as he followed. I turned the light switch on, revealing pottery, Daddy's desk, and a few garden items on the shelves and corner.

"There." I pointed to a vertical closet in the back. I pulled it open, revealing a hole in the bottom where mud and grass had formed.

"How did that get there?" Wheatly leaned in to get a better look.

"I don't know, but daddy never used the closet because of it. I'm going to plant the tree in the hole."

"What if it grows?" Aaron crossed his arms.

"It didn't grow in the cave. I think the darkness kept it tiny. That's why the inside of the shed is the perfect place." I gently took the tree out of the case and unwrapped Wheatly's comic book pages from around it. Wheatly helped me move the roots inside of the hole, then sat the Tiny Tree down, and scooped dirt around it. It sat crooked.

"Now what?" Aaron threw a piece of gum into his mouth.

"What if Daddy decides to fix the hole?" Wheatly probed.

"He's not thinking about this hole," I sneered.

The three of us scrutinized Tiny Tree and wondered if it would survive like that.

"I guess that's it, right?" I shrugged, and they both eyed me wondering what the next step was.

"I guess so. We can check on it tomorrow," Aaron suggested. "I'm sure the roots will dig to find a source…"

"Right!" My brain started to tick again. "All the root has to do is find Fungi underneath the surface, and hopefully the Fungi will connect it to trees to gain nutrients."

Aaron jokingly whispered to Wheatly, "What he said."

"So are we going to keep calling it Tiny Tree or are you going to name it after yourself?" Wheatly excitedly asked.

"Ah, I've been thinking of names that would represent me and the theory of plant intelligence, but I haven't quite figured it out. However, I'll give it a name tomorrow." I closed the closet door, leaving Tiny Tree to rest in complete darkness.

"No one, and I mean no one is allowed in this shed except for me." I gawked down at Aaron and Wheatly. "Especially you, Wheatly."

"Okay," he slurred. "I won't go inside but what if Dad does?"

"Dad only comes inside to read his Bible. If he does, he won't look in the closet. If he does, then I know it's because you said something. Besides, I want to tell Dad about the tree first."

They both followed me out, and I slowly closed the shed's door.

* * *

Night fell, and the breeze through the open window brought fresh air throughout our home. We all sat around the television cooling down from the day's activities. Dad watched the world news, Mama cleaned the kitchen, and Aaron and I played Dominoes on the carpet. BREAKING NEWS: red letters flashed across the television screen catching all of our attention. Mama rushed out of the kitchen to hear what Johnny Roberts, CBS World News anchor, had to say.

"Israel's Prime Minister, Yitzhak Shamir, said a breaking discovery in the Judean Desert could answer questions about the Earth's climate change. This will mark the second biggest discovery there. Craig Folders has the story."

We all glanced at each other and leaned into the television screen.

"Yes, I had the chance to sit down with Prime Minister Yitzhak Shamir and talk a little about the new discovery found by American kids in the Judean Desert."

"Hey, that's us!" Wheatly pointed at the television screen displaying the picture we all took.

"Shush," Dad snapped as he turned up the television's volume.

The Prime Minister sat in a chair surrounded by reporters. "Prophecy?" He chuckled, "The ancient findings in the cave are another case of how Israel is full of ancient hidden treasures. For instance, there are scribbles on the walls that have been studied, analyzed, and compared to historical research about global warming. Scientists discovered that ashes smeared across the walls came from torch-like-sticks that ancient warriors used for war. Therefore, another case of realism," explained Shamir. Video and images taken by an archeologist covered the television screen.

"Archeologist Dr. Frazier from the University of Georgia had more to say about the finding," Craig continued.

"Hey, we met him!" Wheatly shouted.

"Shush!" everyone yelled.

"One thing that's marvelous to me is the soil in the middle of the cave." Dr. Frazier bent down and brushed the dirt gently into a magnifying glass. "We tested it, and it emits a type of radiation that's purer than any soil I have come across. In fact, it might not be soil at all but another substance that's helping these roots and vines grow without sunlight or water."

"That is what I said!" Wheatly yelled.

"BE QUIET!" everyone shouted.

"You're saying that this cave and the findings are not of this world?" Craig questioned as Dr. Frazier chuckled.

"Well, it could be, and it's imperative to handle every part of this discovery with care. We don't know if the soil has any elements that are hazardous or that it might emit poisonous fumes that can harm people. We're hoping for the opposite. However, one thing for sure is it contains a new element that hasn't been seen before."

"This cave seems special. What's going to happen next?"

"Very special and our students at the University of Georgia will study it and try to see if medicine can be made from it. However, we have to work fast because the vines and the soil are dying at a rapid pace, and we don't know why," Dr. Frazier said.

Dad lowered the volume and said, "Wow, boys, you found something special or maybe spiritual that will go down in history, and it's all because of you." He rejoiced, but sadness covered our mood. "What's wrong?" he asked us. Aaron and Wheatly eyes lowered and looked at me.

"He said that the vines are dying and they are missing a source?" Wheatly mumbled.

"Well, that's what happens when things that were untouched get touched. Don't worry. It's a good thing because it may be able to enhance life on earth, and you guys have discovered something that could change the world."

"But…"

"You're right, Dad!" I gushed excitedly and covered Wheatly's mouth.

"He's going to study it at University of Georgia! Maybe we can help?" Aaron announced, and I grabbed his arm.

"Well, it's past our bedtime. Don't want to stay up too late." I headed to the stairs.

"Oh, Son, did you decide on a college yet?" Dad quizzed, and I hesitated.

"I am not going to college. I am going to work for the government once they send me the acceptance letter."

"Okay, but keep it as a plan B. Aaron has a good point about going to UGA."

Aaron blushed, and I snapped, "Okay, Dad!" and stomped up the stairs with Aaron and Wheatly following behind.

"I'm surprised you didn't urge him to choose Morehouse, again." Mama sat down on the couch as Dad grabbed her hand.

"Agh." He twisted in his seat, "As a black man in America today, I feel it's best to be around other strong black men. You know?"

"I understand."

"I didn't have that growing up. My father answered to Mista Billy and Mista Toby as if they were the President of the United States. They were farmers like him. My father never looked them in the eyes because he thought he was less worthy," Dad expressed as Mama held his arms close. "I want him to have confidence and being around people that look like him will give that to him."

"You're talking about our son, Wellington Kole IIII, you know? His brain is big, and his confidence is bigger, thanks to you. Wellington Robert Kole." Mama passionately kissed Daddy.

* * *

Morning broke through the window's curtain. The sun lit the sky, allowing the plants of this earth to submit themselves. "Good morning, Jade." I rolled over to the Jade Plants. "Oh, you want some water? Well, you know you had some yesterday, but I'll give you some if you be nice to Mr. ZZ Plant." I yawned and thought about Tiny Tree in the shed.

I jumped out of my bed, rushed to the window and admired the white shed built like a mini house. The shed was my workshop during the day and Dad's sanctuary at night. He prayed and wrote sermons for most of the night at his small desk in the shed—a place away from family distractions.

I rushed downstairs wearing my pajamas, and I didn't hear pots clicking, water running, and movement on the couch. I slowly entered the kitchen and glimpse inside of the empty bowl. Something was strange.

"Rise and shine!" Wheatly grinned. He and Aaron ate cereal in the dining room.

"Where's Mom and Dad?"

"They left early this morning and said they will be back," Aaron munched.

I headed towards the back door when the front door swung open. Mama and Dad entered holding a few grocery bags.

"You, boys are up early," she said while handing me a bag and proceeding to the kitchen. Dad staggered inside and waited for Mama to make the next move. She shyly grabbed our attention to her unloading the grocery bag

-61-

and motioned for me to place the things into the cabinet. After I helped, I went to the back door.

"Welly. Come in here for a moment." Mama and Dad sat around the dining table. The only time we sat in there together was to eat a fancy meal or discuss serious family business.

My eyes rolled back into my skull. I wondered if Aaron or Wheatly told on me. I shut the back door, and I dragged my feet closer. They appeared sad. Oh, this is serious I felt.

"I'll return it," I sighed.

"Excuse me?"

"The Tree," I confessed, but Aaron shook his head no, and I retracted my statement. "The tree from the neighbor's yard."

"Come in here and sit down, boy," Mama demanded.

I grabbed the bench and sat on it.

"What is this all about?" I demanded.

"Are we going to Disneyland?" Wheatly guessed.

Mama said, "Listen, your father and I visited the doctor today because he didn't feel too well."

That sentence made my heart hit the bottom of my stomach, and I glanced at Wheatly as he and Aaron leaned in.

"The cancer has come back, and his markers are extremely high." Mama held her mouth as Wheatly swished his head to me. My face rested in the palm of my hands.

"What does that mean?" Wheatly shouted. I leaped up from my seat, leaving everyone to talk details.

"Wellington!" Dad chased after me and embraced me as I sobbed.

"I thought that was over," I screamed.

"Son—"

"I should have acted out Chat and Rabbit."

Dad squeezed me tighter. "Son, this isn't your fault. This is life, and God is still in control—"

"God? God did this?"

"No, listen to me. We all knew there was a chance that cancer would return. I'm going to do chemotherapy. However, your mother and I felt it was best to tell you, boys, before we got blindsided with anything."

"Chemotherapy?" Wheatly questioned. "Does that involve chemicals? Maybe I can help." Wheatly ran up to us, and Dad embraced us.

"Wellington, you will have to do more around here now."

"Can the doctors do more?" I sobbed.

"The doctors will do their best, you guys," Mama intervened.

"But you don't look sick," Wheatly said. We lifted Dad's arms and touched his face, hoping they told a cruel joke.

"There is a lot that your mother and I kept from you. Going to Israel with you boys was a major health risk, but I needed to do it for us, and I'm glad we did. Look, you boys are real scientists now. I got to see you discover something that may be big."

Those words from Dad comforted my heart for a moment. Dad widened his arms for Aaron to join and the three of us soaked in his massive arms for almost an hour, crying our eyes out, and asking questions about his health.

Mama made each of our favorite meals that afternoon and encouraged us to get some fresh air. For the whole day, I avoided entering the shed but pounded the baseball against it repeatedly.

"Hey, do you think the fumes from the tree caused this?" Aaron approached, and I ignored him. "Maybe taking the tiny tree was a bad idea and now God is punishing us?"

"Welly, is that true?" Wheatly moaned. "Is God replacing the tiny tree by taking Dad?"

"We have to fix this…" Aaron panicked.

"You guys are stupid. God wouldn't punish us!" I yelled.

"Tell Uncle Robert about the tree so he can help us return it," Aaron suggested.

I rubbed my hand. The scar had faded.

I mumbled, "There is no going back. What is done is done."

"But Welly—"

"Go home, Aaron. There won't be a father here much longer for you to mooch off of." I threw my baseball glove on the ground and ran into the house.

In my bedroom, I dumped all of my various plants into a box. My love for plants came from Dad because he told exciting stories of growing up on a farm.

An unopened letter with a gold seal from The Federal Government sat on my desk. I grabbed the letter, ripped it open, and recited, "Dear Wellington Kole. Congratulations on being a new member of the . . . Or Dear Wellington Kole, you have been accepted to blah blah. Dear Wellington Kole, sorry—" I paused as a large gulp of spit forced itself down my throat. "You have not been selected into the Elite Scientific Program with the United States of America's Federal Government. Thank you for your consideration and please apply again next year." The letter slid out of my hands and on to the floor. A world of pain formed inside of me and one thought exuded my mind and gave me chills; what if Tiny Tree had cursed Dad and me?

Throughout the whole afternoon, I stayed in my bedroom and thought if going to college was the best thing. Aaron sat on the steps all alone. I heard chatter and saw Wheatly had joined him. I wanted to share my rejection letter with Aaron, but when I got the courage, I talked myself out of it. Suddenly, Aunt Pinky ran up the sidewalk from her car and embraced Aaron. He sobbed as she gently soothed him. I realized that I soon would only have one person to hug me when things aren't going my way. Tears filled my eyes as Aaron walked to the car with his mother. He got in, I gently waved goodbye, and he waved back before Aunt Pinky sped off. From that day, I promised myself I would protect my family from Tiny Tree.

«CHAPTER FIVE»

MY MEMORIES faded away, and I stood back in 1999. The black-and-white photo of Dad and us gave me the strength and the motivation to face my biggest secret. I yanked the folder off the couch and sneaked towards the front door when Janice tugged my shirt.

"You're working already?" she complained. I scratched my chin.

"Agh. Just going to review a few things."

"You told me you were not going to—"

"I told you I was going to make peace with my past." I held the green binder up to her. "This is me making peace."

She stepped back and asked, "What do you mean?"

"You know I found soil in the cave, right? Well, when we did the experiments on it, all the results came back negative except for five." I opened the green binder and pointed to all forty-five experimental attempts listed with the word *negative* next to them except for five. "Five test results said the molecules found in the soil could cure various diseases and viruses. However, we ran out of funding, and the SAA refused to give us any more money. If I can prove this theory, baby, I can heal you." She stepped back in awe.

"Why would they stop funding something like this?"

THE REVELATION BEGINS . . .

"I don't know. The school thought it was a hoax after multiple negative results."

"What do you think is missing?"

"I don't know, but I am going to find out. I promise."

"Okay. Okay." She hoped. I closed the folder and kissed her lips.

"Solving this mystery would mean I could save my family and me and not look like a failure."

Janice grabbed my chin.

"Your family is happy that you're home."

"You're right." I took a deep breath.

The front door swung open, and we stepped back.

Aaron stepped through the doorway carrying a grocery bag. He was taller than my five feet seven inches—but then again, most were nowadays—and he obviously lifted weights. He wore a fatigue jacket over a white T-shirt, jeans, and black boots.

I flopped the green binder on to the couch to hug my cousin, but he stepped back. I shoved my hands in my pockets, and he chuckled, "It's really you?"

"You're far from the chubby kid I used to know." I admired his frame.

"And you stopped growing I see?" He frowned. "So, you saved the world, and now you're back? I want to hear all about it. Oh and start with the part with you being too busy to visit home."

An unsettling grin crossed my face. "Work stuff took most of my time," I lied.

"That is no excuse, man. I hope becoming a scientist was worth the lost time," Aaron retorted as he noticed Janice.

"Oh, excuse me, my name is Kingston, but the family calls me Aaron." He stretched his hand out to Janice, and she shook it.

"Oh." I grabbed her by the waist and moved her in front of me. "This is my girlfriend, Janice."

"Forgive me, Janice, for being rude, but Welly was raised better than to abandon his family for all these years . . . So, Wellington has a girlfriend." Aaron stepped back. "A lot has changed, I guess, a lot has changed."

"I said the same thing when Rock Boy had a baby," I mumbled to Janice and Aaron, chin lifted up as he teased, "Okay, Flowerpot Boy."

"Hey, be nice, Aaron." Mama helped carry food wrapped in plastic containers into the house. "We'll have a lot to discuss at dinner."

My Aunt Pinky followed behind her with a bowl of chicken that awoke our tummies.

"Hey, baby. Nice to see you home again." She winked and headed into the kitchen while Aaron followed behind sniffing the scent.

Janice gently wrapped her arms around my waist, and I confessed, "Well, that was unexpected."

"He seemed okay, hurt and shocked, which is normal. Give him some time," Janice comforted me.

"No, I expected this from Wheatly but not Aaron. He's usually chill with things."

"Just be honest and tell them you have been working on the soil project and it has taken years to solve it," she said. "That's not a lie."

I nodded at her.

Mama yelled, "Time to eat!" as I recited the story of why I stayed away for so many years in my mind. Janice pulled my hand towards the dining room.

* * *

Food covered the table like a Thanksgiving feast: macaroni, fried chicken, greens, yams, stew rice, and yellow cake for dessert. Mama's dining room décor reminded me of good and bad memories, and the serious talks around the table and the joyful times we spent together.

My imagination took me back to the days as a young boy sitting around the dinner table with Dad, Mama, and Wheatly. They all listened to me complain about my science classroom debates. My science teacher would ask the class a question about plant anatomy.

Everyone would quickly point to me in the front row, and I'd proudly stand and ask if I could borrow the chalkboard to explain my answer to the class. Impressed, but not surprised, my science teacher would let me teach the lesson. I'd take a few minutes to create a chart and a beautifully drawn flower with 3D layers, which left everyone in awe except for Tommy Lewis. Tommy would always try to challenge my knowledge, and I would have to test his stupidity. Frustrated in explaining that plants are similar to a human body and you can't study the whole anatomy or expect to understand every function, we would argue down the hallway and into the school bus. The conversation would end with me explaining this, again, to my family around the dinner table.

"Just like there are foot doctors, heart doctors, brain surgeons, throat, ear, and nose doctors, there are scientists who focus their studies on each plant's function to understand it completely," I concluded.

Silence dwelled in the air, but in a good way. My parents would smile gracefully and allow me to get all my thoughts out into the open air. Dad chewed viciously on a chicken leg as Mama patted her food with the fork, happy that she raised an intelligent boy.

"You can do anything that you put your mind to," Dad encouraged me.

Where did that passion go? I thought as the cinnamon's scent interrupted my flashback.

Mama passed by with a dish of sweet potatoes, and I wrapped my arms around her and whispered, "This looks amazing, Mom." I kissed her on the forehead, and she wiggled out of my arms to place the dish next to the serving utensil. "This announcement must be big." I rubbed my hands together.

"Mom. I knew you would invite him." Wheatly grunted. He stopped and pouted like a baby.

"Of course she did, why wouldn't she?" I teased.

"Because you're super busy, and I didn't want to bother you with something like this."

"Well, I didn't invite him." Mama giggled.

"Wheatly, come on, man. I love you guys, and I'm happy to celebrate whatever it is with you, especially if Mama was cooking like this," I cheerfully said and pulled Janice's seat out.

"We were going to go to a restaurant for Wheatly to share his announcement, but since all of my boys are home, we are having a feast like old times."

Everyone sat around the table, and Wheatly prayed, "Heavenly Father. Thank you for another day and this amazing food. Most of all, thank you for the unexpected visit from my big brother, Wellington, Amen."

Wheatly's joy brought sadness to me as I thought about being absent from his life for so many years.

"Wheatly, I may have missed birthdays and holidays, but I wasn't going to miss this," I reassured.

"Yep, because Mom was extremely persuasive when she called you," Wheatly grumbled.

"I said I didn't tell him about the dinner," she snapped back at Wheatly.

"Mom, it's fine and don't protect his feelings. She had the right to send me the letter, Wheatly." I pulled the letter from my back pocket and handed it to Mama.

Her expression fell as she accepted it from me while Wheatly said, "I was saving my invite for—"

"I didn't write this letter. This isn't my handwriting." Mama showed it to everyone, and a thick silence covered the room.

"If you didn't write it, then who did?" I turned my attention to Aaron and Aunt Pinky who both shook their heads no. Aaron took a sip of wine, curiosity spread across his face.

"Well, whoever did it, it finally brought you home, and I am grateful. Let's eat." She folded the letter and handed it back to me.

Everyone wolfed down the food, and I sat there lost and confused.

Janice shrugged.

I mumbled to her, "Did you?"

She shook her head no. Everyone chatted amongst each other, and I tapped my fingers against the table. My food remained untouched, and I asked, "So tell us what is so special?"

Mom nudged Wheatly, and he wiped his mouth with a napkin and slowly said, "Okay, Mom and I planned this dinner to tell you guys that I. . . got… accepted into The Elite Scientific Program."

Everyone yelled with joy, except for me. I thought how Wheatly's attention span and intelligence could never compare to mine, and he never showed interest in working for the government or the secret agent's unit.

"Good job, little brother." Jealousy formed in my chest as I raised my glass into the air and nodded at Wheatly.

"Thanks." Everyone patted his shoulder.

"See, I told you that's something worth celebrating," Mama cheered to him.

"So, no college, you're going straight into work?" Aaron paced the floor.

"Both, actually. ESP is paying for me to go to college at National Intelligence University in Washington D.C."

"Man. That's insane! So you'll be working with special agents in the FBI, and you're only twenty-three years old? You must have some serious hot pot of brains." Aaron clapped his hands.

Mama noticed my reaction and spoke up, "Both of my boys are smart." She nodded my way, helping me out of my feelings.

"Of course. But Wheatly, I thought you weren't into college." Aaron sat down.

"I'm not! High school was hard to fit in and . . . I couldn't focus on anything. So when I dropped out, I was determined to give up the science thing."

"Wow, Wheatly . . . I didn't know you had a hard time in school," I grumbled as I played with the peas on my plate.

"Why would you?" Aaron snapped.

"Calm down," Aunt Pinky said. She patted Aaron's hand.

"My girlfriend found the blueprint to my Body Armor experiment and submitted it to the program, and I got in."

"And I am so grateful that she did." Mama kissed Wheatly's cheek.

"Yeah, but I didn't want to leave you. At least, I'll be in D.C. near home, and I can visit everyone on the weekends," Wheatly explained, making me sound like an evil child. I started tapping my feet, and Janice gently touched my thigh.

"Tell them more about the project that they want you to work on," Mama urged him, and then said to us, "This is what sealed the deal."

"When Dad died, it was excruciating for all of us, so I started working on a chemical that will eliminate physical and mental pain from people. Physical pain from accidents and from war."

"So, you've created pain medicine?" I muttered under my breath with an ugly laughter. "Easy, anyone can do that." Jealousy dripped from my face. "Really, anyone," I insisted and shrugged.

"I'm not creating medicine. I'm creating a solution to end war against people by ending pain. I formed a chemical formula that creates molecules that tell irons to protect the skin, bones, and body structure from breaking.

You rub it on your body like lotion, and no bullet, no explosions, and no knife will be able to penetrate the skin." He rubbed his right arm with his left hand. "It's like an unbreakable glove you put on before leaving the house, and I call it I-bonic Armor, and then once I make it consumable it, I will create the first I-bonic Human."

Silence festered as our minds pondered on such a thing.

"That was my pitch," he concluded.

"Wait, this is the same thing you worked on as a kid? Are you serious?"

"Yes, but I changed the name once I started to play with Ions and—"

"That's impossible. Did you test this out? Did you shoot a homeless person as a test subject, Wheatly?"

Wheatly calmly shrugged and said, "All of my answers will be in my book, *The Last One Standing.*" He popped the tension, and everyone laughed.

"That's dope, and I'll be the first to buy your book when you write it," Aaron babbled. Everyone laughed except for me.

"Don't worry, Wellington. I have proof and experiments to back it up." His words were calm as I smashed the peas with my fork on the plate.

"So, Wellington, it's your turn." Aaron changed his position towards me, while Janice rubbed my back encouraging me to give the dinner another chance.

"Oh. Yes, what have you been doing in Atlanta for all these years that you couldn't visit your family?" Aunt Pinky crossed her arms.

"Yes please, cousin, inform us." Aaron leaned fully towards me.

"College took most of my time and work is demanding these days." I rubbed the bottom of my chin as I leaned back.

"Oh, how is work? Are you a plant scientist?" Aunt Pinky asked.

"My baby got a good job working with all types of plants," Mama bragged.

"Really, Welly? What do you do there?" Aaron wondered.

I chewed on the piece of chicken. "Ah, it's nothing. Besides you already know."

"I do? You never told me. Come on man, we want to hear."

"Research."

"Like a scientist?"

"Yep."

"Oh, are you traveling and finding these plants fossils you talked about? Oh, you were so precious back then," Aunt Pinky said.

"Yeah, Aaron what is new with you? Dating anyone?"

"Come on, Wellington, I'm married and my daughter, Dianne, is nine."

"Oh, yeah. That's right, you did marry that girl." Heat rushed to my forehead as I patted it with the napkin.

"Beatrice? And thanks for not attending the wedding," He grunted and said to Wheatly, "Beatrice sends her apologies for not being here. Dianne had a cold so they couldn't make it."

"What about you two?" Aunt Pinky quizzed. "Is there a marriage in the future?" I felt every vessel leave my body.

"Have you been watching my baby for all these years?" Mama interjected.

Janice and I blushed. "Yes, Wellington has been such a blessing." She rubbed my back, and my face turned bronze-red.

"Awe, how sweet. How did you two meet? How long have you guys been dating?" Aunt Pinky's chin sat in the palm of her hand.

"Um, well . . . we met at a coffee shop. I was studying for a big test for my Biochemistry class, and Wellington was writing a research paper. I could tell that he was staring at me for a long time, so I said to him, "If you want to ask my name or for my number, just do it."

Everyone gasped.

"Yeah, tell them what I said next," I chuckled, and Janice giggled and gently shoved me away.

"His eyes got big, and then he pointed to my paper and said, you got answers five and twelve wrong." Everyone laughed as Janice nodded her head up and down with an embarrassing grin. "But he said, 'And I would like your number too,' and now here we are." I kissed her on the cheek.

"Well, how long has it been?" Aunty Pinky asked.

"Oh yeah, it's been the best three years of my life. I don't know what I will do without her." I thought about her being sick, and immediately my heart sank.

"When is the wedding?" Aunt Pinky asked.

"What is with all these questions? Janice and I will be getting married soon." I waved off the questions as Mama clapped her hands.

"Awe. Marian, two weddings in one year would be so cute," Aunt Pinky announced.

"I wouldn't handle that . . . a grandbaby and two weddings."

"Two weddings? Wait, grandbaby?"

Wheatly's head lowered into his hands and said, "That is what I was saving my invite for."

"You're getting married and having a baby?" Humbleness captivated me.

"I was going to tell you later but didn't expect you to be here."

I held my head in my hand and rested both elbows on the table. Janice roamed her hands up and down my back to soothe my hurt.

"I missed so much," I grumbled.

"Well, you're here now," reassured Aunt Pinky. She motioned Aaron to speak up.

"Okay, okay, let's change the subject to me. Wellington, you're going to love this." Aaron waved for everyone's attention. Aunt Pinky drum-rolled on the table.

"Mom, is that necessary?" Aaron asked.

"I'm not going to stop until you tell them."

"Last year, a friend sent me an email to apply for NASA's space mission called Future Eight—a special mission to space that's open to civilian geniuses, and I found out this morning that I've been chosen to study rocks on the moon."

"What?" Wheatly yelled as Mama and Aunt Pinky rejoiced.

"To outer space?" Wheatly pointed up.

"Yes, up there." Aaron pointed.

"Aaron, this is a dream come true. You talked about collecting samples from the moon for years." Wheatly stood and shook Aaron's hand.

Everyone applauded, but I didn't believe it. I burst out in laughter.

"Okay, next joke. You are not going to space."

"I am going to space."

"NASA don't pick random people to go to space, Aaron. You have to be trained for that."

"Well, they picked me, and I have been training for almost a year."

"You didn't finish college."

"Luckily that wasn't a requirement. Face it. I entered and won."

The silence between us lasted for a moment. "I had to write a lot of essays, take a bunch of tests in physics, mathematical astronomy, and I scored higher than anyone. In fact, they were very impressed and begged me to accept the opportunity. You know my passion is to study geology and cosmology, so why does this surprise you?"

"I don't know. Maybe because you're a scaredy-cat. You hated the dark, and you never wanted to go on our adventures."

"That was ten years ago. And from the look of things, I'm much bigger and stronger than you." Aaron and I glared at each other.

"Okay, whatever." I leaned back in my chair.

"Baby, are you okay?"

"No, Mom. I am not."

"What's wrong?"

She hardly got her gentle words out before I interrupted her with mine, "I did everything right. I applied to college and went to college, and I graduated with my masters and a doctorate degree, and now I've been working as an office clerk for six years. Okay, I didn't visit home in ten years, so what? But I still should have gotten something better than Aaron and Wheatly. Wheatly doesn't want to go to college, was a troublemaker, a high school dropout, and gets into the most highly respected program on this earth that rejected me! While Aaron attends college, gets a girl pregnant, has to marry the girl, dropped out of college, and works full time as a plumber, and now he's going to space?"

Everyone's mouth fell open.

Janice patted my hands.

I took a deep breath and relented, "What I mean is Wheatly got the best job where he's actually doing something that he loves, and Aaron is going to a place that he talked about his whole life. However, Wellington here is working at a job that he hates that won't promote him!" I slammed my fist on the table.

"You're a scientist at a plant facility."

"I . . . am . . . an . . . office clerk, mom. I have been for six years, and there is no scientific work involved but conducting data entry on other scientists' work." I pouted and stood up. "I just thought that my life would be special at age twenty-eight, but it's not, just the same old. . . thing.

Everyone goggled in complete silence.

"May I be excused?" I stormed out to the backyard.

My foot touched the pavement, and the cold air surrounded me. The sun had faded away, and the half-moon's light blossomed bigger than ever. The coolness calmed my heart and my head from getting even angrier. Being in the backyard brought back memories of being in my safe haven when life seemed to not go right.

I closed my eyes as I embraced my old outdoor sanctuary. The smell of winter, the leaves from the trees in the distance, and the dirt from the garden made me calmer. I was finally home. Finally back to the place where my desires began. I wiped tears with my shirt and detected how much the backyard had changed.

The garden was made smaller with added tiles for a walkway to the patio deck. The old shed still remained in the corner of the backyard, with dirt stains and old rusted paint peeling off. I remembered when Aaron and I helped Dad build the shed, buying a lot of plywood and a bucket of white paint created something beautiful. Now, the shed wasted away in the back of the house being attacked by the rainy, snowy, and hot seasons.

«CHAPTER SIX»

FLASHBACK TO 1989. I cracked open my fortune cookie and read, "Seasons are symptoms before the change, and it is vital to understand, which season is coming or which season is here." Mama brought Chinese food home after work. It has been two months since Dad's re-diagnosis of lung cancer. I entered the living room where Mama napped on the couch. The light from the television shined on her face creating a glow around her. I grabbed a blanket from out the closet and covered her, just like Dad used to do.

A few months before, Mama was a stay-at-home mom, taking care of us, but since Dad got severely worse and couldn't work, she got a part-time job at the hospital to pay bills. The Olive Baptist Church helped our family tremendously as members rotated daily cooking duties and family activities on weekends.

I made my way up the stairs to a light beaming from under Wheatly's bedroom door. I knocked before entering.

"Hey, little brother." I peeked inside. The experiments kept him locked away from the world these days. Posters of superheroes were on the wall and action figures arranged on his dresser: Superman, Batman, Wonder

Woman, and more. Star Wars on the bed sheets and my *Back to the Future* toolkit, from Israel, on his desk.

He turned around wearing goggles bigger than his head and quickly took them off.

"Hey!" he yelled.

"Shush! Take the ear plugs off." I motioned for him to do so.

"What? Oh." He reached for the plugs. "Hey, I made the same chemical formula I've learned how to do in class. You want to see?" He anxiously waited for a reply.

"No, it's a school night. Remember?"

He hid his face with disappointment.

"I'm close to discovering something new. Adding these two substances will cause a big eruption. Want to see?" He mumbled, but my interest in scientific experiments did not satisfy me anymore.

"Bed. It's close to 10 P.M."

"Welly, I am working on my purpose, my secret powers." He held the cup to his lips.

"Wheatly? You better not drink that mess—"

Green and orange liquid sat inside of his two beakers near a large test tube.

"Come on. It's orange and green Kool-Aid. Mixed with a secret element of mine."

"Wheatly, please."

"But it's called body armor!"

"Wheatly, go to bed!"

He grabbed his Superman action figure and dropped it inside of the green liquid. My eyes rolled away and noticed the handle missing from my *Back to the Future* toolkit. I faintly pointed to it.

"Oh, it fell off. It's somewhere." He pulled the handle from off the floor and fixed it back on top of the toolkit.

I dropped my finger and sighed, "It's yours. I have no use for it." I stepped back to close the door.

"Wellington," Wheatly called out to me. "I'm already losing Daddy. I don't want to lose you too," he sincerely said.

The responsibility I carried now weighed heavy on me. The words from Dad at the campsite, "No more adventure this and adventure that," replayed in my head.

I stuck my chest out and marched to the guest bedroom. My chest sucked back in, and my feet stopped. I tried moving, but my body froze in fear. My chest went in an out as I encouraged my feet to take baby steps towards the open door. I slowly entered the guest room, now a hospice room, and wandered to the medical bed with the Parameter Monitor in the corner.

I listened carefully for sounds of life. The machine that hummed, buzzed, and beeped were connected to a man, a man who used to lift me up in his arms, a man who used to embrace and encourage me, and a man I still called Daddy. It was hard for him to breathe. Every breath was like a miracle and a battle at the same time.

The simplest thing humans do were hard for him now. I examined Dad's frail frame. Last week, he opened his eyes smiling at us, but this week, his eyes remained closed. I touched his warm hands and felt him alive somewhere in there.

"I love you, Pops," I whispered to him. "I decided to not do the Elite Scientific Program, and I rather stay here with Mom because I know she will need help taking care of Wheatly. And I know I would have been miserable working for the FBI. You're the only person that can keep me sane about plant theory." I lied through my teeth and then listened to the machines that helped Dad breathe for a moment. "Besides, plants studies are boring to me nowadays because I know everything about them, right?" I chuckled to myself not wanting Dad to worry about me. "I guess I want to make you proud, Dad." I grabbed his hand. "And don't worry about Mama. I'll take care of her when you're . . . " I paused refusing to say the word gone. "Now that you're transitioning into a better place."

I leaned over and kissed him on the forehead, satisfied that he heard every word from out of my mouth. My hands caught the tears running from my eyes. The promise of staying strong for our family comforted me.

One more glance before exiting Dad's bedroom . . . deep down I knew our encounter would be our last.

My shirt caught the last bit of my tears as I made it back to my bedroom, and it didn't feel like a happy place anymore. It reminded me of my passion and Dad's amazing stories. I flipped on the light switch. A colorful blanket covered all my plants in the far corner of my bedroom. I tried to eliminate how much joy they gave me, but thoughts of growing them danced in my mind.

I climbed into my bed.

My body numbed from worry and stress. I wondered if God heard my plea, and if he existed, if I mattered to him, if he would spare my father's life just this one time for my family and me.

* * *

A car door slammed and woke me up to the sun shining upon my face. Odd. The sun never rose before me. I checked my clock, and it read 8 A.M. I jumped out of bed, grabbed my book bag, and stuffed my books and folders inside of it. Thirty minutes left to be at the bus stop. I dropped my book bag, grabbed my towel, and headed to the shower. Dr. Wilson, my mother, and aunt Pinky stood in the hallway, and I froze wearing only my boxers. Mama's eyes puffed up and sobbed, "Baby --"

"No!" I backed away not wanting to hear the next words.

"Listen. Your, " She stepped closer to me.

I yelled louder, "No! I don't want to hear it."

"Okay." She stopped pursuing me. Helpless pain rose inside of me. My throat could not swallow or form a sentence. I huffed and puffed from the ache that burned inside of me, and I couldn't help but blame Tiny Tree and myself. Again. It made sense that Tiny Tree caused these unfortunate events. I immediately pushed passed the adults and ran downstairs. Wheatly and Aaron sat on the back porch crying. I ran past them and into the shed. They followed behind me. Rage boiled inside of me, pushing me to destroy the mysterious tree. I grabbed a baseball bat from the corner and swung it over my shoulder almost hitting Wheatly.

"What are you going to do with that?" Aaron yelled out.

"This thing has destroyed our lives, and I'm going to destroy it forever."

I took one last breath and opened the closet door where I planted Tiny Tree two months ago. It grew. Our mouths fell apart for the tree wasn't tiny anymore. The baseball bat fell right out of my hands, and I fell on to my knees crying out to God, begging it to remove Tiny Tree from my family.

"Please bring my Daddy back!" I screamed, causing Aaron and Wheatly to weep with me. "Have mercy on me. Mercy please. Give me mercy please," I cried, and Tiny Tree blossomed with colors decorating the shed's walls as if it celebrated my misery.

"Really, what is this thing?" Wheatly cried to me. However, I was too distraught to answer any questions or think about anything other than my pain. Tiny Tree had created its own three-foot dirt hill patching up the hole at the bottom of the shed. The bark of the tree started from my thigh, and the branches stopped at my head.

"I guess the new name is Miniature Tree?" Aaron spoke out.

"No," I quickly said, "Mercy Tree." Mercy Tree's light danced upon my face, and I became calm and then joyful. Slowly, I stood up and stepped closer to it.

"Welly?" Wheatly urged me to back away. I had nothing to lose or to gain. My hand stretched out towards Mercy Tree.

"No! Wait!" Aaron pleaded. Mercy Tree twinkled in our eyes, fear crept back into my mind, and my hands shook uncontrollably with suspense. *What if the Mercy Tree shreds me into tiny pieces?*

My hand slowly entered Mercy Tree's assortment of sparkly light, and its warmth covered me. I kept on pushing, blocking out Wheatly's and Aaron's pleas, and soon their voices faded into the distance.

I touched it.

Warmth and uncontainable motion crawled beneath my hands like a rattlesnake caught in a trap. My emotions attached itself to the good energy and the evil energy that the Mercy Tree concealed from the world, like a pathway for dark and good energy to coexist. From the corner of my eyes, I could see Wheatly and Aaron moved their hands, trying to get my attention. However, Mercy Tree captivated my soul with its swirls of bright colors and glorious music.

"Music?" I mumbled as the shed's roof supernaturally opened up. My body immediately shook with an overwhelming sense of wonder and excitement. A pulling sensation inside of me played tug-o-war, moving me forward, then backward, and then forward again, and then right out of my body. My soul leaped through the open rooftop as my heart sank with fear, and my body, thumped, hitting the ground. Aaron and Wheatly froze, screamed, and ran out of the shed.

I ascended through the shed's roof and floated into the sky, where hundreds of glowing dots soared upward. Fear faded from me as I embraced my newfound flying skills. I flew closer to an oversize diamond sparkling above my home, and then the diamond transformed into Dad hovering over the house.

"Dad, you can fly too!" I floated towards him, and we locked hands. A radiant sensation from him jetted to my soul as we rejoiced.

"The Kingdom of the Lord is at hand." Thousands of flying diamonds glistened and sang praises.

I yelled, "The Kingdom of the Lord is at hand." And held on tight to Dad's hand as he ascended up and yelled, "Ya-hoo!" He released my hand while gazing down at me.

I flapped my arms to fly upward, but I was stuck. I kicked my feet and moved my hands to reach for Dad's feet, but he kept on moving upward while smiling down at me. Then, I slowly began to descend.

"Dad!" I yelled the lower I got. "Dad, I want to go with you! I want to go to Heaven."

He smiled and instructed, "Son, the tree belongs to God! Protect it with all your might!" His voice clapped like thunder, and everything went black. Only my thoughts remained floating in the sky as my soul went searching for my unconscious body.

I mumbled, "Bye, Daddy."

* * *

My body weighed an extra hundred pounds. Well, it felt like it did, and I felt weak and sick, ready to shrivel up and die. I moaned, and pain rushed straight to my head and ached. My lips were dry from lack of water. I finally forced my eyes to open, and Wheatly and Aaron watched me.

"He's alive," Wheatly confirmed.

"Welly, what were you thinking? You could have died," Aaron grumbled.

"What happened?" I sat up in the bed.

"You touched the tree and fell to the ground."

"But I flew into the sky, right? You saw me. Dad saw me?"

"Nope. Dr. Wilson helped carry you to the bed and told mom that you were overwhelmed because of…" Wheatly paused.

"Dad. He's gone?" I interrupted him.

"Yeah." Wheatly whimpered. Still, my head ached as I massaged it. I felt overly small in my own body as if my body was a tiny tin can and God had stuffed my soul into it. Wheatly started to cry, and I hugged him.

The more I thought about my experience of floating in the sky, the more it became less real to me. Aaron stepped forward and rested his hand on my shoulder, and I asked, "I can't fly, right?"

"If you can, we sure didn't see it because you hit the ground pretty hard." Aaron smirked.

"How could that be?" I pondered. "It felt so real."

"What is it, Welly? The tree isn't normal?" Aaron wondered.

"I saw Dad going to heaven, and he said the tree belonged to God," I shyly revealed.

They both froze, and Aaron shouted, "We helped you steal God's tree?"

Aaron stepped back, and silence covered the atmosphere as we all contemplated that thought.

"Oh, boy. Oh, boy." Wheatly shook his head.

"Maybe I heard wrong?"

"We have to return it. Did your Dad say how to?" Aaron panicked. "Maybe you can get help from the Elite Scientific Program once you get in?"

"We can't. Dad also said I need to protect it."

"Protect it from what?" Wheatly stepped forward.

"Do you think that's why bad things are happening?" Aaron loomed. "Wellington! Are we cursed?" Aaron took a deep breath. "You have to tell someone at ESP!"

"I didn't get into the Elite Scientific Program, okay." I pouted.

"What? You didn't tell me?" The same disappointment that covered my face visited Aaron's.

"I didn't tell anyone. I got the letter right after I found out about Dad's sickness."

"Welly, you got into thirteen colleges."

"Fourteen," I corrected him.

"There has to be a big mistake."

"There was no mistake. I'm no good, and I'm cursed, just like you said. The Mercy Tree belonged to God, and I stole it!" I laid back down, blocking tears from streaming down my face. "I am sorry that I got you guys into this situation."

"What about Dr. Frazier? Remember the scientist we met in Israel? Contact him." Wheatly sat on the bed next to me.

"I'm not going to Georgia. That's too far from you and Mama."

"He said you would be working on your own plant discovery. That's got to be better, anyway. Maybe God blocked ESP so you can work on this?" Aaron argued.

"I'm not going to Georgia."

"Okay, pick any of the other colleges . . . Fourteen of them! We have to figure this thing out before we all are doomed." Aaron pouted.

"The deadline to accept them passed. I'm out of luck. Maybe it was meant to be this way."

"You should at least tell Dr. Frazier about the tree," Wheatly shouted, and I grabbed him by the shirt and said, "No . . . one . . . I mean _ro_ one can know about the tree."

"Mom and Dr. Wilson saw it already." Wheatly wiggled from my grip. I covered my eyes with my hands, angry at the confession.

"But they didn't see the glow," Aaron said.

"Guys, if people know about this tree, they will take it away, make a lab rat out of it." I used my wrist as an example. "Cut it open until it bleeds red and blue. We must protect it like Dad said. It is now our responsibility."

"But you said it is God's tree. We have to give it back!" Wheatly yelled.

"Dad also said I have to protect it!"

"This is crazy," Aaron shouted.

They both crossed their arms and angrily stared at me, and I knew if I didn't make amends, they would leak the tree to the authorities themselves.

"Guys, I will fix this. I'll write Dr. Frazier to see if he will honor my scholarships, maybe it is best for me to go away before something else bad happens." I shivered with fear. "I won't forgive myself if something happens to our family. But you have to promise me that you will not go into the shed, _ever_, until I return."

"I won't," Aaron confirmed.

He nudged Wheatly, and he groaned, "But what if—"

"No! Not until I become a real scientist and experiment on it myself."

"Okay." He pouted.

I took a deep breath, accepting responsibility for the major task ahead of me as Wheatly and Aaron loosened up their stature.

"After I get my bachelor's degree, I'll come back and conduct my own experiment on the tree."

"With us, right?" Aaron stepped forward with spread arms, shocked that I didn't include them.

"Of course with you guys. Aaron, you will be my assistant, and Wheatly will be my understudy."

Wheatly's expression changed, and I asked him, "What's wrong?"

"That's like four years. You're not going to visit home at all?"

"Wheatly, coming back and forth from Georgia will cost a lot of money that Mama doesn't have. We'll talk on the phone and write letters, I promise."

"I'll be here by myself then?"

"You'll be helping Mama out."

"Aaron, will you be here?" He turned to Aaron for comfort. Aaron placed his other hand on Wheatly's shoulder. "Sure, buddy, I will be here."

"No, Aaron will not be here. He'll be going to college right after me and will be back later than me. Face it, Wheatly, it's time to grow up. Daddy is gone. I'll be gone. Aaron will be gone. God forbid something happens to Mama. You need to get used to it." I sat up in the bed. Aaron's mouth fell open as Wheatly stepped backward and exited the bedroom.

"Come on, Welly. That was harsh."

"He's my brother, and Wheatly needs to grow up sooner or later."

Mama entered the room holding folded T-shirts in her hand. "Welly, you're awake, my dear?" Her eyes, puffy, as she placed the clothes in my middle chest drawer.

"Yes, I was just overwhelmed, that's all." I rushed to her and hugged her.

"Oh, that's what Dr. Wilson said." She wiped her eyes with the back of her hand. "Your dad is very proud of you, all of you," she said before exiting the bedroom.

Mama brought back sad feelings, and I immediately thought about the glorious dream, or vision, or whatever it was that the Mercy Tree revealed to me only to be woken up by my reality, the world's mysterious existence.

A constant pain hindered me as I lay down and hugged my pillow. I wanted to be alone to remember every detail of my experience. However, fear overshadowed my thoughts, and the feeling of God angry with me for stealing his precious tree kept me on edge.

«CHAPTER SEVEN»

THE BREEZE AWOKE me from my precious memories, and unresolved shame lingered inside of me from my outburst at dinner a few moments ago. I paced and pounded my fist repeatedly in my hands. "You're so stupid," I grumbled to myself. Nevertheless, the cool backyard breeze comforted me, and the rattling of the leaves and twigs on the shed's roof caught my attention. I approached the shed to examine it and wondered if my family's biggest secret remained inside.

I tugged on the door, but a gold lock kept it closed.

"You need a key," a voice insisted from behind me. Started, I turned to Wheatly holding the missing piece to my puzzle.

He dropped it in my hand. "I didn't touch it like you told me to. In fact, I haven't seen it since you left. I locked it to keep it safe from Mom because she talked about cleaning out the shed a few times."

Too embarrassed, I said nothing.

"I couldn't wait to give you this key."

He walked away, and I said, "Wheatly. I am so proud of you. Honestly. Sorry I wasn't here to encourage you or to be here for you at all."

"I got used to it just like you told me to." He nodded and slowly entered the house.

I wanted to apologize for telling him that all those years ago, but I didn't know where to begin. I inserted the key into the gold lock and said a silent prayer to myself.

I slowly pushed, and the shed door creaked open. I fumbled against the wall for the light switch, but the light bulb was blown. I tiptoed into the darkness and examined the ground before I took each step. *An abandoned shed is a snake's dream*, I thought when I finally made it to the back of the shed to the closed closet door.

"Wow." Aaron came out of nowhere. His head poked inside. "Can you believe that our head never used to touch the ceiling? Now we have to bend over." He wobbled inside and asked, "Is it still here?"

I hid my face.

"It's too dark to know. I need a flashlight."

"Uncle Robert used to store one around here, right?" Aaron and I searched the top shelves, and my hand landed on my old *Back to the Future* toolkit. I quickly opened it. "Jackpot." I handed a flashlight to Aaron, and we both tested it.

"It doesn't work." He chuckled.

He found a light bulb still sealed in the box on the shelf. He ripped open the box and replaced the busted one with the box-light bulb, and it turned on and blinked.

I held on tight to the handle to the closet door and took a deep breath.

"Are you nervous?" Aaron asked, and I nodded. However, being in Dad's favorite place where his briefcase sat against the wall gave me the strength.

"Okay, one . . . two . . . three." I opened the closet door.

"The Mercy Tree," we both marveled as if we were seventeen and sixteen again.

"It looks the same," Aaron examined, and I agreed. It did not change or wither. Perfectly positioned. "So what are you going to do with it now?"

"We're going to finally figure out what it is." I turned to him. "Just like we said ten years ago, remember? I have access to equipment and data." My heart thudded fast. My finger tapped repeatedly—I love fieldwork—just the thought of experiments, strategies, formulas, and equations enticed me.

"Now, that I have some experience working with medicine, I know a thing or two."

"No, Wellington. You can't walk up in here expecting things to go back to normal. You abandoned us, and I am not cool with that. What if it curses us again when Wheatly and I finally are doing good for ourselves?" Aaron asked, and my joy dove out the door.

"That is why we need to figure things out now—"

"Now, we are too busy with work. Sorry, cous', but you're too late."

"You're right. I messed up the plan. I'm six years late, but I am the same guy."

"Okay, then old Welly can do it without us. Your brain is big enough, and your confidence is bigger." Aaron smirked. He brought up the old sayings about me, and I remembered being a knucklehead, a know-it-all, and too confident in plant science, but *where did all that confidence go?*

"Aaron, I am sorry about what I said at dinner. It was stupid and uncalled for."

"You have always been a jerk. That is what I know. However, Wheatly is different now. He battled depression for a very long time after you left." Aaron tightened the bulb some more. "You created a dark pit for us all. So, don't come back and shake things up again."

"I-I didn't know things got so bad."

"Because you didn't ask or call. But you made a good point at dinner. I did suck at life in my early twenties." He sat on edge of the dirty desk. "I was so afraid of failing that I didn't try to pursue my dream. That is why I am determined to live my dream this time with no interruptions." Aaron headed towards the shed's exit and stopped. "I can't believe it glows, thought it was our imagination." He pointed at the Mercy Tree. He admired it, and I admired only an ordinary miniature tree.

"You see it glowing?" I reached out my hand to touch it.

"Hey, you remember what happened last time. You hit the ground like a sack of potatoes," Aaron joked, and I quickly moved my hand away. Instead, I examined the healthy green leaves wondering why it hid its radiant glow from me.

"Wellington?" Aaron snapped me out of my focus.

"Why can't I see it?" I wondered.

"I know I am being tough on you, but for the past ten years—" he revealed, and we talked over each other.

"But you can?" I pondered and closed the door to the Mercy Tree.

"Wheatly has become more like my little brother! I don't want you to make him lose his focus," Aaron shouted and went back to the house.

I slammed my fist against the desk and a cup and a few pencils fell off. The thought of Wheatly's depression and the whole family viewing me as a traitor for leaving consumed me. Even the Mercy Tree lost trust in me. My only proof had fallen into my illusion of nonexistence.

I creaked open the closet door and gently grabbed a test tube from my jacket, scraped soil into it and sealed it. Despite my blindness to the Mercy Tree's abilities, I knew that returning home was the right choice for my family's future and my career.

«CHAPTER EIGHT»

THE BIRDS CHIRPING OUTSIDE kept me company all morning until the sunlight graced my face. I studied the past experiments in the green binder by writing down a few notes that caught my attention. I looked at the type of substance that each scientist added to the soil that tarnished it or gave it a negative result, and I compared it to the experiments I conducted with Dr. Frazier in college. The soil, stand-alone, contained notable radiation and our results produced remarkable outcomes but eventually turned the soil hard, and it became useless after three months. *Spoiled,* I thought.

I lay against the headboard, and my feet landed on both sides of my old twin bed. My leg and feet tingled from being stagnated for a long time, so I waited patiently for the numbness to fade away. The small mirror across the room revealed that I had a late, stressful, and restless night. Nevertheless, I picked up the small tube filled with soil that I had gathered, and I poured some into a mug.

KNOCK. KNOCK. The door slowly opened, and Wheatly peeked inside. "What's up, bro? Did you have a good night's rest?"

"As much as I was going to get, I guess," I grumbled, suggesting that the bed was way smaller than I remembered.

"I am surprised you did. I couldn't sleep a wink." He chuckled. "It must know that you're home from the way it beamed from the shed all night."

I squinted at him and grabbed my T-shirt from my suitcase. Wheatly stepped further inside of the bedroom with his hands in his pockets.

"That's hard to believe. It hardly acknowledged me. Only Aaron saw it glow last night."

"Honestly, the beam from the shed is painful to the eyes. That is how I knew it was still alive all these years, but last night, it glowed brighter, and I can't believe the neighbors aren't complaining." He marveled.

"What did Mom do with the plants?" I threw the T-shirt over my head and stretched my arms.

"She placed them in the garden." He stood tense against the wall.

I went to the window. The garden was small, and many of the plants were dead.

"She couldn't even water the plants?" I questioned. I thought about how hard I nursed each plant from seed to sprout.

"Mom called this room her office at one point," Wheatly moved towards the small desk covered with boxes.

"It's small enough. I can't believe how different everything looks."

"Yeah." Wheatly smiled as he crossed his arms and then rubbed his side pocket repetitively. I waited patiently for him to share more.

"So you're going to be a father and get married?"

"I am. I think I owe that to Dad to pass down the Kole's family name," he joked, and I grinned.

"I thought the Elite Scientific Program was rigorous on having a family because of time and commitment?"

Wheatly slowly stepped closer to me and jokingly whispered, "Yeah, I sort of lied on my application and said I only had a girlfriend. They came and interviewed Ma and us to double-check if I had kids. Luckily, we found out about the baby after the process."

"I know you're going to be amazing at it."

Wheatly's smile slowly faded, his hands remained in his pocket, and he rocked forth on his toes.

"Why didn't you really come home after college?"

"I—I started working this job, and I—couldn't find the time." I took out my shirts and pants and aligned them neatly on the bed. I shook off the nerves that shackled my true feelings. "Wheatly, I'm sorry for leaving you and Mama like that, especially after Dad's funeral. I should have stayed and not gone to college, but when Dr. Frazier offered me a full scholarship, I had to take it—"

"I get it, but you should have visited." Wheatly's eyes watered as he turned and stormed to the door.

"Wait. Please, don't be mad at me. This is new for me, and I'm trying to make things right." I grasped my head with my fingers.

His shoulders dropped, he crossed his arms. "When you leave again, take it with you." He jetted out of the bedroom and slammed the door.

Anxiousness represented my body, and I fell to the floor and then crawled to the window. The old white-now-beige shed with broken paint from years of rain and sunlight sat peacefully in the corner of the yard. I thought about how it had taken on so much and was still standing. It gave me the strength to stand on my two feet and to make things right in my life.

I grabbed my sweatpants, pulled them over my legs, and hurried out of the bedroom. I tiptoed all the way to the living room where Janice and Mama sat sipping morning tea and chitchatting.

"Baby, is everything okay?" Mama worried as Wheatly stood behind the couch.

I clapped my hands. "Mom, I am so sorry about last night. It was uncalled for."

"It's fine, baby. We moved past it." She sipped her tea.

"I want to make it up to everyone... Where is Aaron and Aunt Pinky?"

"They left last night," Wheatly grumbled through his teeth.

"Okay. I'll tell them later." My nerves rattled me, and I trembled as I announced, "I decided to move back home." I clapped my hands together as everyone gulped. Wheatly grunted and went back into the kitchen, disgusted by the decision. Janice's mouth fell wide open.

"Baby. You can't do that." Mama shook her head.

"Mom, yes I can. My boss told me to work from home, and I want to. I have some unfinished business that I need to face, and I want to be near Wheatly and you. To catch up. Please?"

"No, Welly, you have to find another way." Mama stood up and waved her hands.

"But Mom?"

Wheatly stormed back into the living room and shouted. "Mom is selling the house."

"You can't sell this house." I held Mama's arm.

"I can't afford it anymore." She touched my chin.

"Then I will pay for it."

"We already started the process and—"

"Where are you going to go?" I frowned.

"To live with your Aunt Pinky—"

"Is this why they're so many renovations?" I spun around, analyzing the newly installed hardwood floors and painted walls. Janice carelessly turned on the television and flipped through the channels.

"Yes. Baby—"

"Mom, it's our family's home and it has so many memories. Why would you just give it up like that?"

"The same reason why you did." Wheatly's nostrils flared as he jerked his head forward. "We want to move on and live our life too, Welly. And this house has nothing but pain residing in the walls." Wheatly turned to Mama. He huffed, "Mom, don't listen to him."

Sweat formed on my forehead and eyebrows, and I wiped it away and said, "Okay. Sell it. I'll buy it. I didn't get the chance to experience living here after Dad's death so let me have that opportunity."

"Bullshit, Welly!" Wheatly shouted, and Mama slapped his backside.

"Wheatly!" she admonished as Wheatly stomped my way.

"You only want to stay because that tree is still alive, that same tree that cursed this family. It killed Pop and kept Wellington away for all these years, Mom!" He revealed and then declared, "And I am going to finally destroy it." Wheatly sprinted towards the kitchen, and I chased after him.

Janice and Mama glanced at each other and quickly followed us to the backyard patio. Wheatly ran down the patio steps to the shed and locked himself inside. I jumped over the rail, yanked the shed door's handle, and repeatedly banged, bruising my fist.

"You boys stop playing and come on inside." Mama fidgeted with her housecoat.

I paced back and forth like a mama lion hunting her prey. I pressed my ear against the shed's door, and then I squinted through the dirty window. Wheatly had a baseball bat behind his head approaching the closed closet door. I screamed, "Wheatly, you're making a big mistake! This tree didn't do this!"

Wheatly slowly opened the closet door where Mercy Tree sat. With sweaty palms tightly grasping the bat, he swung it behind his shoulder and yelled, "Rest in peace." With inner fury built up for all these years, he swung it down.

The Mercy Tree exploded with excessive light, knocking Wheatly down. It shifted everything in the shed. It blasted the door open, and I dove to the ground and covered my head. The rainbow light sparkled like a big diamond against the sunlight. I crawled against the light's pressure on my stomach, army style, to rescue Wheatly, who was cradled like a baby on his side. Various colors radiated from the Mercy Tree, dominating the atmosphere. Janice and Mama stepped back into the house. Miniscule bright light sparkled like stars in the sky.

"Dad. Daddy? I was up there. I flew. . . in the sky." I recounted the old memories the day Dad died.

I got to Wheatly and held him in my arms. The Mercy Tree glowed brighter and brighter, mixed colors, telling an incredible story that had no end. Its presence held us close and warmed our bodies. Then, it shimmered down and twinkled.

"Ah—I think I'm going to be sick." Wheatly wiggled out of my arms and quickly crawled out of the shed. I heard Mama through the open window ask him questions about our action-show she just witnessed.

However, Mercy Tree captivated me. "I'm sorry," I cried. "Please don't take another family member away because I took you away from God." I hoped it heard my plead. I slid closer to the twinkling Mercy Tree and examined its fading glow.

Closer and closer, my hand drew near the last fading ray, and I hoped, with one touch, Dad would appear to me.

"So this is it?" a voice asked. I snatched my hand away and turned to Janice standing wrapped up in a blanket.

"Isn't it precious?" I beamed. She shook her head. "It's just a tree."

I turned back to Mercy Tree, and it twinkled beautifully. "There, look closely. Do you see it glowing?"

"Glowing? Is this the magical tree that you told me about all those years ago? Wellington, we spoke about this, and you finally stopped believing in that mess."

"Wait, you and Mama didn't see anything?"

"No, we heard Wheatly fall and saw you dive on to the ground like an idiot," she shouted.

"Welly, as your lover and part-time therapist, you need to separate fantasy from reality. Glowing trees? Come on!"

I slowly stood. "How do you know which one is fantasy or reality? How do you know that you and I aren't fantasy, and the tree is more real?"

She gawked at me.

I grabbed my head and laughed uncontrollably. Then, the Mercy Tree faded and returned to normal.

"No . . . no . . . no, please come back." I begged the tree.

"Ah—Welly. Let me tell you something that is more real, my cancer."

My joyful laughter halted because Janice made a good point.

"And we have other things to discuss. Like you're moving back here?"

Janice placed her hands on her hips—a disappointed future wife's attitude.

"You're right. It was my imagination. It is not real," I swore to Janice and shook the thought out of my head. "But Wheatly saw it. Aaron did too," I whispered to myself.

"Welly, are you listening to me? You are out of your mind! And you broke your promise … again and again." Janice crossed her arms and stormed out of the shed.

I quickly grabbed her by the waist. "Wait, no. Move here with me so I can test the soil experiment on you—to fix you? The tree may not glow, but it can heal people. It healed me once. I just need time to figure it out." I held her hands.

"Are you insane? My doctors and family are in Georgia. Welly, why can't you put this on hold while I complete chemotherapy treatment? You promised me," she cried.

"Janice, baby. I also promised Dr. Frazier that I would get this done."

"Unbelievable. You said not even a work project would stop you from being with me."

"This is about you, I am doing this only to save you. I love you, Janice."

"No … no, you don't." She yanked her hands from mine.

"We're still going to get married, and if I crack this experiment, you will be healed."

"If you solve this experiment." She left and then turned back. "I drank the tea mixed with the soil that you made for me, and it hadn't worked, yet. How many failed attempts do you need before you get it?"

"Give me a chance to prove that this will work—"

"Welly, life is pretty short when it comes to cancer. It's time for plan B." She stormed away leaving me dumbfounded.

«CHAPTER NINE»

JANICE FOLDED HER T-SHIRT into her suitcase. Her voice shook as she fumbled through her things. "I had always dreamed of being married and having three kids." She added more clothes into her suitcase. The disappointment and hurt covered her face. She continued, "When you said those things at dinner, it reminded me of myself. I did everything right too. I was a good girl, went to college, and fell in love." She paused and said, "And for what? To die at such an early age?"

I stood near the door with the cup of tea mixed with droppings of soil. I couldn't bear to see Janice torn apart. She flopped on to the bed with her face in her hands. I quickly placed the cup down and rushed to her side and embraced her as she moaned, "God, I know I wasn't perfect, but why me?" I lifted my eyes to the ceiling to hold back my tears. I wiped her eyes with my T-shirt and listened to Janice. "I just hope you don't think striving to be the best makes you happy because it doesn't matter at the end of the day." She forced herself out of my arms and finished stuffing her suitcase. "I just pray to God that he gives you the desires of your heart."

Those words were like needles penetrating my skin. "How could you say that?"

"What do you mean? Oh, right because you're having this crazy vendetta against the maker of life."

"Janice, there is so much I want to tell you. Just know that God is after me, not you."

"Wellington!" She threw down a few clothes on to her luggage. "You are not cursed by God. He only wants you to love Him."

"How can you be so sure? Like you Janice, I've put my trust in Him and look at me now."

"Okay, who can I trust, Wellington? Man? Because the man that I trusted broke his promise to me, again," she shouted. Her eyes were red, and she trembled. She grabbed her suitcase, zipped it, and rolled it to the door, but I stopped her.

"One last time. Please try it."

She glared at me and then at the cup in my hand. She clutched it and took a big gulp and left the room.

* * *

The clouds hid the sunlight, and the rain fell to the plants. I stood on the porch, soaked. The taxi driver sped off towards the corner of the street. I slowly lifted my hand and waved goodbye. The taxi turned on to the main, road and my gut nudged me with the thought of losing the one person in my life that I trusted. I slowly stepped back into the house, regretting taking on the assignment, again. I thought about Dad and me discussing formulas and equations at the kitchen table. Us, watching our favorite movie, *Back to the Future*, in the living room and running out the back door with new flowers to plant. He always filled me with hope for tomorrow.

An old picture of Dad working at the factory caught my attention. He was a skinny, energetic and a hardworking man, and a man who was my real hero. However, I needed to be Janice's hero.

I stepped back into my bedroom where all of my dreams of being a plant scientist started and where all of my dreams were lost when Dad died. I rushed to my dresser and opened the drawer with the green binder tucked inside and with its big question mark endlessly waving back at me. "Goodbye question mark," I declared as I slowly sat down on the edge of my bed and flipped to the page with the image of the cave. There were twenty images labeled with descriptions of the inside of the cave. I flipped to the next page, and four pictures of the vines and roots covered the walls. I flipped to the third page where scientist captured the three statues on the cave's wall in a photo. They were less defined than I remembered.

I flipped to the last page, and the number to the Research Department at Pharmaceutical Plant Discoveries stood out to me.

I took the cell phone that Dr. Frazier gave me and dialed the number. It rang twice, and then a deep foggy voice answered, "Pharmaceutical Plant Discoveries' Research Department, who am I speaking with?"

"Ah—my name is Wellington, and I am—"

"Oh, yeah. Dr. Frazier said you'll be calling about this case file," he mumbled to me on the phone. "I pulled the case last week. It was covered with dust, and the notes are hard to read, so bear with me."

"Of course, take your time," I nervously suggested.

"Okay. Basically, the case was discovered in 1970 by government officials and was made known to the public in 1989 by a group of kids."

"Wait? We weren't the first to find it?"

"Sorry to break it to you kid."

"Why didn't the government protect it back then?"

"Well, they probably didn't think kids would mountain climb in the desert."

"What did they say about it? Is there any information on Israel's experiment?"

"Nope. Everything is negative or kept secret from what I can tell. It was discovered in the West Bank, and the only thing the Israeli government is calling it is Mount Hit-ga-lút… yeah, I think that's how you pronounce it."

"Is there anything about the figures on the wall?"

"Figures on the wall? The vines and roots?" He ruffled through the pages. "There's nothing here that says anything about figures or statues on the cave walls. Why do you ask?"

"I remember." I explored my memories of the figures on the wall ten years ago and an image that captured a portion of it.

"You don't have the image B in your notes?"

"A . . . C . . . D? B is missing, but D is a close up on the pile of soil. I have other things to do, but I can give you the number to Israel's Scientific Allegiance Agency office if you would like."

"Yes. Please." I stared at the image in my folder that was not in the primary database.

"Here you go," he started and rattled off a phone number.

"Thanks."

We both disconnected the call. I dialed the long distance number, and a woman answered with a thick accent.

"Israel's SAA Aerology Headmasters. How may I help you?" she asked.

"Umm—ah, Mount Hit-ga-lút's case, please. I need to talk to someone who knows about it."

Silence concealed the phone line for a moment.

"Mount Hitgalút?" she repeated accurately.

"Yes, I am a scientist at Pharmaceutical Plant Discoveries."

She spoke in Hebrew in the background with someone for a moment and said, "Mount Hitgalút is a beautiful mountain located in the West Bank of Israel. If you want more information about it, I can redirect you to our travel guide department—"

"No, wait. A group of kids found a discovery in 1989. I am one of those kids, and I am researching it."

Silence thickened again, and she stuttered in Hebrew to another person as the words American came out, and then said to me with fear shaking in her voice, "Sorry, sir. The Israeli government is privately investigating that discovery. It is not open for discussion."

"But, I have a few questions about the figures or statues on the wall."

"Statues on the wall?" Her voice pitched as she pressed her lips to the phone and whispered, "If you know about the figures on the wall, then you should know that this discovery is top secret. We cannot help you."

"Then who can help me? Can I visit the place myself?"

"Look up Mount Hitgalút prophecy. Goodbye, Wellington."

The phone disconnected.

The phone fell out of my hand. "How did she know my name?"

The front door slammed and startled me.

As I got closer to downstairs, chatter and laughter from Mama and a man calmed my nerves. I entered the kitchen to the two blushing like high school kids. They both placed the groceries from out of the brown paper bag on to the counter.

"Welly? What are you doing home?" Mama asked cheerfully.

"I didn't have anything planned for today." I grinned at the familiar man from the photo on the wall.

"Oh, this is Pastor Al. He's the new pastor over at Olive Baptist Church."

"Pleased to meet you, Wellington. Molly told me so much about you."

He reached his hand forward, and I shook it. "Molly?" My eyebrow rose. That was a personal nickname that the family called Mama. "What happened to Pastor Chris?"

"He moved five years ago to Ohio," Mama placed the groceries on the shelves.

"Your mom tells me that you're a scientist," he mentioned, and Mama glowed with guilt.

"Kind of, if I solve this case." I revealed the green binder in my hand.

"Wow. Molly said it's a big project that could change the world. It's amazing how God uses shepherds in every field to bring glory to His kingdom," he mentioned.

"I doubt I am one of God's shepherds."

"Of course you are. We all are as long as we do right by Him."

"Well, what if you don't or hadn't?"

"Wellington? That is why we have the cross and the blood of Jesus. Repentance is the key son," Mama reassured me.

"But look what happened to Dad . . . And what about Janice? They were faithful to God and look what he did to them."

"Wellington, you know that God did not cause them pain," Mama spoke up.

"I don't want to hear the religious talk. God is—Well, the whole God thing isn't for me."

"My Jesus." Mama turned and threw her hands up in the air.

"Wait a minute, Marian." Pastor Al touched her arm to keep her from walking away.

"Let's listen. Son, what do you believe in?"

"I don't know. I found out God is not what I thought He was. I thought we had a connection when I was a kid, but I realize it wasn't real," I thought about the stolen tree, and God taking Dad and the Elite Scientific Program from me. "Like, wouldn't God stop you from making a big mistake or isn't his job is to heal you from pain?"

"You're a scientist, and usually you guys think evidence and logically," Pastor Al mentioned, and I sort of agreed.

"Wellington Kole the fourth, your father is probably turning in his grave as we speak. I told him this would happen if you started down this scientific road."

"Mom… it's complicated."

Mama threw her hands up in the air and stormed out of the kitchen. Tension rose to a boiling point, and I felt the heat. Pastor Al stepped closer to me with his chest poked out. He jammed his hands into his pockets, deepened his voice. "Son, I get that you are hurt. You lost your father, you didn't get the promotion, your best friends have moved on, and your girlfriend has cancer. You feel abandoned, and you have been asking yourself where is God in this?"

My face clutched as I tried to hold back the anger that boiled deep inside of me, but his gentle voice soothed my pain. However, my chin lowered to my chest, ready to ignore the message that came next.

"But Jesus, the Holy Spirit, and God will never leave you. They will not forsake you, and if you open your spiritual eyes to see what each devastating thing in your life is leading you to do, you will begin to hear God's voice and to accept Jesus as your Lord and Savior," Pastor Al preached. He patted me on the shoulders, went to the living room, and sat on the couch.

"Okay, maybe God can tell me what's on Mount Hit-ga-lút," I sarcastically slurred. I opened the refrigerator and scanned the shelf.

Pastor Al lifted his chin in deep thought and said, "Mount Revelation. I would like to visit that place." He turned on the television.

I immediately said, "What did you say? You know of this place?"

"Nope ... the word hitgalút means Revelation in Hebrew and Revelation means the awakening or the revealing—God's revealing something in your life today. . . that's a good sermon." He took out his notepad and wrote it down.

"Have you heard of the Mount Revelation Prophecy?" I rushed to him.

"Oh, I see that I have your attention now. As a matter of fact, I did. A while ago when I was a young boy during the 1950s, old letters were found in Europe, and it was all over the news and in the church that a woman prophesied a hill with angels praying and protecting something. Then, the next vision was about a tree's root growing from out of the Garden of Eden. The tree kept on growing, and eventually, its branches covered the whole earth—"

"Yeah, well, that's impossible ... it's weird, right? Trees can't cover the whole earth or come out of hills?" I popped open my soda can and slurped desperately to quench the heat from rising from me.

"Well, when it comes to prophecies and dreams, God uses imagery to connect with us so we can apply it to our own life. The tree can mean different things—"

"Pastor Al, can you help me with something?"

"Anything, son," He turned the television off and stood up with his chest poked out and hands in pockets.

I placed my soda down, slowly stepped to him, and showed him images in my green binder. "Umm—Wheatly, Aaron, and I found this cave with special natural substance. However. . . " I flipped to the next page—to an image with the letter 'B' on it.

"This image was taken that day, and these statues surrounded the tre— soil we found. I can't remember exactly, but they had wings and a sword."

"You think it means something spiritual?" He scratched his chin.

"Umm?" I stepped back and shook my head. "I don't know. When I called about it, no one would tell me anything."

"Well, they could be Cherubim. They're angels in the Bible, sent to protect God's special things. God mentioned Cherubim guarding the Garden of Eden." He paused. "Oh and strategically designed the Mercy Seat to have statues of Cherubim."

"Mercy?" My knees buckled like Jell-O, and my breathing became faint. I closed my eyes to regain my balance and to recollect my thoughts on what may be in my shed.

"Son, are you okay." Pastor Al grabbed my arm. "Is that the answer you were looking for?" He moved me to the couch.

"Marian!" he called to Mama, and she rushed in.

"What is going on here," she complained, still angry from what I said.

The missing image bothered me, and the secrecy behind Mount Revelation alarmed me.

"Breathe, Welly. He hasn't had an asthma attack since he was a child," Mama mentioned to Pastor Al.

"I'm okay," I managed to say as my heart repeatedly bounced inside of my chest.

KNOCK . . . KNOCK . . . KNOCK. We all poked up from the unexpected sound.

"What on God's earth is going on?" Mama marched to the door, and Pastor Al held her back and said, "I'll handle this," which made Mama blush.

Pastor Al swung open the front door. Three clean-cut government officers waited eagerly dressed in navy-blue suits, one with sunglasses, the other with a black trilby hat and the other holding his government badge towards Pastor Al.

"Is Wellington Kole here?"

I stepped from behind Pastor Al and said, "Who wants to know?"

"I guess that's you. Can we speak with you?" We moved to the side, allowing the three men to enter our home. The man with the top hat and the sunglasses snooped around the living room. They picked up pictures and opened books, which made Mama uncomfortable.

"You contacted the Israeli's SAA department, and we wanted to know why?"

"I am looking into the soil discovery on Mount Hit-ga-lút."

"Is that so? I thought that discovery was old news?"

I focused my attention towards his men touching Mama's things. He blocked my view and folded his arms.

"It was given to me by Pharmaceutical Plant Discoveries—"

"Ah. Dr. Frazier? That makes perfect sense. Well, son, there's no need to look into it any further. My team and I will take over your case from now on. You can hand over anything regarding the assignment." He held out his hand.

"I don't have anything to give you, other than what I was given by Dr. Frazier." I waved the folder.

"The folder with the question mark is all that I need." He smirked, and his partners surrounded us.

"Of course." I moved it towards him, and he snatched it from me and glued it to his side. He marched towards the front door, and the two guys followed him.

"Excuse me? Who do you work for?" I asked as they headed down the porch steps.

"The United States of America. Good day, sir."

I closed the door, locked every lock, and turned to Mama and Pastor Al who held each other close.

"I think the government is hiding something?"

Pastor Al stepped to me and gripped my shoulder. "Then it's best we mind our own business." He and Mama walked into the kitchen.

My heart raced with excitement as Dad's words rang inside of my head: *Whatever you do, protect the Mercy Tree.*

«CHAPTER TEN»

TOOLS AND MACHINERY from inside of the shed now covered the lawn and patio. I threw an old rusted hammer into the pile of trash and moved the lawnmower closer to the house. The fading junk inside of the shed slowly brought the interior of shed back to life. I scrubbed the dust off Dad's old desk and neatly placed a notebook and a few pencils on top of it.

"Okay, much better." A simple accomplishment made my heart rejoice.

Wheatly and Aaron chuckled and entered the backyard. Nerves overshadowed my joy as I hid behind the shed's door to listen to them gossip about my new plans. However, two birds chirped and at that moment, it reminded me of my father's fictional characters—Chat and Rabbit—and how their bravery saved their farm. I stuck my chest out and exited the shed with extended arms.

"Welcome!"

"There he is." Wheatly motioned.

"You look like a mental patient." Aaron picked up the old baseball bat and slapped it against his hand. I looked at my reflection in the window, seeing an unkempt beard and bushy eyebrow, and I wore a ripped T-shirt.

"Wow, how things have changed." He swung the bat against the air, imagining being in the big league. "This bat won't stand a chance in a game nowadays," Aaron joked.

"I am moving back home to study the tree. I am sure you heard the news." I crossed my arms, and Aaron dropped the bat.

"Wait. I thought Aunt Molly was selling the house and moving in with my mom?" he asked Wheatly.

Wheatly shrugged and said, "Wellington, here, decided to buy it."

Aaron turned back to me and licked his teeth for a moment while he thought hard about his next statement.

"I thought I told you to not cause problems."

"Cause problems?" I stormed towards Aaron as he stepped back. "This is my dad's house. My house. I can choose what I want to do."

"I thought you hated this place. That's why you left and never came back home! If Wheatly's gone, who is going to check on Aunt Molly?"

"I'm staying for good!" I stood on my tippy toes to reach his eye level.

"He won't leave because of what is in that shed." Wheatly pointed. Our attention immediately focused on the shed.

"I thought it glowed," I calmly said to Aaron. "Our imagination got the best of us again." The tension between us slowly disappeared. I approached the shed's dirty window to peek inside.

"Of course it glows? It was never our imagination," Aaron snapped as he rubbed his chin.

"It also has a temper." Wheatly gently stepped onto the grass.

"I know for a fact it glistened in the night. It's beautiful." Aaron stepped inside, and I followed him. I grabbed my white lab coat and put it on. Wheatly waited impatiently for two seconds and then joined us.

The shed's opened door allowed the Mercy Tree, beautifully full of leaves, to enjoy the cool breeze swishing through it.

"Wow. It's even more beautiful during the day," Aaron admired.

"Yeah, I know." I crouched down and analyzed it.

"Maybe you can get some help from Dr. Frazier and figure out why it glows?"

"Trees don't glow. I take this to him, and the whole department will laugh at me."

"You're mad, right? You saw it explode with light the other day!" Wheatly fussed.

"The point of you going to college in the first place was to figure out what it is. You even said it yourself; I need a team to study it. You work at the biggest botanist company in America who develop and research unexplainable species like this, what is the problem?" chimed Aaron.

"The problem is I tried to figure this out! I told Janice, and she laughed at me and said it's my imagination, and she might be right. This is too extraordinary, and I need to know if it is our imagination before I bring other people into it." I bent over to view Mercy Tree some more.

"It is not our imagination. We can prove it!" shouted Aaron.

"How, if we are the only ones that can see it!"

"He has a good point, Aaron. Mama and Janice didn't see it glow."

"Only the three of us can see it. That is why we should put our minds together. Aaron, what if you don't need to go to space. Wheatly, what if you don't have to go to work-college at the ESP, and what if we start our own scientific company in this shed?" I revealed my master plan, but uncertainty filled the atmosphere, and not a peep or a sound lingered.

Aaron clutched his cheekbone and mumbled, "Welly, I'm going to the moon, bro."

"Yeah. The more I think about working for the FBI, the more I want to do it. Sorry," Wheatly added.

"So, The Mad Scientists aren't going to be mad together?" I wiped my forehead with my shirt. "You guys are missing out on a great opportunity."

"Are you serious? Wellington, we waited for you! We both hoped and prayed for five years that you would return with news like this, but you didn't."

"Okay, but I am here now."

"It's not the same. My family needs to eat now. My bills need to be paid now. Wheatly and I stayed here while you went to live your dream as a plant scientist, and we took care of family affairs. I had to put my love for astronomy, physics, and cosmology on the back burner. Not anymore."

Aaron exited the shed as Wheatly agreed, "Wellington, I dropped out of high school to get a job to help Mama pay the bills. Now, it seems like good things are finally happening for us. Please don't ruin it." Wheatly joined Aaron.

A cool breeze shuffled the Mercy Tree's leaves. And I knew what I had to do.

I hurried to stop Aaron and Wheatly from leaving.

"I want to give you guys something." I motioned for them to enter the shed, and they did. "You're right. I broke my promise, and I want to make up for it." I bent down near the Mercy Tree to measure it.

"Stop!" Wheatly yelled. "Are you out of your mind? Don't touch it."

I quickly yanked my hand back. However, I took a deep breath and stuttered, "Don't worry baby brother, and remember, it's just a tree." I grabbed small scissors from my lab coat's pocket and touched one of the tree's branches. Aaron and Wheatly cringed and slowly stepped back. Memories of the light explosion constantly replayed in my mind as I slowly measured twelve inches of the stem and clipped it. A big sigh of relief came from us as well as a satisfying grin. My hands carried the precious Mercy Tree's stem full of green leaves.

"See?" I sighed. I carefully broke it into three pieces and handed one to Aaron.

He took it, cautiously sniffed it and then held it up and away.

"Wow! Ten years ago, you would have killed us if we touched this," Aaron said, and I smirked. I tried to give the other piece to Wheatly, but he stopped me with his hands.

"Wheatly? It's not going to hurt you. Take it."

"How do you know that? I'm the one who threatened it with the baseball bat," he revealed.

I shook my head and laughed. "Do you remember that I did too? After Dad died, I blamed the tree for everything that happened to us." With both hands, I gently toyed with the stems and then pushed it closer to Wheatly.

"You were right to be mad at it." He still refused to take the stem.

"Not quite, but I am learning about forgiveness, and I have forgiven God. Do you guys forgive me?"

Aaron and Wheatly acknowledged each other, wondering if I had a trick up my sleeve.

"I do. That doesn't mean I won't give you a hard time." Aaron smirked.

Wheatly took the tiniest stem from my hand. His fingers rubbed the texture, examining the smooth, pure form. "Give Aaron and me a year to get ourselves together, please."

"I just want you guys to know that it won't be the same starting this without you."

"You're not going to be alone." Wheatly rested his hand on my shoulder and pointed his nose towards Mercy Tree. "I think it may know something about the soil."

Aaron grabbed the broom and swept as Wheatly threw old junk inside boxes. While I admired the tree, I threw empty soda cans into the trash bin.

"Promise me one thing, that you'll be at my space launch?" Aaron said to me as he rolled an old tire on to the grass.

"Of course. It would be an honor to." We shook hands, and Wheatly wrapped his arms around us. "I am glad we can finally support each other." Wheatly sniggered and moved a few smaller things into the corner as I sprayed and cleaned the shed's window.

"I just hate it that Israel's SAA is hiding information from the public," I complained.

"Like you're hiding something from the public?" Aaron nodded towards Mercy Tree.

"Not the same. I'm creating medicine so it can help heal the public, but something is missing from the equation."

"Medicine that you haven't worked on since you've been here?" Aaron teased.

"The feds came up in here without a warrant when I started to."

"Yeah, they took the folder right out of your hands too," Wheatly agreed.

I dusted myself off and crossed my arms.

"Maybe Aaron is right to tell Dr. Frazier about it. We're not kids anymore, and this could be serious," Wheatly suggested.

I grunted, and then Aaron and Wheatly juddered from shock. Amazement lit up their eyes as they gazed at the stems glowing on the table.

"Whoa. . . " Wheatly drifted his hand over it. "It's warm." He chuckled as the sensation sparkled. They laughed uncontrollably.

"What. . . what is happening?" I couldn't see or feel anything.

"The glow, it's beautiful." Aaron slurred.

Their heads went from wall to wall. The beautiful light captivated their attention. They giggled until their face turned red.

"What is happening?" I demanded. "Why can't I see it, again?" I whined louder. They gave me a peaceful look and joy rested in their eyes. Then, it stopped. Aaron and Wheatly came back from the marvelous experience.

"What did you see?" Inches from their nose, I hoped to view a movie of their experience through their eyes.

"We're going to be late." Aaron grabbed the stem, placed it in his pocket, and smacked the dust off his hands.

"Where are you guys going?" I chased after him like a madman.

"I have a dinner."

"Welly, are you okay?" Wheatly wondered.

"I didn't see anything. You guys were kidding, right?"

They both gave each other a long stare, and then Wheatly said to me, "Ah Welly, how will you solve something that you do not believe in?"

His words struck my core.

"You should come with us," Wheatly urged, and Aaron groaned.

"Oh, ah… where?"

"To the NASA's gala dinner in Hampton, tonight. It's going to be about the Future Eight's space mission." He exhaled.

"Oh, I need to study the tree and come up with more reports and data." I didn't want to be a burden on them.

"No, you should come … Scientific Allegiance Agencies from all over the world will be there, and you may find what you're missing." Aaron patted my shoulder.

"Okay… okay! I'll go."

Wheatly checked his shirt. "I have to wash up before we leave. Don't want to look a mess when pitching how the formula that I am working on can sustain human life on Jupiter." Wheatly playfully rubbed his hands together and gave us a proud grin.

Aaron checked his watch. "You two ride together. I have to pick up my mom. Then afterward, I'll take Wheatly to D.C."

Wheatly and I nervously smiled at the idea of being alone in the car for an hour together.

* * *

A few hours later, I leaned against the wall as Mama squeezed Wheatly's cheeks in the palm of her hands. With a runny nose, she sniffed and wiped the tears that streamed down her face.

"Are you sure you want to go right before Christmas?"

"Yes, I want to get settled in," he squealed. "It's okay mom. I'll visit on weekends," Wheatly said through his awkward mom-squeezed duck lips poking out towards her.

Mama released him, and they both turned to me. Wheatly gently massaged his cheeks, and I stepped closer to them with both arms wide opened.

"He's better than me." I hugged and rocked them gently in my arms. Mama latched on to me and sobbed into my chest.

"He's the baby, that's all," she cried as Wheatly grinned.

I rubbed my hands against Mama's back. "Ugh, don't tell him that," I joked. "I'm going to miss you again, brother." We pounded fists.

"Okay, Mom. We have to go before traffic gets too bad." Wheatly grabbed Mama's waist to urge her to let me go. She released me, and we both gathered the bags from the front door.

"I'll be back in a few weeks to pick up Colette, but I have to get settled in first," he informed us.

"You and Colette need to go to the justice of the peace and get married." Mama threw her hands up and then rested them on her hip,

"Mom? Colette wants a wedding after the baby is born. And after I save a few paychecks, we are going to have one soon after. Don't worry," He wiggled her arms to loosen up.

I opened the front door. "Are you ready?"

Wheatly nodded and then kissed Mama on the cheek. "Don't cry. This son of yours will return home," he clowned as he rushed out of the house avoiding a punch from me.

"You drive safe, you hear me?" she called out as she followed us on to the porch to wave goodbye. "Wellington?" Mama called out. "I know you're hurt that Janice left you."

"Mom! Really? Right now?" I grunted.

"I am just saying, come back home! Drive safe, and I love you guys."

I nodded and hurried into the van that had been in our family for over fifteen years.

Wheatly already had his bags in the back seat and was sitting comfortably with his CD player and headphones already in place.

I took a moment to reminisce inside of the old Ford Econoline that Dad used to drive, proud that my brother had taken action to improve his life despite the constant setbacks he faced in high school.

"Why are you smiling at me?" Wheatly grumbled.

"I don't know. I think I am smiling because if Dad were here, he'd be driving you to college right now."

"It's not college. It's work … college."

I grabbed my bag from the backseat.

"Here. I bought you a going away gift slash Christmas present."

I handed a blue gift bag to Wheatly, and his eyes lit up.

"What is it?" He shook it.

"Just look inside," I groaned.

He pulled out a case with a cell phone inside.

"What? Are you serious?"

"Yeah, you need one now that you're going away to college."

Wheatly measured the phone's thickness and weighed the phone in his hand.

"I don't know what to do with it."

"Call home." I revealed mine to him.

"Thanks." Wheatly smiled as he roamed through the new device. We drove through the community and then turned on to the main street where traffic formed behind us. My hands grasped the steering wheel as my finger tapped and tapped, making a melody of their own.

"I figured that we can still work together while you're away," I revealed.

Wheatly rolled his eyes and said, "You really want us to help you with this?" He frowned. "Aaron is leaving! Why do you need us?"

"Because together we are the Mad Scientists. We always did projects together."

"Welly, you have been away for ten years. I am sure you've done projects while you were away." Still focused on the phone, Wheatly entered contacts and asked, "Did you do experiments while you were gone?"

"Only on dumb class assignments."

"You're telling me that I experimented more than you? I successfully sold five different chemical solutions to a cleaning company. The other hundred almost blew up the house." He shook his head. "Welly, I can't believe you gave up on finding a solution to what we found? You were supposed to work with Dr. Frazier in college. That was the plan."

"I did, and then we stopped! Dr. Frazier got so tired of the negative results that he moved on. Now he has to deliver something soon, or the whole company will go under."

"So, us helping you this time may bring different results?" Wheatly stared at me with a you-need-me smile, and I blushed.

"Yes. I need my bros on this."

"Aaron has to go to the moon, and you can't take that away from him." Silence hovered after Wheatly's comment. "And I will help you, but only if I can. I don't want to mess up this job. I have a family to think about now."

"Of course. You got mouths to feed. I will only need your help with research and stuff." I glanced in my rearview mirror and then over my shoulder. I picked up speed and entered the highway. Wheatly went back to playing with the phone.

"So you failed a hundred times? Wow," I pondered. A part of me felt relieved and then the other part of me felt foolish to be afraid of failure.

He nodded, and I read the highway sign to Hampton and turned on the radio.

«CHAPTER ELEVEN»

FROM A DISTANCE, the parking lot was a colorful sea of cars. Near the building, limos and high dollar cars parked at the curb with secret service men and security patrolling the area. Young valet attendants ran back and forth from the parking lot to get keys and to park cars. All of this thrilled Wheatly and I as we followed Aaron to the outside concierge desk.

"Oh, yes. Mr. Kingston Kole, right this way." The man behind the desk pointed to two large doors. Two doormen stood like statues that moved every time a guest approached them, pulling the heavy doors open to a ballroom. Politician's eyes fell upon us as we made our way down the blue carpet.

Civilians greeted Aaron with a nod and a smile. Aaron greeted them back with a salute. Aaron expected this from everyone, and I thought, *who is Aaron to these people?* The four of us headed inside of the Langley Research Center. Minuscule sparkles of light shimmered the ceiling, and the round spotlight moved up and around the walls. We entered the dining hall with thirty tables and ten waiters standing on each side. Men dressed in black attire and the ladies wore beautiful cocktail gowns. People laughed, conversed, and ate.

"It's very fancy in here." Wheatly fixed his tie; he wore white tennis shoes, red slacks, a blue sports jacket with a tie pinned to his collar shirt. I wore brown jeans with a beige sweater, and Aaron wore a black suit with a space shuttle pendant. Aunt Pinky wore a beautiful dark purple dress. She smirked at us and sashayed away as if she didn't know us.

"Well, if it isn't Kingston Kole." A short, stocky guy with blond, wavy hair roared as he reached out his hand to Aaron.

Aaron shook it with a big smile and chuckled, "Ah, hey man. You made it."

"I almost didn't. NASA had that important meeting this morning, which caused a lot of pushbacks in my department, but the show still goes on, I guess."

Delicious hors d'oeuvre taunted my growling stomach. Oysters wrapped in bacon, chicken wings, sliced vegetables, and fruits. I gathered cheese, veggies, and fruit into my plate.

Aaron stepped aside and introduced us. "These are my cousins, Wheatly and Wellington Kole."

"Wait. The Wellington Kole that everyone's been talking about at the SAA?" The guy blurted as he slowly approached me. "It's an honor to meet you. My name is Branch. I am an engineer inside of the Scientific Allegiance Agency, and well, your research and reports are legendary. The Headmaster of Botany has them plastered all over the wall." I stepped back with a half-eaten carrot in my mouth.

"Umm, thank you ... Branch." I shook his hand dropping either a cheese-cube or grape; I wasn't sure which, on to the floor.

"No, it's my honor. My whole office waits for Dr. Frazier to send your reports every month."

My hard work and dedication to the formula for all these years were actually being recognized. "Oh, I didn't know that my reports were being known and shared with the SAA."

Flattered, my face shined with happiness, and then disappointment took over as I recalled Dr. Frazier saying, '*you're no good,*' to me.

Branch turned back to Aaron. "You didn't tell me that your cousin is <u>the</u> Wellington who assisted Dr. Frazier on the soil discovery, which Pharmaceuticals Plant Discoveries was founded upon?"

"Actually, Aaron and Wheatly were a part of that discovery too," I interjected.

"Oh, we are so proud of Kingston here." He placed his arm around him, bringing Aaron further into the circle. "He is the secret weapon on this mission to space."

"Um, a secret weapon?" My happiness, gone. I scratched my chin and stumbled over my words, "Ah, you didn't tell me you're the mission's secret weapon?"

"Well, I didn't want anyone to be worried about me. Besides, we aren't supposed to say anything about our roles in the mission." Aaron grunted at Branch, and he blushed.

"Hey, it's Wellington for goodness' sake. He may know something that we do not."

"Yeah? Try me." My body perked up, and I tilted my head to the side.

"Okay. Um . . . we sought the smartest and greatest scientist in the United States to apply for—"

"Yeah, yeah. Aaron told me about that part. But more about the mission?" My hand waved the overdone flattery off as I leaned in to hear more.

"Oh, of course. We are being sent to study a rapturous glow that is underneath Asia. It is deep inside of the earth's mantle, and now the same glow is forming in North America."

"What do you think it is?" I asked.

"From the satellite images, the glow looks like a red blob as if a volcano erupted underground," explained Aaron.

"But we don't know what it is yet. SAA leaders from the east have been studying it for over fifty years, but now that it popped up in North America, we are taking action and going to study it from above," Branch bragged, and we all stood intensely absorbed.

"Why Aaron?" I asked.

"Well, we needed a young astrophysicist to join our team." He grabbed Aaron again making him red in the cheeks. "And not just any astrophysicist, but someone that has a greater understanding of creation."

"I'm sorry, but Aaron? You know he never graduated college, right?"

"Welly?" Wheatly blurted as Aaron tensed.

"What? This seems like a pretty serious mission, and I wanted you to know the facts."

"Ah, Kingston came highly recommended by a former ESP alum and a few astrophysicist officials, and Aaron proved himself countless times during training, testing, and more. That's what made him first select." Branch winked at Aaron with an *I got you* smile,

"Okay, wow. Yeah, of course, and I double recommend Aaron, better than … who?"

"Gary Foster," Aaron revealed, and chills covered my body. "He willingly wrote my recommendation letter when you ignored my emails multiple times."

"I don't check my emails—"

"And because I dropped out of college doesn't mean I stopped learning about astrophysics. For the past few years, I grew to admire Christian astronomers' views on God and space. So my application essay was very passionate." Aaron slapped my shoulder and walked to Aunt Pinky who motioned for us to sit down.

"Too bad you've declined the mission. Two Koles would have been awesome!" Branch squeezed my shoulder and headed away.

"Wait, declined what?"

Branch stopped. "The space mission. Dr. Frazier said the soil experiment has you tied down these days," he said, and rage masked my face. "Hey, don't feel bad. All of SAA can't wait for the results since PPD evaluation is coming up next year," Branch patted my shoulder and walked away.

"I thought you said Dr. Frazier stopped the experiments?" Wheatly squinted.

"He did until two weeks ago," I snapped.

The Headmasters filled the first fifteen tables, and their scientific agency flags sat in the middle as centerpieces. The title for Headmaster is written *HM.* like *Doctor* is *Dr.* for short.

HM. Bowmen of Space stood on the stage and announced into the microphone, "We have two big acknowledgments to make this evening, but first I want to thank everyone for coming out this evening."

The Headmasters of Armed Forces, Botanist, Space, Earth, Ocean, Human Rights, Medicine, Zoology, Energy/Matter, Govern, Religion, Chemicals, Biology, Culture, and Technology were all present.

A young man walked on to the stage with papers in his hands and waited for HM. Bowmen to recognize him. "A quick acknowledgment, we inducted a new Headmaster this year." He turned to the young gentleman behind him. "Meet Headmaster of Cyberspace." Everyone's gasp fluttered the room as some complained, "The Internet thing? Released mainstream?" and others whispered, "This is ridiculous and childish. It has nothing to do with human beings."

"Settle down now," HM. Bowmen soothed. "This young man was elected and has proven himself in this new growing global communication gizmo." He turned to Headmaster of Cyberspace and clapped.

Applause filled the room, and the Headmaster of Cyberspace bowed his head and said, "Thank you, Headmaster." while giving HM. Bowmen the papers and then leaving the stage.

HM. Bowmen shuffled through the documents. "Secondly, we are here to acknowledge and to congratulate the chosen space cadets who are going to the moon, and to share more information about the mission." Everyone clapped and cheered as he roll-called the eight names. "Adriane Pipe, Damien Lesser, Mark Scott, Kingston Kole. . ." Our table loudly cheered. ". . . Kourtney Miller, Steven Nelson, Branch Smith, and Jordan Foster."

Cheers from all over the room lasted for a few moments as the HM. Bowmen waited patiently to finish the rest of his announcements. "We have a night of encouragement waiting for you. Each headmaster will give a short speech on what it will take to complete the mission ahead of you." All the headmasters, uniformed, lined up at the stage with notes in their hands.

"Gary Foster," I whispered to Aaron.

"Yes, Gary is not so bad, you know. He's been a great help to us for all these years. He wrote the recommendation letter for me and gave Wheatly a tour of the ESP's facility."

"Wow. I guessed I missed out." I leaned back into my seat when suddenly I grabbed their arms. "Wait, you guys didn't tell him about Mercy Tree?"

"Of course not," they both agreed.

"He's only trying to get close to you to ask about Mercy Tree."

"Or maybe he's not. And your mom told me about your struggle with faith." Aaron yanked his arm away.

"After what we all been through, you're not?"

"Wellington, I miss your dad too, but that's life. Romans 8:28 says, 'And we know that for those who love God all things work together for good, for those who are called according to his purpose.' The pain from your father dying and Janice getting sick can be your testimony of how God used you to help others."

"God left me when I went to college. I haven't seen the man since."

"Then whose fault is that? Because it isn't God's."

We listened to the Headmaster of Chemicals give his advice. "Examine, develop, and try each experiment again and again and again. Soon you will become the experiment. Thank you."

I liked it, so I wrote it down in my notepad as everyone clapped.

"All I am saying is back in the day, you were so certain of what God wanted you to be, and I envied that. When you asked me what my purpose was, I said to survive. What kind of answer was that?"

"It was a great one. You've achieved it and—"

"My purpose has to be bigger than survival." He repeatedly shook his head and then craved, "There is so much out there to do, and I want my daughter to be proud of me."

My eyes twitched as my mind filled with Pastor Al's words and memories of Dad. I remembered the day our Mad Scientist team was formed, and our career goals were established to prove God's existence in science.

Everyone clapped. All the headmasters had given their advice, and then HM. Bowmen called all the Future Eight Cadets to the stage to take pictures.

"Hurry cadets." He motioned them to come to the front of the stage as all the headmasters stood in the back.

"Excuse me, Headmaster." A reporter raised her hand from the front table. "The U.S. hasn't been to the moon since Apollo in 1972. Why now?"

"Well, this expedition is important because we're the first to send environmental scientists from every field to study the condition of the earth from the moon."

"So the government approved funding for future moon landings?"

"Not quite." He paused and continued, "This expedition is only to see if everything is in working condition, and to determine if the earth is in good shape." He redirected his attention to the space cadets standing below. "This space mission is extraordinary because we opened submissions to non-traditional scientists, people who are geniuses in their fields, but they had never worked at a scientific company. These men and woman have passed a variety of tests, and we are happy to have the best on our team. Now, this mission has a lot of layers, so I can't share too much. However, what I can share is that America will be the first to study something extraordinary in space for three months."

Everyone cheered and photography flashes ticked throughout the room. A few people shook Aaron's hand and took pictures with him while my mind was still packed with unanswered questions on why I had lost so much hope in the Lord.

«CHAPTER TWELVE»

Wrapped in Mama's colorful handmade quilt on the couch in the dark. The television's light shined on my face as I watched everyone celebrate New Year's Day. The ball dropped, people wore '2000' shaped New Year's Glasses, lips touched, and cheers plastered all of over the television screen. Once again, I thought about how empty and hopeless my life and future had become. I called Janice a few times last week, but her family refused to give her the phone. They were mad that I broke my promise to help take care of her, therefore, they declined to provide me with any information regarding her health. The front door swung open, and Mama pranced in from bringing in the New Year at church.

"Good night, Pastor Al," she flirted as I rolled my eyes back into my head. She turned to me and flipped the light switch on.

"Happy New Year! I figured you were going stay in bed feeling sorry for yourself. I see you moved your sappy show to the living room," she joked as she took her gloves off and placed them in her jacket. "Do you miss your brother?" she asked and stood between the television and me.

I gave her a stone face, but she didn't back down.

"Now, you feel like he did when you left. I couldn't get him off the couch for a month. Cheer up. He's only been gone for two weeks," Mama snapped and stormed away to the stairs.

"Mama?" I groaned. "I need your help." I really did. I honestly didn't know who I was anymore. The only person that knew me the best was Mama. She remained the only person on this earth who I deeply trusted to bring joy back into my life.

"Yes, baby. What is it?" She felt my forehead and sat next to me.

"What if I do trust God, but I am afraid to admit it because I don't want to be hurt again," I mumbled. I rested my head on her shoulder, and she rested her hand on my knee.

"A lot of people have been hurt by things in life, but it's all a part of having faith. Now, do you believe in the Holy Trinity and who God says He is?" She smiled with an I-don't-play-that-mess look on her face.

I grinned and mumbled, "Ah—I think." I couldn't lie to her, so I cried, "Mom. I want to ... I really do, but how could you be so sure?"

Mama stood up and placed her hand on her hip.

"Let's see. You completed over forty-five experiments with this plant project, right?"

"Ah—yes, all but five came out negative." I scratched my head.

"Okay. Why did the experiment work differently from the rest?"

"I don't know, maybe because the soil was fresher in the beginning stages, or we might have done something wrong because we couldn't get a positive again after a month and years. Why are you asking me this?"

She towered over me. "I figure for you to understand what it means to be a Christian and to believe, I have to talk 'sciences' stuff to you." She quoted with bunny fingers, and then rested her Bible on the edge of the couch.

I leaned back into the chair, and she continued, "When did you complete the first experiment on a sick person at school?"

"When I left home, I was so excited about the results that I called you," I smirked.

"What did you do the day before?"

"Umm—I don't remember?"

"You attended a sermon by Pastor Chris. He was in town, and you were so excited."

"Oh, yeah! He was there. It was a great sermon by the way."

"What did you do after you got the results from the experiment?"

"I called you, remember?" I winked.

"I mean 'do' as in where did you go?" she asked.

"I went to a Bible study at Morehouse. Dad wanted me to attend there, so I felt that was the perfect opportunity to see what it was all about."

"Okay. When was the last time you called home?"

"Oh, mom?" I wiggled forward thinking we were about to get back on this subject.

"Answer, boy. This all has a point."

"Mom, I was inducted into Dr. Frazier's scientist fraternity the second semester, and I couldn't call home because I became extremely busy with researching and lab work. I honestly didn't have time to do anything. To talk to you, to talk to Wheatly ... Aaron—"

"And to talk to the Lord," she exposed, and her words shot me in the chest.

"Okay, Mom I see your point. I abandoned my faith." Tears formed in my eyes. "I still have some unresolved issues and guilt from the past."

My heart was still broken by Dad's sudden death. I just knew no one could fix my inner guilt and shame.

Mama lifted my chin and said, "Honey, you're missing the point to this equation. What was missing forty times was your faith. If God ain't in it, he ain't with it." She grabbed her coat and proceeded to the stairs.

"You can't add that to an experiment."

"Yes, you can. If what you found is indescribable, unimaginable and nothing on this earth and no person can explain what it is, then maybe it's better for you to ask God rather than man what His creation means." She walked back to me.

"I don't understand."

"Baby, forgive yourself and then proclaim who God is. He's an amazing, oh so powerful, and awesome God!" she cheered.

I stood up and held Mama's arms down. "Okay, Mom, stop before the neighbors hear you." I blushed.

"You're an amazing God!" She pointed to the roof.

"Okay, Okay. I get it."

"He's powerful and awesome, and I love Him!"

"Mom! Stop." My face, cherry red, ready to pop.

"Wellington, if you want answers, accept Jesus Christ as your Lord and Savior. He'll tell you, baby, what you need to know. Believe and have faith that everything will work out. He will raise you up from out of the dark pit that you are in sooner or later," she said as she went up the stairs.

I shook my head, embarrassed by Mama's praise dance in the living room, but happy that she spiritually spoke life into me like old times. Her Bible sat on the edge of the couch, and I contemplated if I should read it. I struggled with what page to read or where to start, but I felt it in my heart to trust that God would lead me to a scripture that would speak volume in my life.

I flipped to James 1: 2-4. "Consider it pure joy, my brother and sisters, whenever you face trials of many kinds, because you know that the testing of your faith produces perseverance. Let perseverance finish its work so that you may be mature and complete, not lacking anything." My heart raced, and my mouth fell open. *Was He listening?*

* * *

I couldn't stand to walk past the mirrors in the hallways because of my messy hair from lack of brushing and bulgy eyes from lack of sleeping and worrying. It was May, and I still fought restlessly with meaningless ideas and instructions on how to begin the soil experiment.

I hid my face from reflective objects, like glass, when I traveled down the lonely hallway, down the stairs, and into the kitchen.

The sounds that brought life to Mama's house these days were the kitchen's clock and my footsteps. I munched on potato chips as I watched the old raggedy shed stand peacefully in the sunlight.

The sun's ray highlighting the top of the shed intrigued me, and for that moment out of my desperation, I grabbed my notepad from out of my pocket, wiped crumbs on to my shirt, pulled out my cell phone, and dialed a number.

The phone rang for three solid beats before Charlie answered, "Pharmaceutical Plant Discovery, Charlie for Dr. Eric Stein," he slurred the last piece.

"Charlie, my boy?" I rejoiced.

"Wellington? Is this really you?"

"Yes, sir."

He whispered, "Where have you been? I thought you quit or something."

"No, I've been working from home for the last six months."

"You must have some good connections upstairs to do that. Did Janice say yes to the proposal, did you complete the experiment?"

"Sort of."

"We've been picking up your slack here at work, and I'm trying to stop them from hiring another office clerk."

"Charlie, they can replace me because what I am about to solve will allow me to open my own practice."

"That big, huh?"

"Big. And I want you to help me."

"Ah—gee thanks, but I ain't no scientist."

"So what? You can still assist me while you're working for PPD. Just don't tell anybody about it. What do you say?"

"I am quite honored, I guess. What is the catch?"

"The catch is that I trust you."

"Awe—buddy, I got your back."

"What are you doing today?"

"I have to pick up a few samples from the vault for my boss."

"Perfect! So I need you to do some digging."

"Wait, for what? I just got inducted into this thing. Don't I need some training of some sort?"

Charlie rambled on about how he's no good and how he is always messing up at work. I didn't listen too much because the shed caught my attention and motivated me to see the bigger picture, and how discovering the Mercy Tree can be the answer to everything. I'd cut him off.

"Charlie, do you believe in God?"

"Of course. I grew up Catholic and my mom's—"

"Well, this is a God thing. I need you to go to PPD's vault and check out everything regarding the Mount Hit-ga-lút discovery."

"The hi-baba-ta what?"

"It means revelation."

"Umm—"

"Please. I need this. I need your help. I have no one helping me with this," I pleaded.

BEEP BEEP! An incoming call interrupted. I didn't recognize the number so I told Charlie that I'd call him back and quickly answered with a deeper voice. "Hello?"

"Is this Wellington? Welly?" A woman asked.

"This is he."

"This is Janice's mother."

"Oh, Mrs. McCoy, yes."

"Hi Wellington, as you should know, Janice cancer has worsened, and we are calling everyone to come and say their goodbyes this week." My heart sunk. The promise I made to Janice filled my thoughts. "Hello?"

"Umm—I'm here. I've been calling, but no one answered my calls."

She paused and said, "You have been such a pain in our family's life with your broken promises to my daughter. However, inviting you to see her one last time is to satisfy Janice. She made a request for us to reach out to you when the time has come, and I chose to do this for my baby before she leaves this earth."

"Thank you—"

"She's not responsive, and she has a few days the doctor said."

"I'll be there tomorrow." She hung up, and I dealt with a familiar numbness all over my body. I focused on the sunlight glistening on the shed, and I scanned my notebook.

I've written *The Mad Scientist Team* as the header, and numbered members' names from one to five. Wheatly's name pencil in at number two, Aaron at number three, and I added Charlie to number four. I took a deep breath and then like lightning, I hurried out of the house and into the shed. The closet door was open, and the Mercy Tree grew a few inches bigger and more marvelous than before. I grabbed the crate from out of the corner, sat on it, and placed my notebook on my lap. I prepared to go deeper into the Mercy Tree's thoughts as my hands repeatedly tapped the side of the desk to organize the forever-flowing questions in my mind. I wanted to chat with the thing but didn't know how to do it. My hands scratched my forehead as I shook off the pain that was boiling inside of me.

Then, I saw it, in the corner of the shed, covered in dust, laid Dad's old pocket Bible. Memories captured my imagination as though Dad sat at the desk studying and praying. I fell to my knees, grabbed the small pocket Bible, and roamed through the thin pages. Underlined sentences, circled words, and various highlights told his story—the story of how Dad dealt with depression, worry, doubt and how each scripture ministered to him. Tears streamed down my face as I felt a warm presence. Dad's prayer life covered this shed, and his relationship with God had developed here. It was his prayer-war-room, and he fought a good fight. "Who are you? What are you? Why are you here?" I howled to the Mercy Tree.

Those questions rolled out of my mouth, and I waited for a loud voice to clap like thunder. Nothing happened—or had it? Did my blindness to the spiritual realm block it? The cool breeze passed through, and birds chirped. I read the passage when Moses found the burning bush, but still, no sign came from the tree. I slowly tapped the tree and again, nothing.

"I left my family to protect them from you. You didn't have to heal my hand, you didn't have to take my father away because of it. I blame you! . . . I blamed you . . . I blame me." I sobbed. "God, please forgive me for hating you so much for all these years and for giving up on myself, and my family, and my faith. I don't know who I am anymore, but I am willing to learn and to start over. I want to be the man that my dad wanted me to be, strong and courageous."

An unexplainable peacefulness entered my body, and I whispered to myself, "Do not worry," while rubbing my forehead.

I exited the shed and felt relieved for expressing my feelings to Mercy Tree and to God. And I felt that my questions were heard. One battle at a time, I reminded myself as my heart palpitated. Janice's life was slipping away, and I didn't want to lose her. I randomly flipped to Philippians 4:13 in the Bible, and it was highlighted. I read silently, 'I can do all things through Christ who strengthens me,' and then placed the Bible into my pocket.

«CHAPTER THIRTEEN»

No one moved or made a sound once the doctor closed the bedroom door to examine Janice. Aunts, uncles, and cousins sat silently in the living room and watched the small television in the corner. I sat between Janice's uncle and her cousin. They didn't say a word to me for most of the day, but she referred to me when someone asked who I was.

"Oh, that's Janice's fiancé," her cousin stated, and my head quickly turned to her conversation with family members. Proud that Janice told them about the proposal, I waved to them.

"Hmm, where has he been this whole time?" one grumbled and embarrassment formed on my face. I grabbed my collar and wiped the sweat from my forehead.

"So you're a scientist." Her uncle tilted his head towards me.

"Yes. I work at Pharmaceutical Plant Discoveries downtown." I nodded.

"Oh, the big factory that causes all that traffic in the morning on the east freeway. What you do there?" he groaned.

"I—research cures for diseases." My face turned bright red.

"Is that so?" He jutted his chin and swished his head away.

I slightly leaned over into his space. "Yeah. That's why I been away for so long, I was working on helping Janice beat this thing," I explained, and he scooted away. I re-centered myself on the couch and went back to feeling like the hour hand on a broken clock, stuck in the same spot as another hour passed by. My phone buzzed, and I immediately felt saved by the unknown number and rushed outside.

The sun shined bright, the cold air relaxed my mood and the smell of freshly cut grass danced in the wind.

"This is Wellington," I grunted in my deep voice.

"Wellington? This is Dr. Frazier."

"Oh, Dr. Frazier, how are you?"

"Great son. Look, I heard you were in town, and I would like you to come into the office."

I didn't have much to share with Dr. Frazier but the information regarding the possible Angelic beings in the cave or my secret, Mercy Tree.

"Umm, of course."

"I can't wait to hear about the results so far."

"Yes. I found a few things that I would like to share with you." I wondered how Dr. Frazier knew I was in town. The phone disconnected, and I thought for a while and then I realized. "Dang-git, Charlie."

"Wellington?" A soft voice called out behind me, an older woman stuck her head around the door. "Do you want to see her?" Mrs. Joy, Janice's mother, asked.

My heart thudded as I shoved the phone into my pocket. "Yes ma'am." I forced my legs to follow Mrs. Joy inside the house, past everyone in the living room, and to the back of their ranch home. The hallway went from the sunlight shining brightly in the front part of the house to the dim hallway lights leading our way to the furthest bedroom. She pushed the door open, and I spotted pink walls with pictures of Janice's childhood displayed upon them. To imagine that Janice grew up in this room from a newborn baby to a teenager, that it once was used as a weekend getaway during college, and now her hospice room was unbelievable. I thought not only about how many memories her room held, but I thought about my own memories of when I first saw my father in a hospital bed with tubes attached to him. Mrs. Joy and the doctor gave me space. Janice, skin and bone, struggled to breathe. Her hair was completely gone. She didn't look like the woman I loved, the woman I wanted to marry. She was a different person, and despite the way she looked, I still loved her. Tears filled my eyes as I stepped forward. I rested my large hands on to her tiny body and felt the rhythm of the machine helping her to breathe.

"She's strong," the doctor mentioned as he packed away his things. "However, I feel family and friends should say their goodbyes soon."

"How long does she have?" My voice broke.

"I would say a few hours, maybe a few days."

With her weak hand held in mine, I whispered, "Please wait for me to get back."

"I don't understand?" Mrs. Joy inched forward.

"I have to go to Florida."

Mrs. Joy's nostrils flared, and her feet stomped towards me. "Wellington. My daughter chased after you for three years with nothing to show for it, and you're going to go to Florida when she's literally on her deathbed?"

I stood there and cautiously explained, "It's important. My cousin is going to the Moon and—"

"And the one that you were going to marry is dying?" Just like Mama, she threw her hands into the air and headed towards the door where the doctor stood, shocked by our exchange.

"Mrs. McCoy, I really love Janice. She means a lot to me. Everything I am doing is for her, and she knows it deep inside. I will be back before Janice passes away."

Mrs. Joy left the bedroom with the doctor while muttering under her breath. I held Janice's hand, and I hoped she heard every word, and I knew she knew that I loved her. I kissed her on the forehead. "I got my faith back, and I need you to prove to me it works. Wait for me." I slowly got on to my knees.

"God, I know we spoke yesterday, but I need your help. As you know, my girlfriend is—my wife is dying." I wept desperately. To control my weakness, I held on tight to Janice's hand and continued, "I have to be in Florida to send off my cousin. I love them both, and I wouldn't be who I am today without them, so can you please spare my wife's life for a few more days? I know you did it before for other people." My whole body trembled. I searched for a dose of encouragement or something to calm my heart from bursting inside of my chest.

Suddenly, I felt something thick and heavy inside of my coat. I yanked it out. Dad's pocket Bible, as if he knew I would need it. I quickly flipped to a highlighted scripture and read Galatians 2:20, "I have been crucified with Christ, and I no longer live, but Christ lives in me. The life I now live in the body, I live by faith in the Son of God, who loved me and gave himself for me."

I quickly re-centered myself on my knee and locked my fingers together and prayed, "Jesus, please forgive me for my sins against you. I don't understand the things that have happened to me, but I do believe you are a good God and worthy of praise. I believe in you. I believe you came to Earth and saved humanity from our sinful ways. I believe you sent the Mercy Tree to me to show me things . . . Please heal me from this broken heart and please heal Janice."

Prayer was my only solution and the only thing Mama taught me to do when things didn't feel quite right. "You held time for someone in the Bible." I squinted up at the ceiling as I bit my bottom lip. However, my prayers gave me the courage to solve how the soil can cure diseases. My excitement burst through, and I finally convinced myself to share the Mercy Tree with Dr. Frazier for the greater good. Janice peacefully slept, unaware of me, and breathed as if she held on for a miracle.

$$* * *$$

My reflection in the elevator doors stared back at me. The beeping sound of each floor bled through my ears, and I repeatedly tapped the notebook against my hand. The excitement to share this information with Dr. Frazier and to ask for access to Scientific Allegiance Agency's secure database for more technical data and tools gave me courage. The doors slid open, and my foot quickly hit the shiny red floors. I headed straight towards Trixie's desk, and with one glance, she lit up.

"Oh, Wellington, how is the project going?" she flirted.

"Ah, good actually." I was surprised by her concern.

"I know you probably solved something big. Everyone has been talking about how brave you are to take on such a hard case all alone." She leaned forward and poked her lips out.

"It's nothing, really. Is Dr. Frazier in?" I stepped back and loosened my collar.

"Sure." She signaled to his closed door. I quickly walked to his door, held my knuckles up, and Trixie said in a soothing and disturbing tone, "You can go right in, Dr. Kole," that sent chills down my spine. I quickly opened and peeked my head inside of Dr. Frazier's office. It hadn't changed much. Still, papers and binders cluttered his desk, and pictures of him still dominated the walls. I opened the door wider, and Dr. Frazier was already in a meeting, but I didn't know who because the back of the man's head stopped me.

"Oh, yes the man of the hour." Dr. Frazier got up, hurried to me, and patted me on the back.

"You have all of PPD talking about you cracking a piece of the puzzle?" He gripped my hand tightly as if I had a piece of yummy candy to share.

"Ah—I don't know if I did, sir." I stuttered because of the shaking.

He released me and headed back to his chair. I massaged my hand and announced, "Sir, the cave did have something interesting, and it was right in front of our faces this whole time." The back of the man's head became Gary's face. "What is he doing here?" I grumbled.

"He's a part of this project. I thought we spoke about this, Wellington?"

"He's not a scientist." My voice deepened, and my throat muscle quivered.

"Well, Charlie isn't, and you made him a part of this project. So, what do you have to tell us?" Dr. Frazier urged.

I muttered and thought quickly. "Three government officials came to my house and took the green binder—"

"Ah—so I heard. You had the SAA down my throat about that. Wellington, stick to the soil project and don't step in any other territory."

"I was researching the soil project, and I happened to stumble upon something that the government is hiding."

"Well, leave that to Detective Gary. He's a part of the SAA and an excellent investigator."

"Wellington, I only want to help," Gary said.

"Yeah, you've been doing a lot of that lately."

"Oh, so you heard? Wheatly and Aaron needed recommendation letters, so I offered to help."

I loosened up a little and asked, "Do you remember the figures on the wall?"

"Wait a minute before you start spitting out equations and theories. I need you to sign this waiver." Dr. Frazier handed me a stack of paper.

"Every report and research you compile from this day forward belongs to PPD. That includes secret experiments that you've worked on while being employed here."

"What?"

"Everyone signed one this afternoon. New company policy."

"I don't know about this." I tossed the papers on his desk.

"Wellington! You're scared that your figures on the wall theory would be stolen?"

"Umm. No, it just… can I think about it?"

"We need results now. We need a solution now or . . . you're fired!" Dr. Frazier exploded.

My stomach hardened, and a painful tightness fluttered in my throat. The tension was thick, and I headed towards the door.

"I don't remember figures on the wall," Gary calmly reported to me. "But I do remember a glowing tree." My hand stopped from opening the door, and my heart pounded repeatedly.

"Glowing Tree?" Dr. Frazier's interest struck gold. He sat on the edge of his desk, stroking his beard and watching my every move. "What is that? How does it glow? Why…" curiosity and confusion in his thoughts.

"Yes, from what I remember, there was a tiny tree on the pile of soil glowing," Gary spoke up as I slowly turned to face them both.

"Off your meds again, Gary?" I chuckled, and his face became instantly red.

"Crack jokes if you want to Wellington. I'm pretty sure that stealing is a felony in Israel."

"Tell me more about this glowing tree?" Dr. Frazier's eyes twinkled.

"Are you serious? So, you ignore ancient figures on the wall and the government hiding something, but an imaginary glowing tree gets you on the edge of your seat?"

Gary stormed towards the black-and-white picture of the camping trip on the wall and pointed. "It glowed in the complete darkness. Wellington and his family know more about it."

"I don't know what you are talking about."

"You're lying, and I am going to prove it," Gary said.

"So, you're going to investigate me?" My unbelievable laughter broke the tension in the room. Gary glided closer to me.

"Not unless you give me a reason to," he deeply grunted.

Dr. Frazier stepped in between us. "Wellington is this true?"

"Dr. Frazier, right now my girlfriend is dying, and my cousin is about to go to space. I think my focus should go to that for now." I stormed away.

"Wellington, my condolences. I had no idea that Janice was sick," Dr. Frazier sincerely apologized, and I accepted it.

"Aaron is still going to Space? That's impossible," Gary grunted in disbelief.

"You wrote the letter, right? Aaron was selected, and from what I heard, I was too."

Dr. Frazier silently went behind his desk and explained, "Wellington, I knew you were going to be busy on this project, so I declined the opportunity for you."

Gary interrupted, "No, Aaron's trip was canceled due to astonishing new development. They replaced the cadets with professional astronauts."

"Well, I guess, Mr. Investigator, you have your facts wrong. Aaron is still going, and I guess no thanks to you. Dr. Frazier, I am not signing the forms."

"Wellington, if you walk out of this office, you abandon all of your resources. Think about Janice. This can save her."

I stopped and thought for a moment and murmured, "I am." Then I hurried to the elevator, pressed the down button, and the doors quickly opened. Gary stood halfway down the hallway and yelled with both hands outlining his mouth. "Wellington!"

I stopped the doors from closing and listened to him.

"Those weren't the only letters that I wrote. I knew your family would be happy to see you at Wheatly's celebration dinner."

My mouth fell open as the elevator doors closed. *Gary sent me the letter.*

«CHAPTER FOURTEEN»

THE SUN LOOKED like a honeycomb in the middle of a clear blue ocean, no dark clouds or a clap of thunder for miles. May was a perfect month for a space launch at the Kennedy Space Center in Florida. We saw nothing but shiny grass for miles and miles and a gigantic space shuttle in the distance.

I caught a ride from Georgia with Mama and the family early that morning. When we arrived, we joined the other cadets' family members at the reception desk and toured the facility. Once the tour was over, we impatiently waited behind a roped-off designated area for the eight cadets to parade out of the Space Center. Cars parked along the street were filled with bystanders using binoculars. My family stood in the front row holding signs that read: *We Love You, Kingston Kole.* Three news vans rushed on to the field, and reporters raced towards the crowd.

I was writing down a few notes into my small notebook when I got nudged from behind.

"Wow. Aaron is actually going to the moon." Wheatly, filled with joy tossed popcorn into his mouth.

He wore a Future Eight T-shirt from the gift store.

"You sure know how to get into the spirit." I wore my shirt as a scarf around the back of my shoulders.

"Come on, man? Everything isn't about your hopes and dreams. We have to live ours too." Wheatly tossed more popcorn into his mouth and munched.

I waited impatiently until the horn blew, preparing everyone for the Future Eight Cadets to greet everyone. The doors gradually swung open, and families screamed and waved signs with their cadet's name on it. Each astronaut—small to tall—walked in a straight line wearing sunglasses and a beige jumpsuit. They stopped in front of the mini stage and waved. Wheatly elbowed me and said, "Where is Branch?"

I skimmed the line from small too big and from big to small, and Branch was nowhere to be found. In fact, no one from the original list was present, except for Aaron and the woman cadet. They stood as President Bush approached the podium.

"Can we give these cadets some applause?" He clapped and cheered, "We're going to the moon. Again!" He raised his arms into the air as the crowd went wild. "Family and friends, I want to welcome you today at NASA's special moon mission." Everyone clapped again. "These men and woman standing before you today embody special talents, knowledge, and abilities to make the world a better place. We are proud to be Americans during this unique time in history."

"Tell us what makes this space mission so special," one reporter asked.

"NASA and the Scientific Allegiance Agency teamed up to make the Earth a better and healthier place to live. We have the strongest and the toughest men and woman here ready to achieve any mission ahead of them. Each one of them will truly be added to history." Everyone cheered and waved their signs. A burning sensation boiled in my chest as I heard Aaron would go down in history before me. Aaron waved to the crowd and blew kisses to his mother and wife. The President walked down from the small stage, shook all the astronauts' hands, and then headed back into the facility.

Our family rushed to the front line. "Over here." Wheatly waved from the back. Aaron caught his wave, and rushed over to us. He hugged and kissed his wife, Beatrice, and squeezed their daughter, Dianne, in his arms. "Hey, don't turn ten before I get back?"

He kissed her, and she whined, "Daddy!" wiping her face. "Don't forget to bring me something back cool." He released Dianne and nodded okay.

Aaron kissed Aunt Pinky's cheeks as she grabbed his arms and instructed, "Now, be careful and listen to everything that they have to say, you hear me?"

"Mom, I got this." He kissed her again and headed towards us. He opened his arms and gave Wheatly and me a joint hug.

"Man. You got to meet the President of the United States! I am so proud of you," Wheatly beamed with his eyes locked on the president. "Oh, bring me something back too. Something that I can experiment on or add to my collection?"

"Of course! You just promise not to get married until I get back."

"You better be back in time for my wedding."

"This is going down in history? Wow, that's super big." My teeth clutched, and Aaron tilted his head to the side. "Don't worry. Your time is coming, Welly."

My burning jealousy faded away. "Are you sure about this?" I asked.

"Come on man. I am about to get on the shuttle in a few minutes." Aaron agitatedly chuckled and shooed me away. "He still at this?" Aaron motioned to Wheatly.

"I just want to make sure that you're ready. That's all."

They both passed looks to each other and then Aaron loosened up. "Yes, thank you for your concern."

"I went to PPD to tell Dr. Frazier about Mercy Tree and Gary was—"

"You finally told Dr. Frazier about the tree? That's great news."

"Umm. Not quite. There was a little problem when I went to see Dr. Frazier, and I don't know if I can trust him anymore."

"Okay, so you're here to convince me to stay to help you because you don't trust anyone but me?" Aaron stepped back, not interested in what else I had to say.

"Yeah, and I risked leaving Janice on her deathbed too. You get me so much," I sarcastically announced, and Aaron gasped.

"Jeez man, I'm sorry. How is she?"

"She has a few days, maybe a few hours."

"And you came to Florida to see me off? Wow. I don't know what to say?"

"You wanted me to be here, and I wanted to convince you to stay too." I chuckled.

"Welly, I am not trying to argue with you before I leave. I have other obligations, like walking on to that space shuttle and completing a major mission."

"About that, oddly enough, Gary said they suspended your trip and replaced people, and he was pretty shocked that you're still going," I revealed.

Aaron wrapped his arms around our shoulders and pulled us closer as he checked over his shoulder.

"Aaron, what are you not telling us?" I grumbled

"Wow. Are you investigating my every move now? They canceled the original mission, but I kind of sweet-talked my way back into it."

"Aaron, what is happening?" I demanded.

"No one is supposed to know that this isn't the original mission."

"But where is Branch?" Wheatly wondered.

Aaron gently pulled Wheatly and I closer again and whispered, "Please, keep this a secret from my mom." He patted us on the shoulder. Aaron groomed his shirt, and he walked away, but I grabbed his shoulder.

"Wait. Why are you still going if the mission changed?"

Aaron yanked himself from me and demanded, "Wellington, stop asking me about it. Has it ever occurred to you that maybe because I am good at what I do?"

I got a glimpse of his weakening eyes, a secret that he would die before he told me, and because of his treacherous action, I stormed away. However, sorrow attacked my mood, and I darted to Aaron and hugged him.

"Wellington," he grumbled, and I handed him my small notebook.

"What do you want me to do with this?"

"I don't know. Write about your journey while you're gone. I want to read all about your three months in space." I tried to hold back my tears, but they fell onto my shirt.

Aaron wrapped his arm around my shoulder, flipped to the first page and read, "Examine, develop, and try each experiment again and again and again . . . soon you will become the experiment by Headmaster of Chemicals . . . For the Mount Hit-ga-lút equal the Mount Revelation Project." He snickered. "Your way of saying to work on the project while I'm in space?"

"No, rip the page out or do whatever. Now go."

"Naw, I'll keep a piece of you in space with me. Thank you." We released each other. "Go be with Janice." He pointed to me, then headed towards Beatrice, and gave her one last emotional kiss before going inside of the building.

"I'm going to miss him," Wheatly moaned.

"Me too," I mumbled to him.

The Future Eight headed back into the building to adequately prepare for their take off.

* * *

The headmasters shook hands in the crowd and then mingled in their circle. The Headmaster of Botany stood a few feet from me, and I contemplated where should I hide.

"What . . . what's wrong?" Wheatly peeked over my shoulder. "Who are you hiding from?"

"The man in the all blue suit is Headmaster of Botany and Dr. Frazier's boss, and he's the reason why I haven't been promoted," I whispered.

"What! Didn't Branch say that he raves over your published reports each month? You should talk to him."

"And say what?" I grumbled at Wheatly.

"Well, I'll talk to him and tell him about you." Wheatly started to walk over, but I grabbed him by his arm.

"Stop playing games. This is serious."

"Well, stop acting like a kid and ask the man what you should improve on so you can be promoted," Wheatly suggested.

Dr. Frazier's reason why the board never promoted me—because of my cockiness and proud reports—rang heavy in my mind. Then what Branch said about the headmasters rejoicing over my work comforted me. I took a deep breath, marched towards the headmasters' circle. "HM. Trevestor." We shook hands as he squinted, and he seemed to not remember me at first,

"Ah—Well—Wellington. Oh, yes. How are you doing?" He stepped away from the group.

"I didn't think you would remember me."

"I could never forget an intelligent young man like you. You always had the answers, and your research is so delightful. What are you up to these days?" He chuckled.

"Just working hard at Pharmaceuticals Plant Discoveries, and Dr. Frazier has me working on the soil case, again."

"Oh yes, that infinite case. The board can't wait for the results." He shook his head. "I wish Dr. Frazier would accept his fate and give up PPD in peace. Save us all the embarrassment." He sighed. "Listen, son, I know you like working at Pharmaceutical Plant Discoveries and your reports every month are very—"

"Sir, I must apologize for anything that you heard of me. Sometimes I get carried away with scientific talk, and I can come off rude at times."

"Umm, Wellington, what do you mean?"

"Oh, Dr. Frazier told me the reason why I haven't been promoted within the agency."

"Is that so?" His cheeks fell, and a stone expression covered his face. "That explains why you never accepted my job offers to work for me at the SAA. We needed a junior scientist to handle our hydroponics department."

"Excuse me?" My body heated as I fumbled over my words. "You . . . wanted me to work at the headquarters and be in charge of a wide variety of vegetables and plants sent from scientists in the fields so I could test and provide a concrete scientific solution to their theoretical development—"

"Of course!" He stopped me before I passed out, "Your mind is brilliant. But Dr. Frazier said that you and he were reorganizing and rebuilding PPD's brand, and the soil case was the start of that." He noticed my disgusted expression and sighed, "It looks like he lied about that too." He stuck his chest out. "Son, my best advice to you is to find another job. We are closing Pharmaceuticals Plant Discoveries because Dr. Frazier ran through the budget and has not produced anything groundbreaking since you guys found the cave."

"HM. Trevestor, I would love to work for you at SAA if you would give me another chance."

"All the departments are fully staffed," he muttered. "I'll be happy to write a recommendation letter for you." He placed his hand on my shoulder. I slumped over, defeated and confused.

I had nothing to lose but my dignity. "I will take over PPD," I declared like a robot seeking revenge. "No, I will become a Headmaster and lead a whole new division that involves plant science under the SAA." Another crazy thought hit the air.

"I think all branches of science are accounted for, but I am optimistic. Do you have something to present to the board?"

I awoke from my robotic-stillness.

"I—I am close to something… I think." My nerves tingled in my chest as I lied through my teeth.

"Send me a feasible report and sample of your new science, and I will sponsor you at the next Headmaster Induction meeting." He thought for a moment and informed me, "Which is next year, but it's approaching fast, so clean up whatever you have in mind to pitch."

Wheatly cleared his throat from behind me and extended his hand.

"Hi, sir, my name is Wheatly Kole."

"Yes, this is my younger brother. He'll be working with the FBI in the Elite Scientific Program."

"And our cousin is going to space too!" Wheatly rocked on to his tippy toes.

"Really? Wow, I heard these astronauts are trained killers. Whatever they are looking for better be ready." He winked at me, walked away, and said, "Call me Wellington." He pointed at me.

With my arms crossed, I repeated, "Trained killers?"

"Is that all of the headmasters over there?" Wheatly ignored my question and admired the group of headmasters chatting.

"No, but did you hear what he said?"

"About what?"

He suddenly waved to a group of officers.

"Hey! That's Gary." Gary stood twenty feet away wearing a navy blue suit and sunglasses. He lowered the tip of his sunglasses and sneered.

"Why did you call him over here?" I grumbled to Wheatly.

"Why not? We're friends."

Before I knew it, Gary was shaking Wheatly's hand and then held his hand out to me.

"You're following me," I accused him.

"Ah, don't feel so lucky." He folded his arms. "I came to send off the chosen cadets into the sky." He took a deep breath, taking in the misty air.

"Wheatly, meet the guy who forged Mama's letter. The one that asked me to come home."

"What? Is that true?" Wheatly stepped forward.

"Guilty as charged," Gary confessed.

"Thank you so much." He patted Gary on the shoulder.

"Thank you?" I glared at Wheatly. "He lied. He invaded our privacy."

"And he got you home ... And put a smile on Mama's face. You're forever okay in my book." Wheatly shook Gary's hand again and said, "I'm going to say hi to a few of the headmasters."

"Introduce yourself to the Headmaster of Armed Forces, Admiral Clive." Gary winked, and Wheatly hurried away.

"You're sick," I grunted.

"I'm trying to save you from the embarrassment when that little space shuttle lands on the moon and discovers a radiant and marvelous glow coming from North America. Then it will zoom into the United States of America and pinpoints Virginia Beach and then pinpoints Wellington Kole's house. When that happens, I will be ready to take you away in handcuffs for lying to a federal agent," he whispered into my ear and then revealed the badge on his belt.

"Yeah, and I will report you for seducing my brother to get closer to me." I bumped his shoulder, but he quickly stepped in front of me.

"Maybe I did all of it to get you here. When SAA threatened to close down PPD, Dr. Frazier contacted me and asked about the glowing tree I spoke about all these years, and that he brushed off. Now, he's desperate to save his reputation now that the SAA brags about you and your research reports about plant intelligence.

The reports gave them so much hope, and Dr. Frazier never had what it took to be a researcher or developer. He was more of the analytical and adventurous type who did well in the field. That is why he needed you . . . someone who had the brains to keep him at the top while they stupidly scrambled at the bottom. That fraternity that he inducted you into while in college was made up. It was to break you down so you can remain down."

Memories of Dr. Frazier inducting me populated my mind. Dr. Frazier's plot to distance me from my family tore me away from my faith.

I became angry. "Why are you telling me this?"

"Because I like a good challenge, and since I know what is causing the radiant glow, I'm going to have fun taking you down," he whispered.

"What do you have against me?"

"You convinced everyone that I was crazy for seeing a glowing tree, and I made it my mission to ruin you, even if I had my Uncle Clive ask the Headmasters to reject your application to the ESP and accept mine."

I wobbled backward, and he yelled, "Run Wellington, run!" He laughed. "Run Wellington, run."

People threw glances at us as I stumbled close to Mama and the family. Gary's and HM. Trevestor's statement haunted me for the whole day. Aaron's unknown secret mission scared me. The Mercy Tree was the only thing that made sense to me, and even that became a much bigger secret. I hugged Mama's shoulder as she tried to use her binoculars to view the sky.

It made no sense to worry about Aaron's safety and his mysterious journey. His story was not mine to tell. However, I silently prayed, "God, please watch over Aaron and give me a sign that he'll be okay." I sighed and emotionally set aside today's battle to focus on Janice's battle with cancer.

«CHAPTER FIFTEEN»

THE MONITOR BUZZED and beeped. It reassured everyone that Janice's body still lived despite the outer appearance of defeat. For five days, I found refuge in the chair next to Janice's bed. I wanted to be close to her even though it pained me to know how she struggled harder and harder to breathe. My watch beeped, letting me know that noon was near. Since God answered my prayers and spared Janice's life for another day, I held the signed paperwork from Dr. Frazier in my hand to give to him. After all, it was never about me, but about saving the people, I loved. The hospice nurse entered the bedroom with a large bag and flopped it on the stand next to Janice. "You're a doctor?" she asked.

I shuffled the papers and glanced down at my white lab jacket.

"Oh, no, well… I am a doctor of plant science but not a medical doctor."

She smiled and fluffed Janice's pillow and moved her arms up and down. The nurse cared for Janice even though she was dying and that made me want to do the same.

"Excuse me." I leaned forward. "Can I give Janice a sip of tea?"

The nurse cautiously wondered if I made a joke and said, "Umm—I don't understand?"

"I just want to do something special for her. Each morning, I used to make Janice Chai-Tea, and I guess, I wanted to make it for her again before she—well you know."

A happy glow flushed her face. "Yes, of course. She can't really swallow, but we can try to prop her up, and she can taste it."

I clapped my hands twice and pointed to the nurse. "I'll be right back."

I hurried to the kitchen, filled up the kettle, and placed it on the stove. I took the sugar and a mug from out of the cabinet and hesitated to pour sugar or to leave it plain. I wanted this to be perfect, and the pressure of making Janice's last tea troubled me.

A loud whistle broke my concentration, and I quickly turned off the stove. I searched the cabinet for Chai-Tea, but the container was empty. I rumbled through all the shelves, the pantry, and refrigerator desperate to find something. None. I felt defeated when my hands felt something rough and prickly inside of my coat pocket. I slowly pulled the unknown object out, and it was my half of the broken stem from Mercy Tree.

"Oh, my God." A healthy and spotless stem. The cup was empty, so I poured hot water into it. "Why are you still alive?" I questioned the stem. Childlike faith burned inside of me, and the thought of experimenting grew deeper. I laid the stem on to the cabinet and sliced its leaves in smaller pieces. Then I dropped it into the mug. My heart pounded loudly as I took a sip. The watery concoction made my taste buds disapprove. I didn't care. I stood there for a moment with closed eyes and prayed, "God. My faith is stronger, and your power is bigger. Please heal Janice. In Jesus's name." My heartbeat faded, and peace rested on me. I carried the mug like a torch.

The nurse had Janice already propped up and a drinking tube attached to her mouth.

"It's warm," I warned as I took another sip to show her.

She held the tube and motioned for me to slowly pour a few drops into it. My clammy hands shook as I poured into the feeding tube. Janice's eyes gently moved under her eyelids. Fear crept inside of me, and I said, "Okay, that's enough." I moved Janice's hair back.

Inside of the cup, pieces of the leaves were gone.

The nurse laid Janice back into a comfortable position. Doubt tried to dominate my mind, but memories of Mercy Tree's glistening kept me whole.

In the front of the house, the door opened and chatter from the McCoys filled the house.

I followed their voices to the living room and placed the mug on the kitchen table.

"How is she?" her father, Kevin McCoy, asked.

"She's good. Been sleeping." The only signs of life came from the machine beeping.

The nurse joined us, already packed and ready to head out.

"Okay. I'll be back same time tomorrow," the nurse stated, and we all said our goodbyes.

"Game time." Mr. Kevin threw his jacket on the couch and sat down to watch the game.

"Yeah. I'm going to head out for a bit." I checked my phone. Five missed calls from Dr. Frazier. Suddenly, a text message appeared.

'Hope you're not backing out!'

He'd been pressuring me to turn in the papers ever since I left his office, and I wanted to because I urgently needed all the help that I could get. I hurried to the guest bedroom near Janice's bedroom to grab my bag and paperwork. The bedroom belonged to Janice's younger brother. Most of his high school trophies from track and field and basketball championships covered the wall. One picture of him in his Army fatigue uniform with his bunk buddies hung beside a plaque.

"I don't know why you stare at that same photo every time you stay in here," Janice complained.

"Well, I think it sucks that he can't come home to see you before you die."

Janice, pale and weak, folded clothes neatly into my bag.

"Janice?" My mouth fell open. Her eyes were large, and her arms were still skinny. She took a deep breath, soaking in the air without a struggle.

"I told my parents that you were neat. Why do you have your clothes thrown everywhere, Wellington?" Janice grumbled unaware of her fragile appearance.

"Janice . . . how do you feel?" I cradled the side of her head, grabbed her wrist, and checked her pulse.

"What?" She smacked my hands away, and she folded clothes again.

"Janice, do you know that you were sick?" I staggered back, and she stopped folding and slowly analyzed her nightgown. Suddenly, her knees became weak, and I caught her in my arms. "It's okay. You're okay."

"I—was—dying? I don't remember anything."

"Yes. But now you're better."

"But how?"

"I don't know."

Janice moved from out of my arms and twirled around. She stopped and covered her mouth to prevent herself from vomiting. She chuckled, tapped her feet, and wiggled her hands.

Saliva oozed from the corner of her mouth as she drooled, "I have to tell my parents. Where are they?" She fumbled to the door.

"Wait!" But she was gone out of my sight. Screams of joy and horror sounded throughout the home. Mrs. Joy and Mr. Kevin embraced their daughter and cried. I grabbed my papers and briefcase and ran into the living room.

"How could this be?" Mr. Kevin held Janice close to his chest, and then Janice wobbled away.

"Wellington, did it work?" Janice wondered. "Like you said?"

"Ah, I think it did."

"Of course it did! You knew it was possible. You had faith, the glowing tree is real!" Janice screamed.

Mr. Kevin kissed Janice on the forehead and held her close again.

"Did you cure her?" tears slid down his face and onto his shirt.

"Ah—"

"I told you he would keep his promise," Janice bragged to her parents as she wiped his eyes.

"It's a miracle," I spoke up.

Janice wobbled and fell, but we all caught her.

"Take it easy," I warned.

Janice broke away from us and staggered into her mom's arms.

"Mom, Wellington is going to change the world." Mrs. Joy felt Janice's forehead, and Janice grabbed my hand. "You're going to make history."

My ear tingled, and my heart rejoiced. Mrs. Joy gave Janice a big hug, then rushed to the phone and dialed.

I pressed the disconnect button and scowled, "Wait. This must be kept a secret for now, until tests are done." I grabbed the phone from Mrs. Joy and hung it up. No one said a word.

"We have to tell the nurse and the doctor something." Mrs. Joy folded her arms and cocked her head to the side.

I kissed Janice's cheek and headed towards the front door.

"Where are you going?" Janice held on to me.

"To the lab. I'll be back, but I need you to stay here and rest." I looked at her parents. "Please call me if something goes wrong." They were nervous, but they understood what was at stake.

I sat in my car and thought for a moment. I thought about Dad's warning to me all those years ago, Mama's faith talk, and Mercy Tree's massive glow. I thought about my fears that shackled me down for all those years. I took the signed paperwork for Dr. Frazier and threw them out of the window and sped off.

«CHAPTER SIXTEEN»

I PARKED, AND THE ENGINE hummed quietly in front of Mama's home. The nine-hour drive from Georgia made me hot and stinky, but I didn't care. I lounged in the seat and imagined myself accepting awards and telling my story on television. Then an imaginary pin popped my bubble. *Would Janice's healing be enough and would God take away someone I love?*

I quickly turned the van off and grabbed the Headmaster Induction application that HM. Trevestor mailed me and silently read the beginning of my thesis I'd submitted.

'The soil does indeed have healing and restorative power, but faith is the main ingredient. Therefore, without faith, the restoration of one's bodily sickness cannot be healed.' The sharp pain in my mind questioned me, *how could I prove faith as the main ingredient to SAA?*

Inside, Mama rushed to my side and held onto my arm.

"Wellington. Thank God you are home."

"Hey, Mom, I am but can't stay long. I have to go back to Atlanta to work on some things." I rushed out the kitchen's back door, and she followed me to the shed.

"Back to Atlanta? You just got home. Well, there is a man—"

My phone rang.

"Mom, this is Wheatly. I have to take this." I stepped away for some privacy.

"Hey, what did you find?" I whispered into the phone.

Wheatly whispered back, "I managed to get into SAA's classified system." His voice trembled.

"Did you find anything?" I urged him.

I could imagine Wheatly in a dark place with the computer light shining on his face as he intensely skimmed through the classified documents.

"Wellington, there's too much information about Mount Revelation to read. It's over a thousand pages."

"Come on, find something about the soil."

Wheatly typed Mount Revelation in the search bar, and a few pages populated the screen, and he read. "Okay, here is something. In 1990 they dug a thousand feet and found a large amount of roots of some sort and bones. They kept on digging because there was a bright glow from under the surface, but still, they couldn't find out what was making it."

"Anything about a tree?"

"Umm. No, just animals fossils and—"

"And what? What did they find?" Sweat formed between my ear and the phone.

"Elements of The Garden of Eden." Silence. "When they ran a test on the roots and fossils, it came back with a rare genetic substance, and they saw luminous radiation."

Wheatly muttered about chemical facts and analytical information while my mind tried to connect the dots. He finally explained, "It basically says that the fragmented bones match the same animals today, but when they tested their DNA, the results were different. One scientist said that all of the bones were strong and filled with ancient information about the earth's very beginning—"

"Packaged away for all these years for someone to discover, to reveal it centuries later," I mumbled.

"But what does all of this mean?" Wheatly questioned.

"It means that Mount Revelation is not an ordinary mountain. Mercy Tree's roots go over a thousand layers deep into the Earth, starting where Eden is approximately located."

"How do you know that?" Wheatly gasped.

"I don't know." I massaged my forehead's temples.

"This is insane. The document I am reading is called, 'The Signs of The Beginning, The Middle, and The End of the Times,' and you would never guess what image is depicted as the end."

"The Mercy Tree. . . " I gasped as Mama yanked my shirt, "What?" I waved her off.

I heard the door open. "Hey kid, what are you doing on these computers?" a man yelled.

"Wheatly, get out of there!" The call dropped.

I yanked myself from Mama and slowly approached the shed when Mama shouted, "Wellington!"

I cringed and shouted back, "Mom. I am working!"

A short, black hair, and yellow skinned man stood next to her.

"This is the gentleman I have been telling you about. The one who's been coming to our house every day for weeks asking for you," she sneered through the latching of her teeth.

I met him at the bottom of the patio steps and wondered if I knew him.

"Wellington, and you are?" We shook hands.

"Jeong. You can call me Joe, and I am here to answer your questions about the tree inside of your shed."

I staggered backward. I curved my head to Mama, and she shrugged.

"I don't know what you're talking about." My heart quickened as I thought *what if Janice's healing had been exposed?*

"Sure you do. And God sent me here to give you the answers to your questions. You asked who are you? God says it is a symbol. You asked what are you? God said it is a gift, and you asked, why are you here? God says it is my Son's Hit-ga-lút as known as the Revelation because it is the first sign of the beginning." He nodded and headed towards the gate leading to the street.

"Wait. I—but what? Ah, why—why me?"

The man spoke in a soft voice, "Because you chose it, and God says He chose you." He exited quickly.

I tried to organize my thoughts, but he had left me speechless. The man was gone. Mama caressed her cross necklace. My phone rang, and I was relieved to see Wheatly's name. "Hey. What happened?" I stepped away from Mama.

"Ah—I think I'm in super big trouble. I'm only a freshman and not supposed to be on classified governmental computers yet."

"So what is going to happen?"

"I have to plead my case in front of the ESP board tomorrow afternoon."

"Wheatly, I am so sorry. Maybe I can help or Gary?"

"Gary got me this opportunity. I can't count on him to save me from getting caught. Plus he is the one that helped me get into the computer lab . . . and told me to not get caught."

"He did, huh?" I pondered.

"Yeah, now I got to go tell Colette what happened. Talk to you later." The phone went silent.

«CHAPTER SEVENTEEN»

A WEEK LATER, the whole family gathered in the living room with champagne glasses and a slice of pie. Mama wore a pin that read, *The Birthday Girl*. I had everyone sit as I rambled about my success in the lab and complained about the daily frustrating tasks Dr. Frazier made me do. When I was done, I announced, "And I said to Dr. Frazier, I quit."

The announcement dripped from my mouth like sweet lemonade on a Sunday afternoon. Cheers from the whole family packed the room as high fives, and proud glances came my way.

"So what is next?" Wheatly helped his pregnant girlfriend, Colette, up from the couch. She quickly wobbled away to the hallway bathroom.

"I knew you could do it." Mama held my hand in hers. Her rough motherly hands reminded me of how hard Mama worked to provide for Wheatly and me.

"Well, I am going to open my own scientific practice. Hopefully, the SAA will sponsor it."

"Tell us more about the medicine you've discovered," Mama begged.

"First," I held my hand out to Janice, her hair grown to her ears and her health restored. She bashfully stood between my arms. "This leads me to restore one more promise." I bent down on one knee and asked, "Janice Marie McCoy, will you marry me for the one-hundredth time?"

She covered her mouth and nodded yes. I slipped the ring on, and everyone applauded once again. Mama wrapped her arms around Janice and me as Colette wobbled back into the living room.

"What did I miss?" She glided on to the couch with Wheatly's help.

Janice rushed towards her and screamed, "We're going to be sisters-in-law!" She showed off the five-carat ring. The two squealed, and we all covered our ears. Wheatly smirked and brushed himself off trying to ignore the size of the ring.

Janice wrapped her arms around my neck and said, "I owe everything to this man."

"Stop holding back. How did you cure Janice?" Wheatly perched in an empty chair.

I motioned for Janice to sit, and then I sat down on the wooden coffee table to explain everything.

"Years ago, when we found Mercy Tree on Mount Revelation, I knew it wasn't just any tree because it glowed, and only Wheatly, Aaron, and I could see it." Eyes grew larger, and the room became dead silent. "It healed my hand from a puncture wound." I held my hand up. "When I found out that Dad, died and I didn't get into the Elite Scientific Program, I thought I had been cursed. I thought God cursed me for stealing the tree, so before I ruined everyone's life, I left. I stayed away out of fear."

No one said anything for a few seconds.

"That's the reason why you never visited home?" Mama asked.

"Wait. So the tree did heal your hand?" Wheatly interrupted.

"It did, and I wanted to tell you, but I was afraid that the reporters and the scientists would find out—I stole the tree."

"You knew the tree could heal people, and you hid it?"

"Wheatly, I was a kid, and we didn't know what it was or if it was actually a tree."

"You could have saved Dad's life!" He stood and balled his fist. "You could have saved him. What if you found the tree to save him?" he repeated.

Mama embraced him and soothed his rage. "Is this true, Welly?"

My mouth clutched and ran dry. "Mom, I didn't know what it was, and when we got home from Israel . . . and heard all the things on the news, I—I was too afraid to mention it—"

"This whole time you knew." Wheatly continued and paced back and forth.

"Can Wheatly and I be alone for a moment?"

Mama held Wheatly, wiped his eyes, and motioned for everyone to the kitchen.

"Wheatly, I was afraid. We were only boys. We didn't know what it was capable of."

"No! I didn't know what it was capable of, but you did—"

"I thought it took Dad's life because it healed me! It's crazy talk now, but it made sense to me then!"

"I wish Aaron was here to hear this." Still pacing back and forth. "Aaron was right. You came back for yourself. You're too selfish and only care about you and—" He stopped and thought for a moment. "Funny . . . that fear quickly went away when your beloved girlfriend faced death . . . now you can face the Mercy Tree. . . for goodness' sake, you named the damn tree Mercy!"

"I came back because I missed you and Mom."

"How could you? The tree didn't destroy this family. It only tried to save it. You destroyed this family because you're selfish!"

"Wheatly . . . I am sorry. I can't bring Dad back, but I can save many other people's lives. You want to be a superhero; now you can . . . you and I together . . . everything happens for a reason, right? And in God's time?" My eyes, swollen with guilt.

"Our Dad suffered because of you." Wheatly stormed past me, past everyone, and out the back door and to the garden. I grabbed my jacket and cautiously followed behind him.

"I can't stop thinking about how things could have been different if you said something," he mumbled, " to Aaron and me!"

"Me too."

"And I can't help but to think that we let Dad down."

"We're not going to let him down because Dad would have wanted us to help heal the world. This is what being a scientist is really about and Wheatly, I need your brain."

He leaned away from me.

"Your formula side of the brain, not your actual brain. You're a genius, and I need to create medicine for people to consume." I winked at him. "Like a superhero power formula that's called I-bonic armor?" I said.

"An inner armor formula that will protect the inside walls of our body?" Wheatly asked, and I held my hand in front for him to shake it, but he ignored it. "There is no excuse for not saving Dad's life, Welly. However, doing this will save millions, and it will make us heroes in the process . . . well, me anyway." He bumped my shoulders and headed towards the door, but I forced a hug from him. Wheatly gasped as I squeezed him tight. "You must really need my help?" he gasped.

"I want you to help. You're the best at what you do, and Dad would want us to stick together." I released him and held my hand in front of him again.

"For Dad." We shook hands. "There are so many ideas floating around in my head," he rambled.

"Okay, save it for the lab."

"Who am I kidding? I'm getting married, the baby is coming next month, and I am still on probation at work from last week's incident. I don't even have the time to complete the first I-bonic Armor prototype before my next evaluation hearing."

"You have a year—"

"No, I don't. Since I am on probation, they moved it to six months. I won't make it to next year if I don't complete it by December, and then I am out of the program for good."

He fidgeted with his shirt buttons, and I stopped him and reassured him, "My medicine is consumable, that is the first step to your equation. Help me with mine first, and then we'll work on your project next. I promise."

"Welly, you swear?"

"I pinky swear." I held up my pinky, and he wrapped his around mine.

«CHAPTER EIGHTEEN»

FIVE MONTHS LATER.

A gentleman opened my car door, and I stepped out wearing an expensive black suit custom made especially for my pitch meeting. I brushed off my jacket and proceeded into the full-glassed building, surrounded by guards dressed in army fatigue uniform. They stared at me, and I bet they wondered how such a young guy could afford a luxury car and suit. I hadn't released the full medical treatment to the world. I had leaked information about the successful medical trials, and grants and sponsorships poured in, no thanks to Pharmaceutical Plant Discoveries. When the words, "I quit," leaped off my lips, Dr. Frazier was stunned.

Nevertheless, high energy ran through my veins as I contemplated on how to present my pitch. I pumped myself up as I thought about how every science headmaster had waited patiently for me to share what healing elements were in my medicine.

"First, I want to thank God." I took a deep breath. I couldn't forget the Man upstairs for choosing me to deliver people from death. I shook my head repeatedly to remove the irritating thoughts of why me that cluttered my mind day and night. *I chose it, and He chose me,* I answered.

The secretary noticed my inner fight and quickly whispered, "Are you ready? They are inside." She latched on to the door, and I forced an okay signal. We listened for the chatter to die down as beyond those doors, politicians, inventors, and all headmasters of different economic fields assembled.

Charlie, my buddy, rested his hand on my shoulder. "You ready?" he asked with a smile. He held a box filled with documents and products under his arm as he wiped the sweat from off his forehead with the back of his hand. Behind the door, the chatter faded to a halt. One last collar fix to my shirt and the secretary swung open the doors to twelve bodies assembled around a stainless-steel table. I staggered into the huge conference room.

"Hello," I said. Once I got mid-way in, I noticed a few familiar people that sat against the wall: Gary Foster and Dr. Frazier locked eyes with mine, and it sent chills down my spine.

HM. Trevestor grabbed my shoulder. "Wellington, there is nothing to worry about. The people against the wall are guests of SAA." HM. Trevestor turned to me and whispered, "The ones around the table are the most important ones to impress." He winked and directed me to the red chair at the end of the table. I slowly sat in the red chair and took in that very moment. The same red chair that many SAA scientists started in before going to do amazing things.

"Around the table, we have a few guests," Dr. Trevestor, Headmaster of Botany, mentioned. He flipped through the pile of paperwork inside of his folder.

"Today, we have Headmaster Lucas Clive of Armed Forces and his team joining us from the National Intelligence Agency. Headmasters from the United States federal executive departments usually do not attend scientific introduction meetings, but HM. Clive was intrigued by the scope of the discovery."

"Nice meeting you, Wellington." He nodded.

"And this is Ethan Finn the—"

"From the Facts Report." Ethan Finn, a well-known Atheist reporter, lived and breathed facts. He leaned over and shook my hand. It gave me chills as if he dipped it in ice before the meeting. I cleared my throat as I wondered how to restructure my presentation to not sound too churchy, or was it doubt moving in?

After HM. Trevestor introduced everyone, I went to the projector while Charlie handed out the reports.

"Umm—thank you, everyone, for your time." I turned to the projector. "I am excited to share the Kole-mula drug with you all today." I clicked the remote and soil displayed on the screen. "As you should know, my fiancée was diagnosed with Ovarian Cancer. She only had a few days to live when I dropped a piece of soil into her cup, she drank it, and then a few minutes later, she gradually became herself again." I turned back to the rest of the board members. "You see, this formula doesn't only hold soil, it contains prayer and faith mixed together."

Ethan squinted at me, and I quickly turned back to the projector. My chest thudded, and my hands shook. The whole room became silent and airy, and then whispers started. My thumb clicked, and a picture of a man appeared.

"We tested one hundred people with missing limbs: fifty women and fifty men. Most of them chose to consume the Kole-mula in the form of a pill." Charlie brought the tray with a few tiny green pills and a small capsule filled with green liquid. He rested it in the middle of the table.

"Within days, all of their limbs grew back, and they were able to do things that they used to do. Ten of those people from birth never had legs, or arms, or couldn't even see, and they too were healed."

"My God." The Headmaster of Religion rubbed his chin.

"Yes … Yes ." I pointed my clicker at him.

"Side effects?" HM. Clive asked.

"No. It's like God gave them a new body." I clicked the remote and an image of Mount Govermery Hospice displayed.

"God?" The Headmaster of Zoology questioned.

"Yes … Okay. We did our next experiment at a hospice. Twenty people were dying from a sickness or a disease, similar to my wife. We gave them only a taste of the medicine, and over a few hours, they awoke and danced to the jazz music playing through the intercom." Excitement echoed as chatter rumbled through the room.

"Can the medicine bring people back to life?" Ethan wondered.

"No. The medicine does not bring people back to life. It only heals them."

"Can it protect you from injury, like body protection?" HM. Clive interrupted as he rubbed his chin.

"From what we have discovered, it can heal you from any wounds," I answered.

Gary quickly stood up and roughly marched out of the room. His departure caused me to fumbled with the remote.

Click. A woman on the screen appeared.

"The next amazing thing that Kole-mula can do is . . . this is Amber, as you can see, nothing is wrong with her."

Next, the same woman, but older. Everyone gasped, and the Headmaster of Human Rights yelled, "That can't be the same woman?"

"Yes, we have discovered that when a person consumes the medicine, their body becomes more youthful. This can replace plastic surgery and—"

"My God!" The Headmaster of Zoology gasped and huddled excitedly with two headmasters.

"And we have discovered that people have become smarter, more creative, and driven," I gushed with excitement as chatter dominated throughout the conference room.

Tension peaked, and I stacked my folders into my bag. I waited awkwardly for everyone to stop arguing amongst each other, and I overheard the Headmaster of Energy and HM. Trevestor's conversation. "I heard of something like this before," the Headmaster of Energy said. "There's a Guru in India that has the same type of medicine that can heal people too."

I piped in, "Umm. I thought the presentation was pretty clear."

They ignored me and like a whirlwind, everyone argued their viewpoint. One voice roared, "It has high irons or cell T or X, which decreased the diseases."

My knuckles pounded against the table, and I blurted out, "God! God is causing this."

Ignored again.

The headmasters stopped including me in the conversation, and my facial expression revealed the tension I felt.

"God is causing this?" Ethan asked. He heard my cries, and the chatter wavered to a silence. "What is inside of the soil that's making God relevant to this medicine?" he quizzed.

"Soil?"

"Yes, the soil that you've given everyone," Headmaster of Religion asked.

"Oh, yes . . . the soil. Correct." I picked up one pill off the tray. "With the help of my brother, we created the outer layer of the pill to be rich in nutrient while the interior consists of only the . . . soil. . . and we call the soil Mercy because we believe God is giving mankind another chance at life." I turned off the projector.

"Where does this put Jesus Christ?" the Headmaster of Religion asked.

"Umm. I don't understand."

"The Old Testament had the Mercy Seat, The New Testament had Jesus Christ. Now you're saying this medicine replaces Jesus?"

HM. Trevestor intervened, "Let's not say it is a God thing, but a science thing. I am sure we can figure some formula to convince the public there's more to it?"

The whole room agreed.

"No . . . no! It's Jesus . . . and a God thing, and I won't say otherwise."

"So, God is behind this?" Ethan laughed. "I thought your God hasn't intervened with life in over two-thousand years?"

"God still intervenes through the medicine that we discover, through the doctors, and nurses that dedicate their lives to—" I remembered Dr. Frazier and recited, "—to dedicating their lives to the formula."

He surprisingly gave me a proud nod.

"Well, that's preposterous!" Ethan blurted out.

"This is God-made. Like I said, the reason why this experiment failed forty times was because God was taken out of the equation. Each person, given this medicine, had to believe it works by having faith."

"That's insane. People were dying when you gave them the medicine, they didn't have the mental state to believe!" Ethan shouted

"No, but I did, and their loved ones had enough faith to believe."

"Where did you get the soil from?" HM. Clive asked, relaxed and unfazed by the argument.

"Umm. I've been working at Pharmaceuticals Plant Discoveries for—"

"There's no record of you checking out the soil. Ever. How did you test it if you didn't have it?" HM. Clive flipped through PPD's paperwork as HM. Trevestor's eyebrow rose.

"I checked it out for Dr. Wellington." Charlie stepped forward. "He was in Virginia, and when he visited Georgia, I gave it to him."

HM. Clive placed his elbows on the table and explained, "National Security is on high alert because the soil came from the same place where the massive glow is located. Not only that, it's the same place where the prophecy said the tree of restoration will sprout out of—"

"Mount Hit-ga-lút?" I blurted out.

"Correct . . . and that will be the sign that the end is near. There are only roots, for now, no sign of a tree. I just want to make sure this prophecy is false, and the soil isn't dangerous since it is going to the public."

"Well, Dr. Frazier and his team did an outstanding job at analyzing and determining the soil is sterilized, non-toxic," HM. Trevestor announced.

"Right," I agreed with a guilty expression.

"Can we collect more?" Headmaster of Geology asked. "I would love to get my hands on it."

"No, the Israeli's SAA locked it down," HM. Clive answered.

"Maybe the President can make a phone call?" Headmaster of Earth Science suggested.

"I'd rather keep the President out of this." His greed sparkled on his face. "We have more than enough in the PPD vault to run a test," HM. Clive revealed.

"Why you? Why did your God choose you?" Slumped in the chair with his pencil repeatedly tapping against the table, Ethan pressed further, "What makes you so special to have discovered the soil and to bring it to the world?"

"I don't know, maybe because He trusts me like He trusted Moses."

"So, you're like Moses?"

"No, but I am God's servant doing His work. I'm using medicine to spread his Gospel." I said, even though I felt the Holy Spirit guide my words like Moses.

Everyone glanced at Ethan and then at me.

HM. Travestor concluded, "Well you have heard it, Headmaster of Faith and Science." He clapped, and everyone followed. "I think Wellington will truly make the world a better place with his extraordinary view on God and medicine." We shook hands. "We always have been impressed with your work, and we can't wait to see this God medicine take off." HM. Trevestor clapped his hands and applause populated the room. I shook the hands of HM. Clive, Ethan, and a few of the headmasters' hands as some gave me a good job wink and nod.

HM. Trevestor slid a few documents over to me to sign. "Now that you are in the process of being inducted into the Headmasters' Science Coalition, we need you to complete these."

A document read, 'A NEW WORLD' sat in front of me.

"What is this?" I pointed at the document that had a thousand entries of names and one empty slot at the bottom.

"You're in luck!" HM. Trevestor pushed the paper closer to me.

"Or is lucky to have you as a sponsor," the Headmaster of Earth Science joked.

"That too." HM. Trevestor chuckled and then explained, "As a Headmaster, you get life-changing perks and this opportunity is special." He flipped the page over to a space shuttle blueprint. "NASA is working on a space shuttle called Space Chrome-O-Zone that can float in space for two thousand years."

"So, you're moving me to space?"

"Oh no, well not yet. We're just preparing for the future," HM. Trevestor said.

The Headmaster of Earth Science chimed in. "In forty years, NASA hopes to send the first housing community space shuttle into space to live.

It will consist of scientists, politicians, celebrities, and of course everyday people. They will orbit the moon and eventually travel outside of our galaxy. But for now, every twenty years we plan to send a different batch of residents from earth to live in space. For the first trip, we are only taking the best of the best: scientists, doctors, famous singers, actors, and artist who want to make a difference in the galaxy."

"But why?" I asked.

"Well, because of global warming and the intensive growth of the light from Mount Hit-ga-lút—" Headmaster of Earth Science recounted.

"Another measure of security and to ensure that if this light is really the end, we can at least save some of the human race," HM. Clive interrupted.

"I'm not liking space right now. . . " I thought for a moment and then wrote in the blank spot, anyone with the last name *Kole*, who is related to Wellington Kole IIII.

"Only five immediate relatives can go." The Headmaster of Earth Science sincerely insisted.

I replied, "I know." I slid the paper to the middle of the table with my signature.

The headmasters squinted.

"There you have it." HM. Trevestor stood, and we shook hands again. "We'll be in touch." My phone buzzed inside of my coat pocket. I quickly answered Mama's call. "Hello?"

"Welly?"

"Mom? I'm kind of busy."

"Come home quickly, the FBI is here raiding the place." I froze, and I immediately hung up the phone.

"I have to go." I grabbed my bag.

"Wellington is everything okay?" HM. Trevestor worried.

"I have an emergency at home."

My hand clenched the doorknob.

"Before you go, we all wanted to give our condolences." I stopped and slowly turned around to them and nodded, thank you.

Charlie quickly collected the items off the table as Ethan Finn snatched the pills, and I overheard HM. Clive asked, "Is Wheatly his brother?" before the door closed.

* * *

The wind brushed through my hair as I sped down the long narrow road to Mama's house. The window blew through the gigantic trees on each side, and they waved at me. I kept my mind focused on God's faithfulness and hoped that Mercy Tree miraculously hid from the FBI.

Yellow tape blocked off Mama's house. Neighbors stood on their tiptoes, overlooking the police cars. I parked and broke through the barriers, and one police officer held his hand against my chest.

"Stay back!"

"I LIVE HERE!" I snubbed and ran into the house where Mama and Janice, five months pregnant, sat close to each other. Janice immediately ran into my arms, and I held her close.

"It's okay," I soothed disgusted by the countless FBI agents in our home.

"I want every corner of this house searched again and again," Gary yelled and pointed towards the upstairs. In the kitchen, agents dumped things on to the floor.

"My Jesus!" Mama shouted.

"Hey… hey, man." I stepped away from Janice and Mama and into Gary's face. "What is your problem? Any beef you have with me stays with me . . . man to man. Why barge into my mother's house, demanding things and ripping things apart?"

Gary yanked a warrant from his coat pocket and declared, "This gives me the right to search your underwear drawer. Stay out of my way." His shoulder bumped mine, and he headed to the kitchen.

"Why are you doing this? What are you looking for?" I yelled at him. He slowly faced me while supervising his fellow agents.

"It's not more of what I am looking for, it's more of . . . what are you hiding? I am pretty sure you heard about the prophecy during your pitch meeting and the massive glow that is causing chaos inside of the organization. For all these years, people thought I was crazy for seeing a glowing tree until I resurrected the two hundred-years-old prophecy that the Israeli's SAA denied for all these years. Now, it's time for me to prove that the tiny tree is here." He inhaled. "I can smell it."

"That's super crazy and odd to—"

"Odd that you quit Pharmaceuticals Plant Discoveries and then announced that you found a cure for all diseases." He pushed his nose two inches from mine.

"You're right. I was hiding something." I strode towards Mama. Gary's evil grin twisted softly.

"Then show me. Where is the tree?"

"Gary, there is no tree. Yes, we found a tree that day . . . we saw it sparkle, and I did take it, but when I brought it home . . . it died." I lowered my eyes. "You think I wrecked the prophecy?"

"I don't believe you," he grumbled.

"Well, you should. All I can think about is what if I left the tree there and had real scientist study it?" He followed me into the living room.

"Then why quit PPD?"

"Because you were right. Dr. Frazier was holding me back all these years and for what?"

Gary's shoulder lowered. Guilt and shame covered his expression. "I apologize for—"

"Detective Gary! We found something," an agent called from the backyard. Gary's shoulder rose, and his tough demeanor came flaring back. He rushed to the deck where five of the officials surrounded the shed and where soil residue and leaves scattered the grass. I hurried behind him, but two agents kept me on the patio.

"Gary, wait!" Gary examined the lock on the shed.

"Why is this locked?"

"To keep out the snakes and bears," I joked.

"Open it!" His veins popped outward, and his neck became thicker.

I thought about the prayer I said to God in my car of hiding the tree, making it invisible.

I took out my key chain and slowly inserted the key into the lock and twisted it. I stepped away finally feeling caught and ready to accept my fate. As Gary's men searched, he held me captive.

"There nothing in here boss but a pile of dirt." The men walked out and shrugged.

We both rushed inside. Leaves and dirt scattered around, but the tree no longer sat upon its throne. I waved my hand over the soil. Gary came close behind me and asked, "This is the soil you experimented on?"

"Ah-no. This is from my garden."

"Wait, are those leaves glowing?" He tilted his head to the side.

I said, "Glowing? What's glowing? You see a glow?" My voice quivered as Gary called one of the FBI agents.

"Do you see those leaves glowing?" He pointed.

"Nah, they look like regular leaves to me."

"Are … you … sure?" His face, red with tension, and he sneered at the FBI agent.

"It is not glowing, sir. I swear," the FBI agent hesitated, stunned at Gary's boiling rage.

Gary kicked weakly at the leaves and shuffled out the shed and yelled, "That's a wrap. Let's head out."

I waved my hand over the pile of soil again and again. I felt nothing. I rushed out of the shed. *God took back his precious gift because I couldn't keep it safe.*

The FBI agents packed everything and left in a file line. Neighbors came near and peeked through the backyard fence.

"Baby, are you okay?" Mama rushed to me and grabbed me, and Janice helped pull me to the patio stairs and into the house.

"Where—tree?" I murmured.

"Oh, that's what we wanted to tell you but didn't want to say it with all of the agents in the house." Mama smiled. "Wheatly came and took it this morning. He said he needed it to finish his prototype." I sighed with relief, and walked towards the front door.

"Where are you going?" Janice groaned as she rubbed her tummy.

"I'm going to get it back."

"In D.C. tonight?" She complained.

"Welly, be gentle. He's been dealing with a lot of stress at work and with Aaron not returning home." Mama made a good point.

With my head pressed against the door, I contemplated for a moment and said, "I'll be understanding."

«CHAPTER NINETEEN»

KNOCK. KNOCK. My fist pounded Wheatly's townhouse door and made the windows quake. I heard whispers and movement from the other side of the door.

"Open the door!" I yelled. It was nine o'clock at night, and the neighbors peeked through their windows.

The locks clicked as the door slowly opened to Wheatly's eyes.

"Where is it?" I demanded as he opened the door wider. Colette held Mercy Kole, my five-month-old niece.

"Shush! You're going to wake the baby," he snapped at me. I calmed down and then greeted Colette with a warm kiss on the cheek, and she walked away.

I whispered to Wheatly, "Why would you take it without my permission?" I followed him to the back of his home.

"You should be thanking me," he bragged. "I heard Mama house got raided." We entered a secure area down a long hallway.

He opened the huge doors to his lab. Beautiful décor covered the walls, and furniture populated the room.

"Wow, they surely hooked you up with a nice spot," I grumbled. Wheatly closed the doors.

In the corner, there was a small laboratory table with glass bottles filled with red, yellow, and green liquid. Then the mess: books, folders, and paperwork sorted on the desk, floor, and shelves. I tiptoed-marched behind Wheatly avoiding stepping on the cluttered floor. He sat behind his desk and yelled, "Because you promised me half!"

I tiptoed between his research data on the floor to his shelf and shuffled books, microscopes, tubs, and an incubator carefully around.

"Did you experiment on it?"

"No!"

"Are you sure?" I walked to his desk, knelt down in front, and searched underneath.

"Yes!" He pouted.

The overwhelming amount of unkempt hair on his head, chin, and dirty spots on his lab jacket caught my attention.

"Brother, what is really going on with you?" I dusted my pants off as I stood in front of him.

I examined the unknown man who held my confident brother hostage inside.

He snarled at me, "Don't act like you care."

"Wheatly, I do care—"

"No, you don't. I got so caught up helping you create medicine for your experiments around town that I neglected my own project, which I knew I would."

"I told you once we get my experimental treatment out of the way, we would focus on your class project."

"Class project? That's what you think I am doing? What they want me to create will change the world."

"Okay, sorry—"

"And you almost got me kicked out of the Elite Scientific Program, and this project is the only thing that's keeping me in the program. Next month, I have to deliver a prototype."

"Next month! You should have called me—"

"I called you every day asking for your time, and you never called me back . . . not now Wheatly . . . later Wheatly . . . I had to steal this stupid tree for you to acknowledge me!"

I swayed side-to-side wondering what to say next.

"You're right. I am a jerk, and you know that."

Silence.

The clock ticked. Silence. Another tick.

Wheatly twisted in his seat and mumbled, "It's in the closet." He pointed to a closed door to the left of his office. I yanked the door open to the Mercy Tree, peacefully planted in a large flowerpot. My mouth watered with excitement.

"It's a shame that you're pimping the tree out."

Two inches from the tree, my hands stopped.

"Pimping? It's healing people … if that's pimping then so be it."

"Didn't Dad say to protect it and keep it safe? What if you're killing everyone by allowing them to sip from the Tree of Mercy?"

I slammed the door shut leaving the Mercy Tree back in the darkness.

"Are you freaking kidding me right now?"

"What? All I am saying is what if you're missing the bigger picture here?" Wheatly wondered.

"What are you trying to say?"

"You're manufacturing the Mercy Tree as a gift for people. Soon it will be in groceries stores, department stores, on the corner block. You're destroying it."

My heart sank. Tongue dry and speechless.

"All of this because you can't actually create a prototype that can give mankind superpowers. Blame the tree and me for your lack of reality. Oh, give me a break." I chucked.

Wheatly went to his window. His gesture reminded me of Dr. Frazier's office. How he gazed at the unknown and masked his thoughts.

"Spit it out, Wheatly!"

"It's everything! The whole SAA, FBI, NSA, ESP, government thing! I think they know about Mercy Tree, and maybe Dad was warning us about this very moment—"

I grabbed Wheatly shoulders and pressed my forehead against his. "Calm down. NASA is still investigating Aaron's disappearance." He pulled away from me. "And we can't become crazy now, we must stay on top of the case," I yelled.

Wheatly lowered his head. "I don't get it. Why are you so calm? It's like our life is being ripped from us and we can't control it. Maybe you're right about being cursed every time we mess with the Mercy Tree. It isn't meant for mankind. What if we missed the bigger picture?" Wheatly held his head, and his breathing became shorter.

"Wheatly, sit down." I gestured to his chair. "One thing I have finally come to realize is when God's servants are doing his work, we are going to be spiritually attacked. Also, we can't stop the world from being dangerous or evil; we only can control ourselves from participating in worldly sinfulness. Jesus came to save us so we can have a choice. He's our source and our communicator to God, so if you feel afraid or have a problem lean on Christ."

"Not that easy. That's all that Aaron did and look what happened to him."

"Aaron said his purpose was to survive and well, I believe he is doing it. You got to believe too."

"Mama has you on all this religious talk now."

"No, it's from spending time with the Mercy Tree. I feel as if I am in the Lord's presence," I expressed.

"I don't know about that, but I can tell you this, remember that random guy that showed up to Mama's house and said that the tree was a symbol, right?" Wheatly opened his notebook with scribbles of scriptures on it.

"Okay?"

"I had a dream… about Dad and me fixing a car."

Wheatly rushed to me and held my arms.

"Mercy Tree was there . . . but much bigger . . . and it wore two chains and one said 'the sister to the Tree of Life.'"

Wheatly went back to his seat and said, "Dad said to me when the fall came, it sparkled like stars and rained down on the left side of the Tree of Mercy."

"Wheatly, what does that mean?"

"Dad said The Fall. When the fall of man happened, they were immediately disconnected from the innocence and the pure substance that The Garden of Eden embodied. God protected the garden from mankind by placing two Cherubim. Just like we saw on the cave's walls. If the roots of the tree were believed to develop from out of the Garden of Eden, then that means the Mercy Tree is pure in nature ... right?" His breathing quickened.

"Maybe Dad was saying, the fall of mankind repeats itself every day as a reminder of how much we need God's Mercy," I suggested and waved off his hypothesis. "Wheatly, you need to get some sleep, and we can hash this out tomorrow."

"No." Wheatly rushed over to his laboratory table. "This is my point. God hid the Garden of Eden for a reason, right? Mankind sinned and ate from the Tree of Knowledge, Good and Evil. God said if they did, they would die. So, they couldn't live in the garden because the Tree of Life was there." He placed his white gloves and goggles on.

"Yes, but Jesus wiped our sins away." I leaned against the door.

"Correct. So, if all things were good in the Garden of Eden." He poured yellow colored chemicals into a jar. "And if Adam and Eve were kicked out of the Garden because they sinned." He poured the green liquid into another jar.

"Okay?"

"Then how can sin and holiness cohabitate?" He poured both the yellow and green liquid into one jar, and foams aggressively grew and crackled. My hand held on to the door as a massive white cloud formed, bubbles oozed on to the table and spilling on to the floor. Wheatly watched excitedly as my heartbeat echoed my ears. Past explosions that Wheatly caused populated my thoughts. I waved for Wheatly to stop.

"Jesus became our mediator, right?" he yelled as he poured the orange liquid into the same beaker of the mixed yellow and green, and it caused the big bubble cloud to settle. He took off his goggles and watched my expression. My hands clawed at the door, and one foot pressed against the knob. "What if you're forcing top-notched holiness into sinful human beings? The two don't mix well if the human being is living in sin. They will go ... POP ... Therefore, you need to make sure that each person knows Jesus before they explode. Have them get save or something before accepting the medicine. Then we will know the Holy Spirit will handle the rest."

The boiling water sizzled to an end, and I felt comfortable enough to release the door. I clapped slowly at Wheatly's theory.

"Who's doing the religious talking now?" I laughed. "This is why you wanted me over here? To hear this?"

"Yes, I sent emails of my research and called you, but you did not respond!"

I took out my cell phone and thumbed through. "Well, these last few months have been super busy for me."

"Yeah, once I gave you the Kole-mula prototype, you disappeared."

"I've been crazy busy preparing for the SAA's induction ceremony, which happened today."

"Oh, did you get your 'Headmaster' title?" His fingers bounced like bunny ears.

"I don't know yet." I grabbed the flowerpot with Mercy Tree inside. Wheatly threw his gloves and flopped into the chair.

I sighed, "Give me a week or two to get settled in with SAA, and then we'll work on your assignment."

"Everyone at the ESP depend on me to create something magnificent, and I will disappoint them."

"Hey, you're a Kole, and we are inventors and scientists. A Kole went to space, a Kole found a Holy tree. So, if there is one thing that a Kole can do, it is solving problems. Plus, you're meant to be a superhero, right?" I left Wheatly's office and my mind fell on Mama's advice, *be gentle*. I turned to him, but something already had captivated his attention.

"What are you staring at?" I wondered.

He slowly said, "The twig you gave me." He pointed at the bright green stem framed on his mantle, and we both admired it.

I could tell his brain was ticking, and I winked at him. "See, we solve problems."

«CHAPTER TWENTY»

I BANGED MY TOE on the wooden desk, and excruciating pain crawled all over my foot. Again, another reminder that Mama's home was not big enough for my presence. The old house was a diary that held memories of the past and secrets to the future, and I needed to buy a new diary with new pages to make new memories.

Thoughts of getting accepted into the SAA and a fifty million dollar check to start Kole's Pharmaceutical Discovery with the slogan *Adding Faith to The Formula* made me smile as I limped to the window.

"A black-owned scientific facility." I pointed to the stars, through the drizzling rain, that conquered the darkness. *"We will shine a light on the inner darkness?"* I bragged. I took out my notebook and wrote the job title next to each name.

1) *Wellington CEO and Head of Biology*
2) *Wheatly Head of Chemistry*
3) ~~*Aaron, Head of Geology*~~
4) *The Mercy Tree*
5) *Charlie, Executive Secretary*

Rain trickled against the window of Wheatly's old bedroom, which I used for an office. My future office would be big or bigger than Dr. Frazier's office in Atlanta. With my own green shiny floors that said a world-renowned scientist works here and pictures of my awards nailed to the walls. With my shoulders shifted backward, and with my feet on top of my desk, I came up with the solution that would end my cramped problem—I needed to move away again. Suddenly, I noticed a warm presence at the door.

"What are you up to?" Janice asked.

"Umm. Just thinking?"

"About what?" She stepped forward, grabbed my hand, and rested it on her belly.

I smiled. "Ah, what if we moved?" I said, and Janice smacked my hand away. "Into a bigger place for you and the baby?"

"What about your mom? You bought this place because she couldn't afford it, now you want to move?"

"You're right, but I just need a real home office?" I pouted, and she gently touched my face.

"I thought you wanted to make this your office?"

"I do, but it's too small." I shook my head, then grabbed my notebook and flipped pages over while changing the subject. "Do you feel different after being cured?"

"Ah, here we go again. I'm rounder?" Revealing her belly poking out.

"I know that. Do you feel mentally . . . different?" I hopelessly stared into her beautiful brown eyes.

"I am more active and creative. I feel anything is possible. And of course, I feel God is working inside of me to keep me safe from doing wrong." She giggled.

"Okay. Interesting." I drew a line through 'Happiness' and 'Healthy' in my notebook and reviewed answers from everyone my team examined.

Janice tried to see what I wrote down and then she asked, "Is that what you wanted to hear?"

"Not exactly." I turned to her.

"From you, yes, but I'm getting different answers from other people." I showed the long list of people with words that said dreams of completing a task, visions of new ideas, second chances, inventions that could advance life on earth. "Everyone seems to have a creative drive like they are meant to advance the world somehow or have a God-given mission."

"That's a good thing, right? We are here to live in the abundance of God and to do his will?"

We both smiled.

"It's just … never mind."

"No, tell me."

"Okay. It's like no one is acknowledging God or doing His will but their own will."

"When your hand was healed, you ran away in fear of what happened. Maybe that is a side effect," Janice suggested.

"No, that was different." I pointed to the entry in my notebook. "Look here. People are led by their own desires and purpose as if they healed themselves. At least I knew something supernatural healed me."

"But still, you wanted to discover your own formula and to do your own will until you realized that God was a part of that will."

"Good point." I slouched.

"Now that you have a better understanding of this whole process," she touched my face and continued, "You can help people to avoid the fear of getting a second chance at life. You can show them that God chose them to be fearless in His name."

"You're right. I just hope the SAA approves it," I confessed.

I checked the clock. **1:45 P.M.**

"We'll find out soon if we go public."

My phone buzzed. "Ugh. Wheatly," I slurred and pressed ignore.

"Are you two mad at each other, again?"

"No, he just has a theory that I think he's right about." I kissed Janice on the lips and headed towards the door. "I'll be back in a minute."

"Wellington, don't mess this up."

"What do you mean?"

"Everything is going well for us," she expressed. "You're back on track with your family, and now you're beginning to push them away . . . again."

"It's just Wheatly. He needs to grow up and stop calling me every day about foolishness."

Suddenly, Mama bust through the bedroom door.

"Wheatly said he's been trying to call you and you're not answering him." Her eyebrow rose and arms crossed.

"Mom, I've been busy and I—"

"You have a lot of nerve talking about you been busy. Call your brother!" She slammed the door.

Janice wobbled up to me, patted me on the shoulder, and whispered, "Call him." She left me alone.

I picked up my phone. Seven missed calls from Wheatly. I pressed dial. It rang once, and he quickly answered

"Wellington, I need your help."

"What now! I sent you all the data that my team and I collected about the tree. What else do you need to finish your project?" I walked to the window and gazed at the street.

"Whatever man! I think I made a—wait, why are you so mad?"

"I don't know, maybe because you have been calling me like an insane person," I shouted.

"Answer your phone, and I wouldn't have too," he shouted back. "Never mind. I guess, when you need something, I have to help. But when it comes to me, it doesn't matter." His voice broke. "You're right. You sent me everything that I needed, and I don't need any more help from you . . . ever again. Later."

"Wait, don't hang up. I've been stressed because I'm waiting on the call from the Scientific Allegiance Agency. This call can change our family's life . . . so tell me what you need help with," I calmly said as I noticed a familiar person walking a dog.

"Ah—it's—umm, I created a prototype formula, and the ESP board loves it. Now they want me to sell it to the U.S. Armed Forces, and I'm not ready to give it up so soon . . . you know?" The person in the beige rain gear got closer to my house. Wheatly continued, "It can be dangerous, and I just don't agree with it being released without proper care, that's all."

"Wheatly, you can't call me every time you have to make a decision at work. For eleven years I did things that I didn't agree with at my job, and I didn't quit." I brushed Wheatly's statement off. The person's dog stopped and used the bathroom.

"I know," Wheatly softly replied.

"Look, this is the moment to be braver than me, okay? Handle your situation yourself, and we'll talk and laugh about it during Christmas dinner. I have to run, keep your head up," I hurried and hung up the phone.

"It's him," I whispered to myself.

..*

I ran on to the lawn where the man stood. Rain drenched my shirt as I waved.

"Excuse me." I approached the man. He stopped and revealed a full beard. "Oh, I am sorry, I thought you were someone I knew."

"You do know me. We spoke regarding the Mercy Tree."

I took a deep breath.

"Are you like an Angel?"

He laughed. "No. I live two blocks down the street. However, I do believe people can be angels in each other's life."

"Oh, so you're a pastor? Or—"

"Nope. I own a construction company."

"Okay, are you a prophet? I don't understand how you would know about the tree."

"Of course not."

Silence gloated between us formed.

"Joe is it?" I scratched my chin. "Are you following me? Are you my long-lost brother . . . uncle?" I tried to get to the bottom of him knowing who I was.

"Listen, son, I can't explain it. I saw your picture on the news eleven years ago, and a voice popped in my head and said to write down a message: a symbol, a gift, and the revelation and to tell you that message on May 25th 2000. I eventually went on with my life, but the message was loud and clear when eleven years came. I searched for your name in the phone book, and your house happened to be on the next block."

"Wow." I took a deep breath. "What does the message mean?"

We walked on to my patio from out of the rain. Joe thought for a moment and pondered, "Well, a symbol indicates a sign, right? A gift represents a kindly gesture, and the revelation means the awakening. Usually referring to Christ and since you have a holy tree, I believe so."

"Yes, the tree is Holy. That is why I named it Mercy?"

"God named it Mercy long before you existed."

Speechless, goose-bumps covered my arms.

Joe leaned in closer. "It's what God said it was to you all those years ago."

His statement rang like bells in my heart. I remembered the moment that the word Mercy leaped from my lips on the saddest day of my life.

"Son, don't be sad. The tree represents mercy, which is a good thing." He patted my shoulder, pulled his dog, and left.

"Are you sure you're not an angel or prophet?" I followed him from a distance.

"No, I just owe my life to the Lord. I was a selfish man, but I got in a terrible car accident eleven years ago that tore me in two, and I was pronounced dead." He drew a line across his stomach and tears formed in his eyes. "I saw death, and it was dark and lonely. I never wanted to see wherever I was again." He paused and shook his head. "I couldn't take the stench from burning flesh, so I pleaded, 'God if you rescue me, I will help rescue the whole world." His hands faced the sky. "Then I woke up in a hospital bed with tubes going in and out of me, and your discovery was all over the news that day."

My mouth fell open, and air-cooled my flesh. The word 'selfish' froze my speech and my legs shook. Joe walked away again, and I stumbled behind him like a lost puppy.

"Joe, can you answer one more thing for me?"

He turned around and nodded.

"Is making the Mercy Tree medicine for people harming them? Like, mixing sin with holiness? Darkness with light?" I desperately waited for a reply.

He gazed into the sky, then at his feet. He scratched his head and then said, "I don't think so . . . because God is bigger than any sin, and if the Mercy Tree represents mercy then what better way to experience God's love. The Gospel of Christ is being shared through this medicine, and that is a good thing."

A sigh exploded from me as I had something that proved Wheatly wrong.

"But—"

Joe's *but* gutted my stomach.

"The tree is a part of God and because it contains God's holiness, whoever consumes or touches it, touches God. Therefore, judgment is much greater than the one that hears the word of God because the one who touches God touches heavenly places."

My balance became weaker, I sat down on the sidewalk as Joe whistled to his dog and they walked off again.

"So if this was going to happen, why didn't God warn me? He gave me something that basically can harm mankind without instructions!"

Joe stopped. He stared long and hard at me. "From what I know, you disobeyed your father and snuck away from the campsite and found the soil. However, you found and stole the Mercy Tree too, which belonged to the Earth, not mankind. It's a *symbol* to the earth that Christ is coming soon so that the earth can stop the restless moaning and groaning in natural destruction. It's a *gift* of Mercy because, at this rate, mankind's ungodly energy will destroy it. And it's the *Revelation* because the future of the awakening and the unseen will be seen. Your pride and ego have caused you to chop it up and give it to mankind like a prize. Don't blame God for your wrongdoing."

Joe stormed away. I slowly picked myself off the ground, and my ears rang with fear from his words.

BEEP. BEEP.

I answered my phone and hesitated. "Wheatly? We just spoke buddy."

"I know. I just want to say thank you and that you are right. I need to loosen up and—"

"No . . . no, you listen to me Wheatly. You're the most honest, humble, and morally compassionate person that I know. If your gut says no then live by that. Plus, Dad said to protect the tree. It's up to you to do it because I failed."

"Welly, what's going on? I don't like how you are sounding."

BEEP BEEP. An unknown number appeared.

"Wheatly, we'll talk later. I have another call on the line." I clicked over. "Hello?"

"Good Day, Scientific Allegiance Agency calling for Dr. Kole?"

"This is he." My heart leaped into my throat.

"Your discovery has been approved by all SAA worldwide. Welcome to the team Headmaster of Faith and Science."

"Actually, that's okay. I rather wait to run more test in case there are unknown side effects."

"I don't understand?"

"Can we hold off on making it public for now? I have a few tests to run."

"Oh, a scientist's work is never complete. Now, the Headmaster of Faith and Science, welcome to the Scientific Allegiance Agency team—"

"Wait! Can I at least change my title."

"Oh. What would you like to be called? The Headmaster of–" She waited for my answer.

"Of The Revelation. The awakening of what's coming because it's about to go down," I implied.

"Umm, okay. I wrote that down and don't worry HM. Kole, after reviewing the results, we decided that this needs to be available as soon as possible. Again Dr. Wellington Kole, welcome to the Scientific Allegiance Agency, and your induction ceremony will be in two weeks."

The phone disconnected and rain poured viciously on me.

«CHAPTER TWENTY-ONE»

I SAT IN THE SHADOWS of my office. My feet propped on the desk and my shoulder pressed against the back of the chair as I thought about my next step. My only light source came from my desk lamp showering its light on the desk surface. The lamp cast shadows in my work dungeon. I banned everyone from entering as I sorted through reports, data, and my thoughts about the Mercy Tree. Papers scattered all around the floor, and on the desk next to my feet, beer bottles and a half-eaten sandwich with flies buzzing around it.

I listened to the rain trickle down the roof. The earth was patient while it served God's purpose. From listening to Joe that day, I realized that God not only gave mankind warnings and signs but gave the earth and animals signs, too. I wondered, *Why me? Why did God give me the passion for plants?* I thought about Dad's message to protect it. I thought about my failure of not knowing the instructions. I wondered if the SAA would tear me into pieces if they found out that the prophecy was real and that I harbored the Mercy Tree?

Nevertheless, they did not know about the tree. My nerves made sweat drip from my forehead as I scribbled reluctantly in my notebook. A soft knock echoed the office slash bedroom, and I shuffled reports and drawings into my drawer.

Charlie peeked his head inside "Is it cool to come inside HM. Kole," he joked, and I smiled.

"Come inside, friend."

Charlie flipped the light switch, and I squinted.

"Let's start with business. The Scientific Allegiance Agency approved our new headquarters, and we can move in next week." He scanned the mess on my desk and floor.

"Okay," I sighed.

"Oh, and they are sending over a Time Capsule box to bury in the courtyard. We need to gather materials to put inside."

"Great!" I grabbed the picture of the logo, W.K.D. standing for Wellington Kole Discoveries, from Charlie's hand. "Nice," I admired.

"Umm, and the Department of Trade and Services called back." He held up a sticky note.

I dropped the photo, snatched the number, and dialed.

"Oh, for your ceremony next week." He smiled. "The event coordinator is asking for your guest list."

"Ah. My mom, Janice, Aunt Pinky, you, and Wheatly."

I heard it *RING…*

"Speaking of Wheatly, he called for the hundredth time," he joked. "Please call him back. He left a ton of call-me-back messages." Charlie grinned, and I rolled my eyes.

RING again …

"He wants to know what the prophet, Joe, said, and I am not ready to tell him yet."

RING…

"He called me at midnight last night. If Wheatly calls again, tell him I will see him at the ceremony next week."

RING …

"How can I direct your call?" The Department of Trade and Services operator answered.

"Hi, my name is Headmaster of … ah … Dr. Kole—Wellington Kole."

"Hold please." Immediately, the power of my name took me straight to the head person. As I waited for them to pick up, my office door swung open, and Janice wobbled in while Charlie snuck out. Her hands rested on her belly. I held up one finger and spun my chair away.

"HM. Kole. How can I help you?"

"Yes, I wanted to put an emergency halt on the distribution of the Kole-mula. It has an unexpected kink we need to sort out here in the lab."

"Any terrible side effects we should note?"

"Ah. If used with ungodliness, then yes." I chuckled.

He laughed.

"I am sorry, HM. Kole, the Kole-mula have been distributed, and there is nothing that we can do to stop it at this moment from going overseas. For us to stop it, we will need a written petition with signatures from every Headmaster and The U.S. President and Congress. That process is very lengthy and can take up to a few years since we consider the medicine new science." My heart lapsed as I hung up the phone.

Janice, seated and out of breath, puffed, "No luck?"

"They are not stopping it." I shook my head.

"Well. I have some good news." Janice embraced me. "I think we're having a baby tonight." She smiled as my anger softened to a stew of happiness. I quickly leaped up to her and touched her stomach. "Are you sure?"

"I hope so, or I am having serious back pain." She kissed me, and I helped her walk to the door.

"Okay, okay. Our bags are packed, and we just need to get there," I announced.

Charlie rushed into my office with the phone in his hand.

"Ah, umm. Welly, Dr. Wellington … It's Wheatly."

"I told you what to tell him, Charlie."

"No, you need to take this call."

"No, we're having a baby." Laugher echoed the bedroom.

"Wellington, this is serious. As serious as having a baby," he panicked.

I grabbed the phone out of his hand. "This is Wellington." Silence filled the room.

"Hi Wellington, this is HM. Clive, Headmaster of Armed Forces. We met at the—"

"Yes, where is Wheatly?"

"There has been a robbery last night at Wheatly's residence and—"

I closed my eyes.

"We recovered two bodies, and we need you to identify them."

My knees buckled as Charlie and Janice rushed to hold me up.

"It can't be my baby brother." An unbearable emotion broke through.

"We need you to come—"

"It can't be? I—he called me last night." I held my forehead in disbelief.

"He did?" HM. Clive's nerves shook. "What did he say?"

The room got smaller; my sight became black.

«CHAPTER TWENTY-TWO»

Unsolicited crime scene photos littered my memory from last week, dazed from the gunshot to Wheatly's chest and head, shots to Collette's chest, broken glass everywhere, and no evidence of baby Mercy.

"Wellington," I heard in the distance. "Wellington," I heard a second time but much clearer. My thoughts were in another dimension. "WELLINGTON!" A shout snapped me out of my daze, and I finally acknowledged thirty or more civilians' concerned faces. They mainly hoped that I would accept the award.

Janice touched my leg, and I rocked my head to her beautiful smile, and our baby tucked in her arm. She swayed her finger to the podium.

I stood, and cheers populated the room.

"Come on, Wellington and get your Headmaster's Pin,"

Headmaster of Earth Science exclaimed as he held up a gold 'H' pendant.

Whistles and applause continue to fill the air as I staggered to the podium. I scratched my days-old beard, and I cleared my groggy throat and had nothing to say. Not one peep about finally being promoted and recognized for my work. I was speechless because the three people that wanted me to succeed more than me were no more: Dad, who believed in me, Aaron, who always had my back, and Wheatly, who always looked up to me.

"I can't accept this." I choked on my words and rushed into the hallway. My head pounded and swirled with thoughts. My knees weakened, and dizziness blurred my vision.

"I'm sorry," I confessed to Dad. "Sorry I ruined everyone's life."

I held on to the cool walls, and it calmed my nerves. Janice rushed to me and gently felt my face with the back of her hand.

"Sorry that I'm a failure to our son," I sobbed.

"Baby, you were never a failure, and our son will always look up to you as his hero."

I removed the blanket that gently covered our baby's face. His tiny hands gripped my finger. We named him, Wheatly Aaron Kole, and he was the only thing that made me proud to exist.

Janice grabbed my hand, and we walked towards the exit when HM. Trevestor called, "Wellington." The Headmasters lined up in the hallway facing us.

"Can we speak with you, privately?" He pointed to an empty room across from the auditorium.

Janice touched my face and said, "Go."

They silently entered the room and sat around the table, and I stayed close to the door and acknowledged items on shelves that I could use to protect myself.

"Please sit," HM. Trevestor pleaded, but I crossed my arms instead. "Do not do this. You have worked your whole life for this moment. Why give it up now?"

"I worked to prove to myself and people like you that I had something to offer to the world. That doesn't matter now when I don't have a family to share it with."

"Wellington, you knew that becoming a part of such an elite society, things could get dangerous. However, your discovery is changing the world, and you will go down in history."

The word 'history' did not bring me joy.

The clock ticked. The Headmasters sniffed and shuffled themselves in their seat.

"We understand that you have been through a lot this year. Regardless, if you accept becoming a Headmaster, Wellington, you have proved something that has never been proven before," Headmaster of Earth Science spoke up. "You have proven that there is a God and that faith in Him is truly the key to all things." He slowly stood up and pressed his hands against the table.

They waited for me to budge because I was a statue examining each Headmaster's inner desire.

"My father once told me that the beautiful treasure a teenage boy stores in his heart will only be uncovered by a greedy old man ready for war."

They pondered, wondered, and scratched their chin.

"It means that I have nothing else to give. I don't want to be a part of the Scientific Allegiance Agency. You can reopen Dr. Frazier's practice." I opened the door, and saw HM. Clive approaching.

"Wellington, before you go, we need to discuss what happened to your brother." HM. Clive announced as he stepped aside and revealed an ashamed Gary following behind. At first, I felt ambushed, but sincere faces around the room calmed my mood.

"Please come back inside." HM. Trevestor motioned for us to close the door.

"Please have a seat," HM. Clive suggested as he pulled out his notepad and pen.

I sat.

"Did they find the guys who did it?" Hot again, I fanned myself and tried to stay cool.

"I am afraid not, but it will happen as long as I am in charge." HM. Clive leaned into me. "Wheatly was hardworking and dedicated to the program, and to his project."

Sweat and tears formed on my face as I tried to avoid entering the dark place that Mama and I experienced last week.

"We want to let you know that Wheatly Kole will be given an honorary award from the SAA and will be given a Nobel Prize in Chemistry. He solved a problem that will change the world, and it's called I-bonic Armor," HM. Clive explained.

I sobbed into my hands because Wheatly worked his whole life on that experiment, and would never see it manifest. Someone handed me a tissue, and I wiped my eyes.

"There's one problem though. Whoever raided Wheatly's home took the formula. It is precious and can harm a lot of people. Did Wheatly give you a backup?" HM. Clive tapped his pen against the table.

I slowly wiped the last bit of tears from out of my eyes. They silently waited and waited. No movement or sound, but the hour hand on the clock ticked.

"You want to know how to duplicate my brother's invention?" I rotated my head and cracked my knuckles. "He didn't give you the prototype weeks ago? None of it?" I asked.

"He was going to but had to add something to the data. Then some evil people broke into his home and stole it. Is that right, Gary?"

Gary stayed silent.

"So, it is gone?" I questioned.

"We only want to know what is in it just in case, just to be ready if the bad guys sold it to a U.S. enemy—"

"Wow, how about this … FIND MERCY!" I slammed my hands down.

Everyone turned to HM. Clive. They whispered, asking what I meant.

"I don't understand." HM. Clive slowly stood up.

I slowly became his equal and said, "Oh, you don't? I find it very interesting that everyone has something to say about how Wheatly and his wife died, but my niece's body has not been recovered. I filed a report and got no response from the FBI," I grunted.

HM. Clive's face immediately turned red. He spun to Gary who was equally shocked.

"I reviewed all of Wheatly's personal documents in the Elite Scientific Program. It said nothing about him having a child." Gary stepped forward and explained.

I slammed my fist on the table.

"FIND MY NIECE!" A big roar echoed the room.

"Are you saying this is a kidnapping case, too?" HM. Trevestor questioned, and Headmaster of Human Rights panicked, "We have to alert the Headmaster of Federal Law."

They were more concerned than the rest.

"No need to worry, men." HM. Clive reassured and then turned to me. "Wellington, you have my word that Detective Gary will be dedicating his whole career to tracking down your niece," He then grumbled to a pale, Gary. "If he ever wants to work for this organization again."

The Headmasters' disappointment made the atmosphere troublesome.

I stormed out, and Gary followed me. "Welly, I promise. I didn't know he had a child."

I held Janice's arm, and we headed towards the exit.

"Wellington!" HM. Trevestor called and marched to us.

"I am so sorry about that. I had no idea HM. Clive was going to ask that." I ignored him and kept walking. "Wellington please let me help you. You are a bright kid, and I want to see you succeed."

Without thinking, I demanded, "I need access to my brother's home. I tried going by there, but it's locked up, and officers are surrounding it."

"Done." He patted me on my shoulder.

«CHAPTER TWENTY-THREE»

Mama and I held hands and consoled each other as we stood on Wheatly's porch. The police officer opened the door, and HM. Trevestor and Clive, and Detective Gary waited for us inside. Crime Post-Its and tape outlined where blood fell. I slowly bent down to view the chalk outline that the forensic team wrote, *head, arms, and legs* where Colette was found dead. She was in the living room, probably enjoying a good show on television when the gangster busted through.

HM. Clive watched us closely as we wandered around. "Be careful not to touch anything. Everything is still under investigation," he told Mama, and she placed the framed picture back on to the shelf. Mama took out her handkerchief and sobbed into it.

I held her close.

"Can we have a moment alone?" I requested.

HM. Trevestor nodded to HM. Clive, and he sighed and told everyone, "Let's clear out." He motioned.

"They're treating us like we are the enemy here." She wiped her eyes and followed me down the long hallway and to a huge closed door with yellow tape on it.

"This is Wheatly's laboratory."

I opened the door as Mama rambled, "What is going on? Why are there police officers and FBI agents guarding his home?"

"Wheatly discovered a formula that can help the government, and some bad people may have stolen it, but I am pretty sure there is more to the story, and Wheatly is the hero somehow."

Folders and books still populated the floor, and pictures of family Christmas dinners and vacations hung on the wall.

"This is where they found Wheatly's body." I signaled to the tape that read, *Male head, arms, and legs*, and Mama sobbed.

I opened the closet where he hid The Mercy Tree from me and found his daughter's, Mercy's, baby bottle, glowing, inside of a basket.

I picked it up. "Ma! Do you see this?"

She rushed to my side.

"Awe." She sniffled, "The baby's bottle."

"Yeah, is it glowing to you?"

"No. I don't see anything." She gasped, "Could it be?" She wiped her eyes with her handkerchief.

"That's a very good sign." I twisted open the bottle and it smelled like chemicals and milk—rotten.

"He did it," I whispered."

"He did what?"

"I think Wheatly created I-bonic Armor to be consumable . . . Mercy was his first test."

Mama puffed, "Lord, Jesus. I told him to not drink that mess!"

"No, Mom. He created superpowers . . . Mercy is I-bonic . . . Armor Woman or I-bonic Girl?"

Unimaginable joy rested between us as we heard the door creak open, and I quickly hid the bottle into my back pocket as HM. Clive and Gary marched inside and scanned the room.

"This part of the house is off limits." HM. Clive proclaimed.

"We are leaving." I moved Mama towards the door.

We stepped out of Wheatly's office, and Mama and I grabbed our things to leave.

"That, in your back pocket?" HM. Clive pointed at the bottle, and I revealed it.

"Oh, umm, it's something to remember my niece by."

"It's still evidence."

"My son is dead, and my grandbaby is missing! And all you care about is a damn baby bottle!" Mama threw her jacket down to draw attention away from the baby's bottle.

HM. Clive held both hands up. "I apologize, ma'am."

Mama picked up her jacket and stormed out of the house.

HM. Clive sneered at his men, and they quickly got back to work while he left the room.

Gary stepped forward. "We are actively looking for her. Look, I have a son, and this case is close to my heart."

I shiftily placed the bottle into my coat pocket. Gary grabbed my arm; he had puffy red eyes. "Wellington, I want you to know that Wheatly was like a little brother to me too." I yanked my arm away, and he said, "We became really good friends, and even though you and I fight, you guys are like family to me."

"Prove it by finding my niece and Wheatly's murderers." I scorned Gary, but I felt convicted. I took a deep breath, and said, "Gary, I don't blame you."

I walked off when Gary exposed, "Wellington," I turned to him, and he whispered, "It always had a beautiful glow." He pointed to the bottle in my pocket, and I grinned.

«CHAPTER TWENTY-FOUR»

THE VOICEMAIL message from Wheatly played on repeat. At first, I listened intently at his every word for a few times and wrestled with my own thoughts about what happened the moment the message stopped.

However, listening to his voice comforted my soul as I imagined him across the room, chitchatting about his heroic ideas. The recording started over. I closed my eyes to listen another time of him whispering into the phone.

"Hey, Wellington, I finally know my purpose. Well, I did know, but now I know how it's going to happen. It is time to save the world. Like a superhero, I guess?" He chuckled, and I did too. "Yeah, a hero! Because there are bad guys out there that want to do bad things and I can't let that happen." He rambled on as if he wanted to build up his courage. "And, what am I supposed to do? Let them do what they want?" A knock sounded in the distance, and I pressed the phone closer to my ear. "Who is that?" he asked Collette, "Anyways, I'll catch you at your ceremony. Good night."

I snapped the phone shut and threw it to the floor. A soft knock echoed in my office. Charlie poked his head in, and he eyed the mess on the floor.

"Umm. Thought we cleaned the office yesterday." He giggled and then cleared his throat. "Hey, there's a guy here that says he's your angel?"

I slowly stood up, and Charlie shrugged. "Should I call the police?"

"No, let him in," I shouted.

Joe entered. He didn't even acknowledge the mess on the floor. He admired me as if I was an award. I motioned Charlie to leave us alone.

"Mr. Joe, how are you? Please sit." I pushed the things on the chair to the floor. I sat and slid the pile of paperwork out of view.

"Thank you. I don't want to take too much of your time. Ah, I know you have been going through a lot, and I wanted to check in on you."

"Oh, yeah, a lot is kind of an understatement." We both exhaled, and I leaned forward longing for a definite answer from God. "I just want to know why God hates me so much."

"Remember, God loves you and adores you. The world is the one that hates you."

"I understand that but why me?" My voice cracked as a big gulp of spit slowly slid down my throat. I didn't want to be weak, but my spirit was defeated, and I had no more to give.

"That question is much better. Let's identify why God chose you. But first, I want to apologize for what I said the last time we spoke. I shouldn't have said that you stole the tree."

"But I did, and you were right. That's why I am in this mess."

"I was half right. It revealed itself to Wheatly when it glowed from the other side of the cave's wall, and Wheatly being Wheatly, followed it. Maybe the Mercy Tree was waiting for you guys."

"Umm, what?"

"Well, the tree is a symbol and God chose you to protect it." He leaned forward and said, "The scripture, Psalms 37:4, says, 'Delight yourself in the Lord, and He will give you the desires of your heart.' Because you loved God, His desires became your desires; to study plants was all from God, all for God to lead you to that particular place and time. Your disobedience to your Earthly father was a blessing to your Heavenly Father. All because you listened to what God planted deep inside of you."

"But why me? Why Wheatly? Why Aaron?"

"People have been studying the glow for years on that mountain. They've dug, but no one found what had been causing the glow or how it had begun. Until now, you guys discovered it. The Mercy Tree sprouted above the Earth, and its root manifested from The Garden of Eden, and you know that."

"Yeah, but why us? Is that why God is killing everyone around me? Are we cursed, again?" I slammed my hand on the table.

Joe rested his hand on top of mine. "You are a perfect match for God's plan because you're stubborn, very passionate, a procrastinator, but a go-getter at heart. By the time you got the courage to believe in yourself, you had out waited God's season of patience. Now, God is ready to use you and your family."

I slowly moved my hand from his.

"That is my point! At this rate, I will have no more family left: my Dad, Aaron, and Wheatly are gone." Tears formed in my eyes.

"Ah, let God be the judge and the ruler of life." Before I could respond, Joe continued, "Listen to what is in your heart. Allow the Holy Spirit to guide you."

"Are you sure you're not an angel?"

"Nope, I just have a strong sense that your spiritual gift will brighten God's plan in the years to come."

"So, I'm not cursed?"

"Of course not, but I'm going to leave you with this fundamental message from God; before a woman gives birth, there are signs that a new beginning of life is forming. There is no period, her backaches, her feet swells, and her belly pushes forward. These signs are the reassurance that a baby is forming, and a miracle is in progress. Just like it takes time for a baby to form, signs of disasters, discoveries, and creations will form and produce a new beginning for us on another earth."

"Okay, but after nine months, a baby is revealed. What will be revealed in my case?"

Joe quickly stretched his arm forth, pointing to the window and recited Revelation 1:7, "Look, He is coming with the clouds, and every eye will see Him, even those who pierced Him; and all tribes on Earth will mourn because of Him. So shall it be! Amen."

Drums played within my ears. I sought for the sky through the window, stuck in a trance, as Joe's words recurred over and over. Joe slowly headed towards the door of my office without making a sound, but he stopped and turned to me and mentioned, "Wellington, you may not have gotten into the Elite Scientific Program, but you have made it into The Elite of the most Elite Programs." He pointed up and then headed out of the office, but I stopped him.

"It's killing me to know that I caused harm to Aaron and Wheatly. How can I go on with that thought?"

"I'm sorry for your lost, Wellington, but look at it from this way, Wheatly became a real-life hero and unlocked spiritual powers. His purpose was fulfilled, maxed out to infinity, and that hasn't been done since Jesus died for our sins. As for Aaron, he deeply always wanted to discover something for his own. Maybe he did. Clean yourself up and complete your task." He left.

An indescribable feeling danced upon my gut, and I instantly knew the Kole Mad Scientist legacy had just begun.

* * *

Clean-shaven and in a custom-made suit, I nervously waited patiently inside of the elevator as it beeped while ascending to each floor, which made heat rush to my forehead. Therefore, I patted my handkerchief repeatedly across my neck and head.

"Tenth floor," the auto female voice announced. My reflection doubled opening to the name Wheatly, Wellington, and Kingston
Kole's Pharmaceuticals Discoveries with the slogan, 'Adding Faith to The Formula' splashed on the walls leading to the executive suites.

The grand Kole Pharmaceutical building explicitly designed to suit my taste with green floors, red and yellow walls, and bright brown carpet.

I walked down the hallway towards my office and admired my framed awards, pictures of me accepting awards, and old book reports displayed on the shelves. My office's wall showed an image of a magnificent, colorful tree with a unique sparkly bark. I touched it and imagined the Mercy Tree.

Charlie rushed in and yelled, "Okay, it's finally done. The Time Capsule is sealed with your journals, reports, and pictures of this era. Man, I wish I were going to be alive when they open it in two hundred years. A lot of good stuff in there."

"And the initials?" I took out my pen and started jotting a message down.

"Yep, the initials W.W.K.K. Mad Scientist. By the way, your brother's and his wife's funeral was beautiful."

"Thank you for coming."

"Of course." He examined my office.

"We have been in this building for three weeks and they didn't finish decorating?" He rumbled through the boxes in the corner.

I stopped writing and locked my fingers together.

"Charlie, you're free to go. I placed enough money in your bank account that should last you for a very long time. Go be a filmmaker, live your dream."

"Wait, what?"

"W.W.K.K.P.D. will be closed for a long time as I focus on family matters."

"Wait, what about the Scientific Alliance Agency? They are going to freak out when they find out you're closing after spending all this money for this building. They will raid this place and tear it to pieces to get what they want." He panicked and then whispered, "And they will take the spiritual tree."

"Thanks to you, every formula and research is locked away with the tree for two hundred years."

"You're kidding me?" Charlie stumbled to the wall to catch his breath. "Don't worry, we still have lots of soil that will last us for many years, so we are fine." Charlie reassured himself.

"No, the Mercy Tree gave the soil life."

"Why are you doing this? Okay, I get it. You lost your brother, his wife, and your cousin, but—"

"Don't worry, we have particles of the Mercy Tree that could last us for the next two-hundred years." I slid a bowl of teeny clippings from the Mercy Tree in Charlie's view. "These are smaller than a muster seed, and they could heal a whole human's body. The future will need the tree more than us."

Charlie scratched his head and sat back down.

"So, that's it? You're going to run away like you did all those years ago because you thought God cursed you for being healed?"

"Charlie, I am not running, and believe me when I say that I know God's sovereignty is love. I am not going to put His majestic creation in the hands of greedy and heartless people." I took a walk to the beautiful depiction of the Mercy Tree on the wall. "Therefore, what I have learned in twelve years is God did not choose these things to happen to me. He chose me because these things were going to happen. He knew my humility would outweigh my selfishness."

"Welly, please don't close the practice." Charlie stood up; knees bent, "You have so many people writing thank you letters to you." He rushed behind my desk, clicked around on the computer, and with shock, hissed, "When was the last time you read your emails?"

Thousands of bolded unopened emails with the subject, *Congratulations* or *Thank you* popped up.

"They all read the same. Thank you for creating something that healed my mother from lupus, father from cancer, sister, or brother from leukemia. Congratulation for making the world a better place. Then I would have to explain that it wasn't me but God. I just stopped opening them after a while."

Charlie shook his head and hung it low.

"How do you communicate with the SAA when your inbox is cluttered like this?"

"Believe me, if the SAA wants to reach me, they will call. Plus, this cyber communication thing is too overwhelming for me."

Charlie shook his head and grumbled, "But you told me that you would handle your emails, and I was to handle the calls?"

"Well, I underestimated the number of emails that I would get. Don't waste time trying to convince me otherwise. However, I need you to do one more thing for me." Folded pages were on my desk with a golden seal on them. I motioned for him to pick it up.

"The Revelation Begins." Charlie read, *"The Take Over Volume 1,"* in big red letters across the pages. He went down the list of odd names. "I-bonic Woman, B.A.D, A Place Called Earth, Slave Princess. What is this about?"

"Just send it to the SAA's publishing house as soon as possible with the release dates," I calmly explained, and he marched to the door.

Before he left, he demanded, "Well, do one last favor for me, read your emails to see how much you have done for people." He slammed the door with my reports in his hand.

I went back behind my desk.

I slowly opened my desk drawer to a notebook filled with a thesis report, which one page read, 'Do I have the same gift of Mount Revelation's prophet?'

I closed the drawer. I tapped my mouse, and thousands of unopened emails appeared. I played with the organizing tool, recent to older and scanned twenty-five unopened emails. Clicked alphabetical order and read *Congratulations* all the way down until one seemed out of place. I fell back into my seat as I fought an unbelievable thought. Email COO-Cadet Space0305 in the subject line. My heart thudded. I moved closer and clicked the message.

Would you believe me if I told you that I'm staring at Mercy Tree right now? I wish you guys were here to witness this.

Ps. I heard I-bonic Armor was stolen. How is Wheatly handling that?

K. Aaron K.

My hair stood up all over my body. Shivers danced on my skin. "Charlie!" I screamed, and he rushed in with a box in his hand.

"Yes?" He hurried to see my computer screen, and I moved for him to sit.

"Aaron, he sent me an email. Recently, before Wheatly's death."

We both paused and gave each other a weird look.

"When did he disappear?" Charlie asked.

"Four months ago." We sat in silence. "But he sent this email to me a month ago." I grabbed my jacket.

"What are you going to do about it? Are you going to confront the SAA? They seem like dangerous people," Charlie warned.

"Oh, you think they're dangerous? There is nothing worse than a mad scientist with a God-given dream. Print me a copy of the email."

I stormed out of the office and heard Charlie yell, "Go be mad!"

«CHAPTER TWENTY-FIVE»

HM. Bowmen of NASA burst through his office doors with fury as his assistant tried to stop him. He turned to me, an unknown civilian, admiring the images on his office's wall.

"Excuse me?" HM. Bowmen barked, and I turned around with a saturated grin.

"Oh, yes, the man I've been waiting for." I motioned for him to sit behind his desk.

He leaned towards his assistant, and she whispered, "HM. Kole, sir."

She closed the door.

HM. Bowmen quickly fixed his coat and may have thought, Wellington Kole, a household name.

"What do I owe the pleasure of having the Scientific Alliance Agency's golden child in my office?" He slowly sat behind his desk with his chest poked out, but his hand nervously twitched.

"You know, my father died twelve years ago. That's when I left home to not return after ten years." I sat down. "I guess I was afraid. I blamed God and ruined my faith in the process." My leg sat on my knee, and I dusted my shirt off. "Then my fiancée was diagnosed with cancer. I wanted to run away again, but I knew I couldn't. It would be so wrong on so many levels if I did."

"But you cured her with the medicine that you created?"

I stood up and walked to the pictures of HM. Bowmen in a space shuttle and of him speaking at Yale University.

I shared with him, "Recently, my brother was murdered, but he did fulfill his God-given purpose, which was to be a hero." Then I cupped my mouth and whispered at HM. Bowmen, "Or to create one."

He raised his eyebrow and said, "Dr. Wellington, what is the meaning of this?"

"Oh, I am getting there." I walked to a picture on HM. Bowmen's desk and he sat up.

"What happened to the mission? And why did six cadets return?" I pointed at the Future Eight Cadets' class picture.

"That's top secret. I am sorry, HM. Kole, not even someone with your caliber can know that information." He tapped his pen against his desk.

"Is that so?" I placed a copy of Aaron's email on his desk, and the pen fell out of his hand.

"Then why am I getting emails from Kingston that is dated weeks ago? You told my family that he went missing four months ago because there was an explosion that pushed him and a few cadets into the Ozone layer," I grunted

The blood along with his mouth rushed downward.

"Ah, umm." He tried to maintain his composure, but he became pale.

"Tell me about the mission." I leaned closer.

"Wellington, Kingston was not supposed to be on that mission. He lied to us, to all of us and put himself at risk."

"You're lying. Kingston has a daughter and a wife. He would never put himself at risk."

"What I am saying to you is the truth."

I took a deep breath and marched to the exit when he disclosed, "But there was an explosion, and Kingston did go into outer space."

I slowly faced him, and he struggled with his words.

"But on a different spaceship or shuttle, much larger and more advanced than ours."

"You're saying he was abducted?"

"No. What I am saying is . . . something was found on the moon, and it didn't belong to us."

We dwelled in each other's silence.

"We tried every navigation and tracking device to find him. It's like he vanished or traveled faster than light. He's gone."

"I don't believe you."

"We tried to stop him, but he was too curious. One cadet died trying to save him. That is why only six cadets returned. To be safe, we had to make something up. So we said he died too."

"So you're just going to leave him up there while you guys play with your fingers?"

"No, we are trying our best to find him. We have been monitoring the surrounding areas of the galaxy and the moon. We even put it on the Voyager's radar. The whole department has been swamped because we recently discovered a third glow in Canada. It's spreading all over North America, and if we don't find out what it is, we may be facing a world epidemic of some sort." I counted on my fingers the number of glows that have been found: one from Mount Revelation, the one at my home, and now a glow in Canada.

He spun the globe as I paced back and forth.

"What do you think it is?" he asked.

"Mercy ... It's Mercy." I leaped forward with joy dancing in my belly and then out of the office.

"Dr. Wellington?" HM. Bowmen called, and he followed me in the hallway.

I turned and ordered, "Send that report to Detective Gary. ASAP!"

"Yes, sir." He nodded.

Overwhelmed that my niece could lead us to Wheatly's murderers. I imagined Wheatly doing what any father would do to protect their child. Wheatly pouring I-bonic Armor—a holy substance—into Mercy's mouth so that the power of the Mercy Tree lived inside of his daughter.

I needed to catch my breath. I reached into my pocket for my car keys when my hands fell on Dad's pocket Bible. I randomly flipped to Philippians 4:13. "I can do all things through Him who strengthens me." This made me smile as I walked out of NASA's building and wondered if God gave me the strength to figure all these things out.

I read another verse out loud, "Zechariah 4:10–Do not despise these small beginnings, for the Lord rejoices to see the work begin, to see the plumb line in Zerubbabel's hand." I reached my car, opened the door, and sat down letting the bible slide out of my hand and onto the floor. There, I noticed Dad's written notes on the back page that read:

The blessings of the Tree of Mercy are like fruits to my lips and joy to my spirit. It is a reminder to my soul to give thanks and to repent. Praise the Lord for He has told me the Kole name will rise, the Kole name will fall and then rise again. But as long as we don't disrupt the fallen stars on the left foot of Mercy, but bear fruit from the right foot of Mercy where everlasting life lives, we all will be saved.

I sat in silence and meditated on the meaning of Dad's words. I wiped the corner of my eyes and placed the pocket Bible back into my coat. I knew God would heal my broken heart, Wheatly's murderers would be caught, and Aaron would safely find himself home again because he was a survivor.
However, yesterday's memories couldn't prepare me for the future.

TO BE CONTINUED

NEXT . . .

THE REVELATION
BEGINS ...

with

ANOTHER
EARTH

AARON DIDN'T KNOW THAT IN
ORDER TO SURVIVE, HE HAD TO ARRIVE.

Book Two of "The Revelation Begins ..."

A STORY WRITTEN BY

SHIMIRA COLE

Share your thoughts with the author:
Your comments will be forwarded to the author
when you send an email to
TheRevelationBegins@MiraColeMedia.com

For more news about the author, visit
www.shimiracole.com

www.ingramcontent.com/pod-product-compliance
Lightning Source LLC
Chambersburg PA
CBHW071236250626
47163CB00001B/207